PENGU

RUMPOLE'S LAST CASE

John Mortimer is a former barrister and the author of many novels, stage and television plays, film scripts, and plays for radio, including six plays on the life of Shakespeare, and the Rumpole plays, which won him the British Academy Writer of the Year Award. He has also translated Feydeau for the National Theatre and Johann Strauss's *Die Fledermaus* for the Royal Opera House, and adapted *Brideshead Revisited* for television.

Six of Mortimer's books of Rumpole stories (*Rumpole of the Bailey, The Trials of Rumpole, Rumpole's Return, Rumpole for the Defence, Rumpole and the Golden Thread*, and *Rumpole's Last Case*), all available from Penguin, have been collected into two volumes, *The First Rumnpole Omnibus* and *The Second Rumpole Omnibus*. Penguin also publishes *Rumpole and the Age of Miracles*, the seventh Rumpole book; *In Character and Character Parts*, interviews with some of the most prominent men and women of our time; *Clinging to the Wreckage*, his celebrated autobiography, which won the 1982 *Yorkshire Post* Book of the Year Award; and a volume of plays including *A Voyage Round My Father*. His best-selling novel, *Paradise Postponed*, published in Viking and Penguin, was a much-acclaimed television series in 1986. The sequel, *Titmuss Regained*, was published in Viking in 1990. Another recent novel, *Summer's Lease* (Viking, 1988), was published in Penguin in 1989. His early novels, which are also now available from Viking, include *Charade* (also Penguin) and *The Narrowing Stream*, first published here in 1986 and 1989 respectively. *Like Men Betrayed*, originally published in 1954, was reissued in the U.S. by Viking in 1989.

Rumpole's Last Case

JOHN MORTIMER

Penguin Books

PENGUIN BOOKS
Published by the Penguin Group
Viking Penguin, a division of Penguin Books USA Inc.,
375 Hudson Street, New York, New York 10014, U.S.A.
Penguin Books Ltd, 27 Wrights Lane, London W8 5TZ, England
Penguin Books Australia Ltd, Ringwood, Victoria, Australia
Penguin Books Canada Ltd, 2801 John Street, Markham, Ontario, Canada L3R 1B4
Penguin Books (N.Z.) Ltd, 182-190 Wairau Road, Auckland 10, New Zealand

Penguin Books Ltd, Registered Offices:
Harmondsworth, Middlesex, England

Published in Select Penguin 1988
Published in Select Penguin 1989

3 5 7 9 10 8 6 4 2

Copyright © Advanpress Ltd, 1987
All rights reserved

(CIP data available)
ISBN 0 14 01.2695 3
Printed in the United States America

Set in Times Roman

To all the friends, learned and otherwise,
I made down the Old Bailey
and especially to the criminal defenders
Jeremy Hutchinson who, like me,
has done his last case and Geoffrey Robertson
who certainly hasn't.

Contents

Rumpole and the Blind Tasting

'Rumpole! How could you drink that stuff?'

'Perfectly easy, Erskine-Brown. Raise the glass to the lips, incline the head slightly backwards, and let the liquid flow gently past the tonsils.' I gave the man a practical demonstration. 'I admit I've had a good deal of practice, but even you may come to it in time.'

'Of course you *can* drink it, Rumpole. Presumably it's *possible* to drink methylated spirits shaken up with a little ice and a dash of angostura bitters.' Erskine-Brown smiled at me from over the edge of the glass of Côte de Nuits Villages '79, which he had been ordering in his newly acquired wine-buff's voice from Jack Pommeroy, before he settled himself at the bar; I couldn't help noticing that his dialogue was showing some unaccustomed vivacity. 'I fully appreciate that you *can* drink Pommeroy's Very Ordinary. But the point is, Rumpole, why should you want to?'

'Forgetfulness, Erskine-Brown. The consignment of a

day in front of his Honour Judge Bullingham to the Lethe of forgotten things. The Mad Bull,' I told him, as I drained the large glass of Château Fleet Street Jack Pommeroy had obligingly put on my slate until the next legal aid cheque came in, 'constantly interrupted my speech to the Jury. I am defending an alleged receiver of stolen sugarbowls. With this stuff, not to put too fine a point on it, you have a reasonable chance of getting blotto.'

It is a good few years now since I adopted the habit of noting down the facts of some of my outstanding cases, the splendours and miseries of an Old Bailey hack, and those of you who may have cast an eye over some of my previous works of reminiscence may well be muttering *'Plus ça change, plus c'est la même chose'* or words to the like effect. After so many cross-examinations, speeches to the Jury, verdicts of guilty or not guilty, legal aid cheques long-awaited and quickly disposed of down the bottomless pit of the overdraft at the Caring Bank, no great change in the Rumpole fortunes had taken place, the texture of life remained much as it always had been and would, no doubt, do so until after my positively last case when I sit waiting to be called on in the Great Circuit Court of the Skies, if such a tribunal exists.

Take that evening as typical. I had been involved in the defence of one Hugh Snakelegs Timson. The Timsons, you may remember, are an extended family of South London villains who practise crime in the stolid, hard-working, but not particularly successful manner in which a large number of middle-of-the-road advocates practise at the Bar. The Timsons are not high-fliers; not for them the bullion raids or the skilled emptying of the Rembrandts out of ducal

mansions. The Timsons inhabit the everyday world of pur-
loined video-recorders, bent log-books and stolen Cortinas.
They also provide me and my wife, Hilda (known to me,
quite off the record, and occasionally behind the hand, as
She Who Must Be Obeyed), with our bread and butter.
When prospects are looking bleak, when my tray in the
clerk's room is bare of briefs but loaded with those un-
pleasant-looking buff envelopes doshed out at regular intervals by Her Majesty the Queen, it is comforting to
know that somewhere in the Greater London area, some
Timson will be up to some sort of minor villainy and,
owing to the general incompetence of the clan, the male-
factor concerned will no doubt be in immediate need of
legal representation.

Hugh Snakelegs Timson was, at that time, the family's
official fence, having taken over the post from his Uncle
Percy Timson,* who was getting a good deal past it, and
had retired to live in Benidorm. Snakelegs, a thin, elegant
man in his forties, a former winner of the Mr Debonair
contest at Butlin's Holiday Camp, had earned his name
from his talent at the tango. He lived with his wife, Hetty,
in a semi-detached house in Bromley to which Detective
Inspector Broome, the well-known terror of the Timsons,
set out on a voyage of discovery with his faithful Detective
Sergeant Cosgrove. At first Inspector 'New' Broome had
drawn a blank at the Timson home; even the huge coffin-
shaped freezer seemed to contain nothing but innumerable
bags full of frozen vegetables. The eager Inspector had the
bright idea of thawing some of these provisions however,

*See 'Rumpole and the Age for Retirement' in *The Trials of Rumpole*,
Penguin Books, 1979.

and was rewarded by the spectacle of articles of Georgian silver arising from the saucepans of boiling peas in the manner of Venus arising from the Sea.

The defence of Hugh Snakelegs Timson had not been going particularly well. The standard receiver's story, 'I got the whole lot from a bloke in a pub who was selling them off cheap, and whose name I cannot for the life of me recall', was treated with undisguised contempt by his Honour, Judge Roger Bullingham, who asked, with the ponderous cynicism accompanied by an undoubted wink at the Jury, of which he is master, if I were not going to suggest that there had been a shower of sugar-sifters, cream jugs and the like from the back of a lorry? Anyway, if got innocently, why was the silverware in the deep-freezer? I told the Jury that an Englishman's freezer was his castle and that there was no reason on earth why a citizen shouldn't keep his valuables in a bag of Bird's Eye peas at a low temperature. Indeed, I added, as I thought helpfully, I had an old aunt who kept odd pound notes in the tea-caddy, and constantly risked boiling up her savings in a pot of Darjeeling. At this the Mad Bull went an even darker shade of purple, his neck swelled visibly so that it seemed about to burst his yellowing winged collar, and he told the Jury that my aunt was 'not evidence', and that they must in reaching a decision 'dismiss entirely anything Mr Rumpole may have said about his curious family', adding, with a whole battery of near-nudges and almost-winks, 'I expect our saner relatives know the proper place for their valuables. In the bank.'

At this point the Bull decided to interrupt my final speech by adjourning for tea and television in his private room, and I was left to wander disconsolately in the direction of Pommeroy's Wine Bar, where I met that notable opera buff and wine connoisseur, half-hearted prosecutor and inept defender, the spouse and helpmeet of Phillida Erskine-Brown, Q.C. Phillida Trant, as was, the Portia of our Chambers, had put his nose somewhat out of joint by taking silk and leaving poor old Claude, ten years older than she, a humble Junior. So there I was, raising yet another glass of Château Thames Embankment to my lips and telling Claude that the only real advantage of this particular vintage was that it was quite likely to get you drunk.

'The purpose of drinking wine is not intoxication, Rumpole.' Erskine-Brown looked as pained as a prelate who is told that his congregation only came to church because of the central heating. 'The point is to get in touch with one of the major influences of western civilization, to taste sunlight trapped in a bottle, and to remember some stony slope in Tuscany or a village by the Gironde.'

I thought with a momentary distaste of the bit of barren soil, no doubt placed between the cowshed and the *pissoir*, where the Château Pommeroy grape struggled for existence. And then, Erskine-Brown, long-time member of our Chambers in Equity Court, went considerably too far.

'You see, Rumpole,' he said, 'it's the terrible nose.'

Now I make no particular claim for my nose and I am far from suggesting that it's a thing of beauty and a joy forever. When I was in my perambulator it may, for all I can remember, have had a sort of tip-tilted and impertinent charm. In my youth it was no doubt pinkish and healthy-looking. In my early days at the Bar it had a sharp and inquisitive quality which made prosecution witnesses feel they could keep no secrets from it. Today it is perhaps past its prime, it has spread somewhat; it has, in part at least, gone mauve; it is, after all, a nose that has seen a considerable quantity of life. But man and boy it has served me well, and I had no intention of having my appearance insulted by Claude Erskine-Brown, barrister-at-law, who looks, in certain unfavourable lights, not unlike an abbess with a bad period.

'We may disagree about Pommeroy's plonk,' I told him, 'but that's no reason why you should descend to personal abuse.'

'No, I don't mean *your* nose, Rumpole. I mean the wine's nose.'

I looked suspiciously into the glass; did this wine possess qualities I hadn't guessed at? 'Don't babble, Erskine-Brown.'

'"Nose," Rumpole! The bouquet. That's one of the expressions you have to learn to use about wine. Together with the "length".'

'Length?' I looked down at the glass in my hand; the length seemed to be about one inch and shrinking rapidly.

'The "length" a great wine lingers in the mouth, Rumpole. Look, why don't you let me educate you? My friend, Martyn Vanberry, organizes tastings in the City. Terrifically good fun. You get to try about a dozen wines.'

'A dozen?' I was doubtful. 'An expensive business.'

'No, Rumpole. Absolutely free. They are blind tastings. He's got one on tomorrow afternoon, as it so happens.'

'You mean they make you blind drunk?' I couldn't resist asking. 'Sounds exactly what I need.' At that moment the promise of Martyn Vanberry and his blind tastings were a vague hope for the future. My immediate prospects included an evening drink with She Who Must Be Obeyed and finishing my speech for Snakelegs to the Jury against the Mad Bull's barracking. I emptied Pommeroy's dull opiate to the drains and aimed Lethe-wards.

It might be said that the story of the unknown vendor of
Georgian silver in the pub lacked originality, and that the
inside of a freezer-pack was not the most obvious place for
storing valuable antiques, but there was one point of significance in the defence of Hugh Snakelegs Timson. Detective Inspector Broome was, as I have already suggested, an
enthusiastic officer and one who regarded convictions with
as much pride as the late Don Giovanni regarded his con-
quests of the female sex. No doubt he notched them up on
his braces. He had given evidence that there had been
thefts of silver from various country houses in Kent, but all
the Detective Inspector's industry and persistence had not
produced one householder who could be called by the Prosecution to identify the booty from the freezer as his stolen
silverware. So where, I was able to ask, was the evidence
that the property undoubtedly received by Snakelegs had
been stolen? Unless the old idea that the burden lay on the
Prosecution to prove its case had gone out of fashion in his
Lordship's court (distant rumblings as of a volcano limber-
ing up for an eruption from the Bull), then perhaps, I ventured to suggest, Snakelegs was entitled to squeeze his way
out of trouble.

Whether it was this thought, or Judge Bullingham's
frenzied eagerness to secure a conviction (Kane himself
might have got off his murder rap if he'd only been fortu-
nate enough to receive a really biased summing up), the
Jury came back with a cheerful verdict of not guilty. After
only a brief fit of minor apoplexy, and a vague threat to
bring the inordinate length of defending counsel's speeches
to the attention of the legal aid authorities, the Bull released the prisoner to his semi-detached and his wife Hetty.
I was strolling along the corridor, puffing a small cigar

with a modest feeling of triumph, when a small, eager young lady, her fairly pleasing face decorated with a pair of steel-rimmed specs and a look of great seriousness, rather as though she was not quite certain which problem to tackle first, world starvation or nuclear war, came panting up alongside.

'Mr Rumpole,' she said, 'you did an absolutely first-class job!'

I paused in my tracks, looked at her more closely, and remembered that she had been sitting in Court paying close attention throughout *R*. v. *Snakelegs Timson*.

'I just gave my usual service.'

'And I,' she said, sticking out her hand in a gesture of camaraderie, 'have just passed the Bar exams.'

'Then we don't shake hands,' I had to tell her, avoiding physical contact. 'Clients don't like it you see. Think we might be doing secret deals with each other. All the same, welcome to the treadmill.'

I moved away from her then, towards the lift, pressed the button, and as I waited for nothing very much to happen she accosted me again.

'You don't stereotype that much, do you, Mr Rumple?' She looked as though she were already beginning to lose a little faith in my infallibility.

'And you don't call me *Mister* Rumpole. Leave that to the dotty Bull,' I corrected her, perhaps a little sharply.

'I thought you were too busy fighting the class war to care about outdated behaviour patterns.'

'Fighting the *what?*'

'Protecting working people against middle-class judges.'

The lift was still dawdling away in the basement and I thought it would be kind now to put this recruit right on a few of the basic principles of our legal system. 'The Timsons would hate to be called "working people",' I told her. 'They're entirely middle-class villains. Very Conservative, in fact. They live by strict monetarist principles and the free market economy. They're also against the closed shop; they believe that shops should be open at all hours of the night. Preferably by jemmy.'

'My name's Liz Probert,' she said, failing to smile at the jest I was not making for the first time. At this point the lift arrived. 'Good day Mizz'—I took her for a definite Mizz —I said, as I stepped into it. Rather to my surprise she strode in after me, still chattering. 'I want to defend like you. But I must still have a lot to learn. I never noticed the point about the owners not identifying the stolen silver.'

'Neither did I,' I had to admit, 'until it was almost too late. And you know why they didn't?' I was prepared to tell this neophyte the secrets of my astonishing success. That, after all, is part of the Great Tradition of the Bar, otherwise known as showing off to the younger white-wigs. 'They'd all got the insurance money, you see, and done very nicely out of it, thank you. The last thing they wanted was to see their old sugarbowls back and have to return the money. Life's a bit more complicated than they tell you in the Bar exams.'

We had reached the robing-room floor and I made for the Gents with Mizz Probert following me like the hound, or at least the puppy, of heaven. 'I was wondering if you could possibly give me some counselling in my career area.'

'Not now, I'm afraid. I've got a blind date, with some rather attractive bottles.' I opened the door and saw the gleaming porcelain fittings which had been in my mind since I got out of Court. 'Men only in here, I'm afraid,' I had to tell Mizz Probert, who still seemed to be at my heels. 'It's one of the quaint old traditions of the Bar.'

The surprisingly rapid and successful conclusion of the *Queen* v. *Snakelegs* had liberated me, and I set off with some eagerness to Prentice Alley in the City of London, and the premises of Vanberry's Fine Wines & Spirits Ltd, where I was to meet Claude Erskine-Brown, and sample, for the first time in my life, the mysterious joys of a blind tasting. After my credentials had been checked, I was shown into a small drinks party which had about it all the gaiety of an assembly of the be-reaved, when the corpse in question has left his entire fortune to the Cats' Home.

The meeting took place in a brilliantly lit basement room with glaring white tiles. It seemed a suitable loca-tion for a post-mortem, but, in place of the usual de-ceased person on the table, there were a number of bottles, all shrouded in brown-paper bags. It was there I saw my learned friend, Erskine-Brown, already in place among the tasters, who were twirling minute quantities of wine in their glasses, holding them nervously up to the light, sniffing at them with deep suspicion and finally allowing a small quantity to pass their lips. They were mainly solemn-looking characters in dark three-piece suits, although there was one female in a tweed coat and skirt, a sort of white silk stock, sensible shoes and a monocle. She looked as though she'd be happier judging hunters at a country gymkhana than fine wines, and she was, so Erskine-Brown whispered to me, Miss Honoria Bird, the distinguished wine correspondent of the *Sunday Mercury*. Before the tasting competition began in earnest we were invited to sample a few specimens from the Vanberry claret collection. So I took my first taste and experienced what, without doubt, was a draught of vin-tage that hath been 'Cool'd a long age in the deep-delved

earth, Tasting of Flora and the country green, . . .' And it
was whilst I was enjoying the flavour of Dance, and
Provençal song, and sunburnt mirth, mixed with a dash
of wild strawberries, that a voice beside me boomed,
'What's the matter with you? Can't you spit?'

Miss Honoria Bird was at my elbow and in my mouth
was what? Something so far above my price range that it
seemed like some new concoction altogether, as far removed from Pommeroy's Very Ordinary as a brief for Gulf
Oil in the House of Lords is from a small matter of indecency before the Uxbridge Magistrates.

'Over there, in case you're looking for it. Expectoration
corner!' Miss Bird waved me to a wooden wine-box, half-
filled with sawdust into which the gents in dark suitings
were directing mouthfuls of purplish liquid. I moved away
from her, reluctant to admit that the small quantity of the
true, the blushful Hippocrene I had been able to win had
long since disappeared down the little red lane.

'Collie brought you, didn't he?' Martyn Vanberry, the
wine merchant, caught me as I was about to swallow a
second helping. He was a thin streak of a chap, in a dark
suit and a stiff collar, whose faint smile, I thought, was
thin-lipped and patronizing. Beside him stood a pleasant
enough young man who was in charge of the mechanics of
the thing, brought the bottles and the glasses and was referred to as Ken.

'Collie?' The name meant nothing to me.

'Erskine-Brown. We called him Collie at school.'

'After the dog?' I saw my Chambers companion insert
the tip of his pale nose into the aperture of his wine glass.

'No. After the Doctor. Collis-Brown. You know, the
medicine? Old Claude was always a bit of a pill really. We
used to kick him around at Winchester.'

Now I am far from saying that, in my long relationship
with Claude Erskine-Brown, irritation has not sometimes
got the better of me, but as a long-time member of our
Chambers at Equity Court he has, over the years, become as familiar and uncomfortable as the furniture. I
resented the strictures of this public-school bully on my
learned friend and was about to say so when the gloomy
proceedings were interrupted by the arrival of an unlikely
guest wearing tartan trousers, rubber-soled canvas shoes
of the type which I believe are generally known as
'trainers', and a zipped jacket which bore on its back the
legend MONTY MANTIS SERVICE STATION LUTON BEDS. Inside this costume was a squat, ginger-haired and youngish man who called out, 'Which way to the anti-freeze?
At least we can get warmed up for the winter.' This was
a clear reference to recent scandals in the wine trade, and
it was greeted, in the rarefied air of Vanberry's tasting
room, with as much jollity as an advertisement for con-
traceptive appliances in the Vatican.

'One of your customers?' I asked Vanberry.

'One of my best,' he sighed. 'I imagine the profession
of *garagiste* in Luton must be extremely profitable. And
he makes a point of coming to *all* of our blind tastings.'

'Now I'm here,' Mr Mantis said, taking off his zipper
jacket and displaying a yellow jumper ornamented with
diamond lozenges, 'let battle commence.' He twirled and
sniffed and took a mouthful from a tasting glass, made a
short but somehow revolting gargling sound and spat into
the sawdust. 'A fairly unpretentious Côte Rotie,' he announced, as he did so. 'But on the whole 1975 was a disappointing year on the Rhône.'

The contest was run like a game of musical chairs. They
gave you a glass and if you guessed wrong, the chair, so to

speak, was removed and you had to go and sit with the
girls and have an ice-cream. At my first try I got that distant hint of wild strawberries again from a wine that was so
far out of the usual run of my drinking that I became
tongue-tied, and when asked to name the nectar could only
mutter 'damn good stuff' and slink away from the field of
battle.

Erskine-Brown was knocked out in the second round,
having confidently pronounced a Coonawarra to be Châ-
teauneuf du Pape. 'Some bloody stuff from Wagga,
Wagga,' he grumbled unreasonably—on most occasions
Claude was a staunch upholder of the Commonwealth,
'one always forgets about the colonies.'

So we watched as, one by one, the players fell away.
Martyn Vanberry was in charge of the bottles and after
the contestants had made their guesses he had to disclose
the labels. From time to time, in the manner of donnish
quiz-masters on upmarket wireless guessing-games, he
would give little hints, particularly if he liked the con-
tender. 'A churchyard number' might indicate a Graves,
or 'a macabre little item, somewhat skeletal' a Beaune.
He never, I noticed, gave much assistance to the *garagiste* from Luton, nor did he need to because the ebul-
lient Mr Monty Mantis had no difficulty in identifying
his wines and could even make a decent stab at the vintage year, although perfect accuracy in that regard wasn't
required.

Finally the challengers were reduced to two: Monty
Mantis and the lady with the eyeglass, Honoria Bird or
Birdie as she was known to all the pin-striped expectorat-
ing undertakers around her. It was their bottoms that hov-
ered, figuratively speaking, over the final chair, the last
parcelled bottle. Martyn Vanberry was holding this with

particular reverence as he poured a taster into two glasses. Monty Mantis regarded the colour, lowered his nose to the level of the tide, took a mouthful and spat rapidly.

'Gordon Bennett!' He seemed somewhat amazed. 'Don't want to risk swallowing that. It might ruin me carburettor!'

Martyn Vanberry looked pale and extremely angry. He turned to the lady contestant, who was swilling the stuff around her dentures in a far more impressive way. 'Well, Birdie,' he said, as she spat neatly, 'let me give you a clue. It's not whisky.'

'I think I could tell that.' She looked impassive. 'Not whisky.'

'But think . . . just think . . .' Vanberry seemed anxious to bring the contest to a rapid end by helping her. 'Think of a whisky translated.'

'Le quatre-star Esso?' said the *garagiste,* but Vanberry was unamused.

'White Horse?' Birdie frowned.

'Very good. Something Conservative, of course. And keep to the right!'

'The right bank of the river? St Emilion. White Horse? Cheval Blanc . . .' Birdie arrived at her destination with a certain amount of doubt and hesitation.

'1971, I'm afraid, nothing earlier.' Vanberry was pulling away the brown paper to reveal a label on which the words Cheval Blanc and *Appellation St Emilion Contrôlée* were to be clearly read. There was a smatter of applause. 'Dear old Birdie! Still an unbeatable palate.' It was a tribute in which the Luton *garagiste* didn't join; he was laughing as Martyn Vanberry turned to him and said, icily polite, 'I'm sorry you were pipped at the post, Mr Mantis. You did jolly well. Now, Birdie, if you'll once again accept the certificate of *Les Grands Contestants du Vin* and the com-

plimentary bottle which this time is a magnum of Gevrey
Chambertin Clair Pau 1970—a somewhat underrated vintage. Can you not stay with us, Mr Mantis?'

But Monty Mantis was on his way to the door, muttering
about getting himself decarbonized. Nobody laughed, and
no one seemed particularly sorry to see him go.

There must be no accounting, I reflected on this incident,
for tastes. One man's anti-freeze may be another's Mouton
Rothschild, especially if you don't see the label. I was
reminded of those embarrassing tests on television in
which the puzzled housewife is asked to tell margarine
from butter, or say which washing powder got young Ron-
nie's football shorts whitest. She always looks terrified of
disappointing the eager interviewer and plumping for the
wrong variety. But then I thought that as a binge, the blind
tasting at Vanberry's Fine Wines had been about as successful as a picnic tea with the Clacton Temperance Society
and the incident faded from my memory.

Other matters arose of more immediate concern. One
was to be of some interest and entertainment value. To deal
with the bad news first: my wife, Hilda, whose very name
rings out like a demand for immediate obedience, announced the imminent visit to our mansion flat (although
the words are inept to describe the somewhat gloomy and
cavernous interior of Casa Rumpole) in Froxbury Court,
Gloucester Road, of her old school-friend Dodo Mackintosh.

Now Dodo may be, in many ways, a perfectly reasonable and indeed game old bird. Her watercolours of Lan-
worth Cove and adjacent parts of Cornwall are highly
regarded in some circles, although they seem to me to have
been executed in heavy rain. She is, I believe, a dab hand

at knitting patterns and during her stays a great deal of fancy work is put in on matinée jackets and bootees for her younger relatives. Hilda tells me that she was, when they were both at school, a sturdy lacrosse player. My personal view, and this is not for publication to She Who Must Be Obeyed, is that in any conceivable team sent out to bore for England, Dodo would have to be included. As you may have gathered, I do not hit it off with the lady, and she takes the view that by marrying a claret-drinking, cigar-smoking legal hack who is never likely to make a fortune, Hilda has tragically wasted her life.

The natural gloom that the forthcoming visit cast upon me was somewhat mitigated by the matter of Mizz Probert's application to enter 3 Equity Court, which allowed me a little harmless fun at the expense of Soapy Sam Bollard (or Ballard as *he* affects to call himself), the sanctimonious President of the Lawyers As Christians Society who, in his more worldly manifestation, has contrived to become Head of our Chambers.

Sometimes after the end of *Regina* v. *Snakelegs* (not a victory to be mentioned in the same breath as the Penge Bungalow Murders, in which I managed to squeeze first past the post *alone and without a leader,* but quite a satisfactory win all the same), I wandered into the clerk's room and there was the eager face of Mizz Probert asking our clerk, Henry, if there was any news about her application to become a pupil in Chambers, and Henry was explaining to her, without a great deal of patience, that her name would come up for discussion by the learned friends in due course.

'Pupil? You want to be a pupil? Any good at putting, are you?' This was the voice of Uncle Tom—T. C. Rowley— our oldest member, who hadn't come by a brief for as long as any of us can remember, but who chooses to spend his days with us to vary the monotony of life with an unmarried sister. His working day consists of a long battle with *The Times* crossword—won by the setter on most days, a brief nap after the midday sandwich, and a spell of golf practice in a corner of the clerk's room. Visiting solicitors occasionally complain of being struck quite smartly on the ankle by one of Uncle Tom's golf balls.

'Good at putting? No. Do you have to be?' Mizz Probert asked in all innocence.

'My old pupil master, C. H. Wystan,' Uncle Tom told her, referring to Hilda's Daddy, the long-time-ago Head of our Chambers, 'was a terribly nice chap, but he never gave me anything to do. So I became the best member at getting his balls into a waste-paper basket. Awfully good training, you know. I never had an enormous practice. Well, very little practice at all quite honestly, so I've been able to keep up my golf. If you want to become a pupil this is my advice to you. Get yourself a mashie niblick . . .'

As this bizarre advice wound on, I left our clerk's room in order to avoid giving vent to any sort of unseemly guffaw. I had a conference with Mr Bernard, the solicitor who appeared to have a retainer for the Timson family. The particular problem concerned Tony Timson, who had entered a shop with the probable intention of stealing three large television sets. Unfortunately the business had gone bankrupt the week before and was quite denuded of stock, thus raising what many barristers might call a nice point of law—I would call it nasty. Getting on for half a century knocking around the Courts has given me a profound distaste for the law. Give me a bloodstain or two, a bit of disputed typewriting or a couple of hairs on a cardigan, and I am happy as the day is long. I feel a definite sense of insecurity and unease when solicitors like Mr Bernard say, as he did on that occasion, 'Hasn't the House of Lords had something to say on the subject?'

Well, perhaps it had. The House of Lords is always having something to say; they're a lot of old chatterboxes up there, if you want my opinion. I was saved from an immediate answer by Mizz Probert entering with a cup of coffee which she must have scrounged from the clerk's room for the sole purpose of gaining access to the Rumpole sanctum. I thanked her and prepared to parry Bernard's next attack.

'It's the doctrine of impossible attempt of course,' he burbled on. 'You must know the case.'

'Must I?' I was playing for time, but I saw Mizz Probert darting to the shelves where the bound volumes of the law reports are kept mainly for the use of other members of our Chambers.

'I mean there have been all these articles in the *Criminal Law Review.*'

'My constant bedtime reading,' I assured him.

'So you do *know* the House of Lords decision?' Mr Bernard sounded relieved.

'Know it? Of course I know it. During those long evenings at Froxbury Court we talk of little else. The name's on the tip of my tongue . . .'

It wasn't, of course, but the next minute it was on the law report which Mizz Probert put in front of me. ' "*Swinglehurst against the Queen* . . ." ' Of course. Ah, yes. I've got it at my fingertips, as always, Mr Bernard. "*Doctrine of impossible attempts examined—R.* v. *Dewdrop and Banister distinguished*".' I read him a few nuggets from the headnote of the case. "All this is good stuff, Bernard, couched in fine rich prose . . .'

'So how does that affect Tony Timson trying to steal three non-existent telly sets?'

'How does it?' I stood then, to end the interview. 'I think it would be more helpful to you, Mr Bernard, if I gave you a written opinion. I may have to go into other authorities in some depth.'

So it became obvious that, as far as I was concerned, Mizz Liz Probert would be a valuable, perhaps an indispensable, member of Chambers. When I asked her to write the opinion I had promised Bernard, she told me that she had been the top student of her year and won the Cicero scholarship. With Probert's knowledge of the law and my irresistible way with a jury, we might, I felt, become a team which could have got the Macbeths off regicide.

A happy chance furthered my plans. Owing to the presence on the domestic scene of Dodo Mackintosh (not the sort of spectacle a barrister wishes to encounter early in the mornings), I was taking my breakfast in the Taste-Ee-Bite, one of the newer and more garish serve-yourself eateries in Fleet Street. I was just getting outside two eggs and bacon on a fried slice, when Soapy Sam Bollard plonked himself down opposite me with a cup of coffee.

'Do you read the *Church Times,* Rumpole?' he started improbably, waving a copy of that organ in the general direction of my full English breakfast.

'Only for the racing results.'

'There's a first-class fellow writing on legal matters. This week's piece is headed VENGEANCE IS MINE. I WILL REPAY. This is what Canon Probert says . . .'

'Canon who?'

'Probert.'

'That's what I thought you said.'

'Society is fully entitled to be revenged upon the criminal.' Ballard gave me a taste of the Canon's style. 'Even the speeding motorist is a fit object for the legalized vengeance of the outraged pedestrian.'

'What does the good Canon recommend? Bring back the thumb-screw for parking on a double yellow line?'

'"Too often the crafty lawyer frustrates the angel of retribution",' Ballard went on reading.

'Too often the angel of retribution makes a complete balls up of the burden of proof.'

'You may mock, Rumpole. You may well mock!'

'Thank you.'

'What we need is someone with the spirit of Canon Probert in Chambers. Someone to convince the public that lawyers still have a bit of moral fibre.' Ballard's further mention of this name put quite a ruthless scheme into my head. 'Probert,' I said thoughtfully, 'did you say Probert?'

'Canon Probert.' Ballard supplied the details.

'Odd, that,' I told him. 'The name seems strangely familiar . . .'

Later, when Mizz Probert handed in a highly expert and profound legal opinion in the obscure subject of impossible attempt, often known in the trade as 'stealing from an empty purse', I had a few words with her on the subject of her parentage.

'Is your father,' I asked, 'by any chance the Canon Probert who writes for the *Church Times?*' And then I gave her an appropriate warning: 'Don't answer that.'

'Why ever not?'

'Because our Head of Chambers is quite ridiculously prejudiced against women pupils whose fathers aren't canons who write for the *Church Times*. You may go now, Mizz Probert. Thank you for the excellent work.' She left me then. Clearly I had given her much food for thought.

So, in due course, a meeting was called in Sam Ballard's room to consider the intake of new pupils into Chambers. Those present were Rumpole, Erskine-Brown and Hoskins, a grey and somewhat fussy barrister, much worried by the expensive upbringing of his numerous daughters.

'Elizabeth Probert,' Ballard, Q.C., being in the Chair, read out the next name on his list. 'Does anyone know her?'

'I have seen her hanging about the clerk's room,' Erskine-Brown admitted. 'Remove the glasses and she might have a certain elfin charm.' Poor old Claude was ever hopelessly susceptible to a whiff of beauty in a lady barrister. 'I wonder if she could help me with my County Court practice . . .'

'That's all you think about, Erskine-Brown!' Hoskins sounded disapproving. 'Wine, women and your County Court practice.'

'That is distinctly unfair!'

'So far as I remember your wife didn't care for Fiona Allways.' Hoskins reminded him of his moment of tenderness for a young lady barrister now married to a merchant banker and living in Cheltenham.

'Yes. Well. Of course, Phillida can't be here today. She's got a long firm fraud in Doncaster,' Claude apologized for his wife.

'She might not take to anyone who looked at all elfin without her glasses.' Hoskins struck a further warning note.

'It was just a casual observation . . .'

'And I'm not sure we want any new intake in Chambers. Even in the form of pupils. I mean, is there enough work to go round? I speak as a member with daughters to support,' Hoskins reminded us.

'Thinking the matter over'—Erskine-Brown was clearly losing his bottle—'I'm afraid Philly might be rather against her.'

It was then that I struck my blow for the highly qualified Mizz. 'I would be against her too,' I said, 'if it weren't for the name. Ballard, isn't that canon you admire so tremendously, the one we all read in the *Church Times*, called Probert?'

'You mean she's some relation?' Ballard was clearly excited.

'She hasn't said she isn't.'

'Not his daughter.' By now he was positively awestruck.

'She hasn't denied it.'

Then Ballard looked like one whose eyes had seen his and my salvation. 'Then Elizabeth Probert comes from a family with enormously sound views on the religious virtue of retribution as part of our criminal law. I see her as an admirable pupil for Rumpole!'

'You think he might teach her some of his courtroom antics?' Erskine-Brown sounded sceptical.

'I think she might'—Ballard spoke with deep conviction —'just possibly save his soul!'

So it came about that I was driven to my next conference at Brixton Prison in a very small runabout, something like a swaying biscuit box, referred to by Mizz Probert as her *Deux Chevaux*, and I supposed there was something to be said for having a pupil on wheels. Apart from the matter of transport, there was nothing particularly new or unusual about the conference in question, for I had once again been summoned to the aid of Hugh Snakelegs Timson who had, once again, been found in possession of a quantity of property alleged to have been stolen. Once again, D.I. Broome and D.C. Cosgrove had called at the Bromley semi to find the Cortina parked out in the street, and the lock-up garage full of cases of a fine wine, none other than St Emilion Château Cheval Blanc 1971.

'Hugh Timson seems to be always getting into trouble.' Mizz Probert was steering us, with a good deal of dexterity, round the Elephant and Castle.

'I suppose he takes the usual business risks.'

'Have you ever found out the root of the problem?'

'The root of the problem would seem to be Detective Inspector Broome who's rapidly becoming the terror of the Timsons.'

'I bet you'll find that he comes from a broken home.'

'Inspector Broome? Probably.'

'No. I meant Hugh Timson. In an inner-city area. With an anti-social norm among his peer group, most likely. He must always have felt alienated from society.'

Was Mizz Probert right, and is it nurture and not nature that shapes our ends? I suppose I was brought up in appalling conditions, in an ice-cold vicarage with no mod cons or central heating. My old father, being a priest of the Church of England, had only the sketchiest notion of morality, and my mother was too occupied with jam-making and the Women's Institute to notice my existence. Is it any real wonder that I have taken to crime?

When we had met Mr Bernard at the gates of Brixton and settled down with the ex-Mr Debonair in the interview room, I thought I would put Mizz Probert's theories to the test. 'Come from a broken home, did you?' I asked Snakelegs.

'Broken home?' The client looked displeased. 'I don't know what you mean. Mum and Dad was married forty years, and he never so much as looked at another woman. Hetty and I, we're the same. What you on about, Mr Rumpole?'

'At least you were born in an inner-city area.'

'My old dad wouldn't have tolerated it. Bromley was really nice in those days. More green fields and that. What's it got to do with my case?'

'Not much. Just setting my pupil's mind at rest. Why was your garage being used as a cellar for fine wines?'

'Bit of good stuff, was it?' Snakelegs seemed proud of the fact.

Didn't you try it?'

'Teetotal, me. You know that.' The client sounded shocked. 'Although the wife, she will take a drop of tawny port at Christmas. Not that I think it's right. It's drink that leads to crime. We all know that, don't we, Mr Rumpole?'

'So *how* . . . ?'

'Well, I got them all a bit cheap. Not for myself, you understand. They'd be no good for Hetty and me. But I thought it was a drop of stuff I might sell on to anyone having a bit of a wedding—anything like that.'

'And *where* did you get it? The Judge might be curious to know.' I felt a sudden weariness, such as whoever it was among the ancient Greeks who had just pushed a stone up a hill, and seen it come rolling down again for the three-millionth time, must have felt. It was one thing to win a case because the prosecution evidence wasn't strong enough for a conviction. It was another, and far more depressing matter, to be putting forward the same distinctly shop-worn defence throughout a working life. I just hoped to God that Snakelegs wasn't going to babble on about a man in a pub.

'Well, there was this fellow what I ran into down the Needle Arms . . . What's the matter, Mr Rumpole?'

'Please, Snakelegs'—my boredom must have become evident—'can't we have some sort of variation? Judge Bullingham's getting tremendously tired of that story.'

'Bullingham?' Snakelegs was understandably alarmed. 'We're not getting him again, are we?'

'Not if I can help it. This character in the Needle Arms —not anyone whose name you happen to remember?' I lit a small cigar and waited in hope.

'Afraid I can't help you there, Mr Rumpole.'

'You can't help me? And he sold you all these crates of stuff. Who's got the list of exhibits?' Mizz Probert handed it to me immediately. 'Cheval Blanc. St Emilion . . .'

'No. That's wasn't the name. It was more like, something Irish . . .' Snakelegs looked at me. 'What's our chances, Mr Rumpole?'

'Our chances?' I gave him my considered opinion. 'Well, you've heard about snowballs in hell?'

'You saw me right last time.'

'Last time the losers didn't come forward to claim their property.'

'Because of the insurance.' Liz filled in the details.

'Mizz Probert remembers. This time the loser of the wine is principal witness for the Prosecution.'

'Martyn Vanberry.' Bernard was looking at the prosecution witness statements. First among them was indeed the proprietor of Vanberry's—purveyors of fine wines, Prentice Alley in the City of London—not a specially attractive character, the highly respectable public-school bully.

Back in the *Deux Chevaux,* I felt a little guilty about disillusioning Liz Probert and depriving Snakelegs of an unhappy childhood. I complimented her on her runabout and asked if it weren't by any chance a present from her father, the Canon. It was then that she told me that her

father was, in fact, the leader of the South-East London
Council widely known as Red Ron Probert. He was a man,
no doubt, whose own article of religion was the divine
right of the local Labour Party to govern that area of London, and he frequently appeared on television chat-shows
to speak up for minority rights. His ideal voter was apparently an immigrant Eskimo lesbian, who strongly supported the I.R.A.

'Is there anything wrong with Ron Probert being my father?'

'Nothing at all provided you don't chatter about it to our
learned Head of Chambers. Do you think you could point
this machine in the general direction of Luton? I'm going
to take a nap.'

'What are we doing in Luton?'

'Seeing a witness.'

'I thought we weren't allowed to see witnesses.'

'This is an expert witness. We're allowed to see them.'

Luton is not exactly one of the Jewels of Southern England. American tourists don't brave the terrorists to loiter
in its elegant parks or snap each other in the Cathedral
Close, but its inhabitants seem friendly enough and the first
police officer we met was delighted to direct us to the
Monty Mantis Service Station. It was a large and clearly
thriving concern, selling not only petrol but new and sec-
ondhand cars, cuddly toys, garden furniture, blow-up pad-
dling pools, furry dice and anoraks. The proprietor
remembered my face from Vanberry's, and when I gave
him a hint of what we wanted, invited us into his luxur-
iously appointed office, where we sat on plastic zebra-skin
covered furniture, gazing at pictures of peeing children and
crying clowns, while he poured us out a couple of glasses

of Cheval Blanc from his own cellar, so that I might understand the experience. When I made my delight clear, he said it was always a pleasure to meet a genuine enthusiast.

'And you, Mr Mantis,' I ventured to ask him, 'I've been wondering how *you* became so extraordinarily well informed in wine lore. I mean, where did you get your training?'

'Day trip to Boulogne. 1963. With the Luton Technical.' He refilled our glasses. 'Unattractive bunch of kids, we must have been. Full of terminal acne and lavatory jokes. Enough to drive "sir" what took us into the funny farm. We were all off giving him the slip. Trying to chase girls that didn't exist, or was even fatter and spottier than the local talent round the Wimpy. Anyway, I ended up in the station buffet for some reason, and spent what I'd been saving up for an unavailable knees' trembler, if you'll pardon my French, Miss Probert. I bought a half bottle. God knows what it was. *Ordinaire de la Gare,* French railways perpetual standby. And there was I, brought up on Tizer and Coke that tastes of old pennies, and sweet tea you could stand the spoon up in, and it came as a bit of a revelation to me, Mr Rumpole.'

'Tasting of Flora and the country green... Dance, and Provençal song, and sunburnt mirth!...'

'Shame you can't ever talk about the stuff without sounding like them toffee noses round Vanberry's. Well, I bought four bottles and kept a cellar under my bed and shared it out in toothmugs with a chosen few. Then when I started work at the garage, I didn't go round the pub Friday nights. I began investing...'

'And acquired your knowledge?'

'I don't know football teams, you see. Haven't got a clue about the Cup. But I reckon I know my vintages.'

'Such as the Cheval Blanc 1971.' I sampled it again.

'All right, is it?'

'It seems perfectly all right.'

'You're sure you won't, Miss Probert?'

'I never have.'

Liz Probert, I thought, a hard worker, with all the puritanism of youth.

'This is better, perhaps'—I held my glass to the light—'than the Cheval Blanc round Vanberry's?'

Monty Mantis looked at me then and began to laugh. It was not unkind, but genuinely amused laughter, coming from a man who no doubt knew his wines.

Our clerk, Henry, is a star of his local amateur dramatic society, and is famous, as I understand it, for the Noël Coward roles he undertakes. Henry's life in the theatre has its uses for us as a fellow Thespian is Miss Osgood, who, when she is not appearing in some role made famous by the late Gertrude Lawrence, is in charge of the lists down the Old Bailey. Miss Osgood can exercise some sort of control on which case comes before which judge, and when the wheel of fortune spins to decide such matters, she can sometimes lay a finger on it. I had fortunately hit on a time when Henry and Miss Osgood were playing opposite each other in *Private Lives* and I asked our clerk to use his best endeavours with his co-star to see that *R*. v. *Snakelegs Timson* did not come up for trial before Judge Bullingham. On the night before the hearing, Henry rang Froxbury Court to give me the glad news that the case was fixed to come on before a judge known to his many friends and admirers as Moley Molesworth.

'A wonderful judge for us,' I told Bernard and Liz Probert as we assembled at the door of the Court the next morning. 'I'll have Moley eating out of my hand. Mildest-mannered chap that ever thought in terms of probation.'

'For receiving stolen wine?' Bernard sounded doubtful.

'Oh, yes. I shouldn't be at all surprised. Community service is his equivalent of dispatching chaps to the galleys.'

But just when everything seemed set fair, a cloud no bigger than a man's hand blew up in the shape of Miss Osgood, who came to announce that his Honour Judge Molesworth was confined to bed with a severe cold and would not, therefore, be trying Snakelegs.

'A severe cold? What's the matter with the old idiot, can't he wrap up warm?'

'It's all right, Mr Rumpole. We can transfer you to another Court immediately.' Miss Osgood smiled with the charm of the late Gertrude Lawrence. 'Judge Bullingham's free.'

Why is it that whoever dishes out severe colds invariably gives them to the wrong person?

'Mr Rumpole. Do you wish to detain this gentleman in the witness-box?'

The Bull had clearly recognized Snakelegs, and remembered the antiques in the frozen peas. He looked with equal disfavour at the dock and at defending counsel. It was only when his eye lit upon young Tristram Paulet for the Prosecution, or the chief prosecution witness, Martyn Vanberry, who was now standing, at the end of his evidence-in-chief, awaiting my attention, that he exposed his yellowing teeth in that appalling smirk which represents Bullingham's nearest approximation to moments of charm.

'I have one or two questions for Mr Vanberry,' I told him.

'Oh'—his Lordship seemed surprised—'is there any dispute that your client, Timson, had this gentleman's wine in his possession?'

'No dispute about that, my Lord.'

'Then to what issue in this case can your questions possibly be directed?'

I was tempted to tell the old darling that if he sat very quietly and paid close attention he might, just possibly, find out. Instead, I said that my questions would concern my client's guilt or innocence, a matter which might be of some interest to the Jury. And then, before the Bull could get his breath to bellow, I asked Mr Vanberry if the wine he lost was insured.

'Of course. I had it fully insured.'

'As a prudent businessman?'

'I hope I am that, my Lord,' Vanberry appealed to the Judge, who gave his ghastly smile and murmured as unctuously as possible, 'I'm sure you are, Mr Vanberry. I am perfectly sure you are.'

'And how long have you been trading as a wine merchant in Prentice Alley in the City of London?' I went on hacking away.

'Just three years, my Lord.'

'And done extremely well! In such a short time.' The Bull was still smirking.

'We have been lucky, my Lord, and I think we've been dependable.'

'Before that, where were you trading?' I interrupted the love duet between the witness and the Bench.

'I was selling pictures. As a matter of fact I had a shop in Chelsea; we specialized in nineteenth-century watercolours, my Lord.'

'The name of the business?'

'Vanberry Fine Arts.'

'Manage to find any insurance claims for Vanberry Fine Arts . . . ?' I turned to whisper to Bernard, but it seemed he was still making inquiries. Only one thing to do then, pick up a blank sheet of paper, study it closely and ask the next question looking as though you had all the answers in your hands. Sometimes, it was to be admitted, the old-fashioned ways are best.

'I must put it to you that Vanberry Fine Arts made a substantial insurance claim in respect of the King's Road premises.'

'We had a serious break-in and most of our stock was stolen. Of course I had to make a claim, my Lord.' Vanberry still preferred to talk to his friend, the Bull, but at least he had been forced by the information he thought I had to come out with some part of the truth.

'You seem to be somewhat prone to serious break-ins, Mr Vanberry,' I suggested, whereupon the Bull came in dead on cue with, 'It's the rising tide of lawlessness that is threatening to engulf us all. You should know that better than anyone, Mr Rumpole!'

I thought it best to ignore this, so I then called on the Usher to produce Exhibit 34, which was, in fact, one of the bottles of allegedly stolen wine.

'You're not proposing to sample it, I hope, Mr Rumpole?' The Bull tried heavy sarcasm and the Jury and the prosecution counsel laughed obediently.

'I'm making no application to do so at the moment,' I reassured him. 'Mr Vanberry. You say this bottle contains vintage claret of a high quality?'

'It does, my Lord.'

'Retailing at what price?'

'I think around fifty pounds a bottle.'

'And insured for . . . ?'

'I believe we insured it for the retail price. Such a wine would be hard to replace.'

'Of course it would. It's a particularly fine vintage of the . . . What did you say it was?' The Bull charged into the arena.

'Cheval Blanc, my Lord.'

'And we all know what you have to pay for a really fine Burgundy nowadays, don't we, Members of the Jury?'

The Members of the Jury—an assortment of young unemployed blacks, puzzled old-age pensioners from Hackney and grey-haired cleaning ladies—looked at the Judge and seemed to find his question mystifying.

'It's a claret, my Lord. Not a Burgundy,' Vanberry corrected the Judge, as I thought unwisely.

'A claret. Yes, of course it is. Didn't I say that? Yes, well. Let's get on with it, Mr Rumpole.' Bullingham was not pleased.

'You lost some fifty cases. It was insured for six hundred pounds a case, you say?'

'That is so.'

'So you recovered some thirty thousand pounds from your insurers?'

'There was a considerable loss . . .'

'To your insurance company?'

'And a considerable profit to whoever dealt with it illegally,' the Bull couldn't resist saying, so I thought it about time he was given a flutter of the cape: 'My Lord. I have an application to make in respect of Exhibit 34.'

'Oh, very well. Make it then.' The Judge closed his eyes and prepared to be bored.

'I wish to apply to the Court to open this bottle of alleged Cheval Blanc.'

'You're not serious?' The Bull's eyes opened.

'Your Lordship seemed to have the possibility in mind...'

'Mr Rumpole!'—I watched the familiar sight of the deep purple falling on the Bullingham countenance—'from time to time the weight of these grave proceedings at the Old Bailey may be lifted when the Judge makes a joke. One doesn't do it often. One seldom can. But one likes to do it whenever possible. I was making a *joke*, Mr Rumpole!'

'I'm sure we're all grateful for your Lordship's levity,' I assured him, 'but I'm entirely serious. My learned pupil, Mizz Probert, has come equipped with a corkscrew.'

'Mr Rumpole!'—the Judge was exercising almost superhuman self-control—'may I get this quite clear. What would be your purpose in opening this bottle?'

'The purpose of tasting it, my Lord.'

It was then, of course, that the short Bullingham fuse set off the explosion. 'This is a court of law, Mr Rumpole,' he almost shouted. 'This is not a bar-room! I have sat here for a long time, far too long in my opinion, listening to your cross-examination of this unfortunate gentleman who has, as the Jury may well find, suffered at the hands of your client. But I do not intend to sit here, Mr Rumpole, while you drink the exhibits!'

'Not "drink"'—I tried to calm the Bull—'"taste", my Lord. And may I say this: if the Defence is to be denied the opportunity of tasting a vital exhibit, that would be a breach of our fundamental liberties! The principles we have fought for ever since the days of Magna Carta. In that event I would have to make an immediate application to the Court of Appeal.'

'The Court of Appeal, did you say?' I had mentioned the only institution which can bring the Bull to heel—he

dreads criticism by the Lords of Appeal in Ordinary which
might well get reported in *The Times*. 'You would take the
matter up to the Court of Appeal?' he repeated, somewhat
aghast.

'This afternoon, my Lord.'

'That's what you'd do?'

'Without hesitation, my Lord.'

'What do you say about this, Mr Tristram Paulet?' The
Judge turned for help to the Prosecution.

'My Lord. I'm sure the Court would not wish my learned
friend to have any cause for complaint, however frivolous.
And it might be better not to delay matters by an application
to the Court of Appeal.' Paulet is one of Nature's old Eton-
ians, but I blessed him for his words which were also welcomed by the Bull. 'Exactly what was in *my* mind, Mr
Tristram Paulet!' the Judge discovered. 'Very well, Mr
Rumpole. In the quite exceptional circumstances of this
case, the Court is prepared to give you leave to taste . . .'

So, in a sense, the party was on. Mizz Probert produced
a corkscrew from her handbag. I opened the bottle, a matter in which I have had some practice, and asked the Judge
and my learned friend, Mr Paulet, to join me. The Usher
brought three of the thick tumblers which are used to carry
water to hoarse barristers or fainting witnesses. While this
operation was being carried out, my eye lighted on Martyn
Vanberry in the witness-box—he looked suddenly older,
his expensive tan had turned sallow, and I saw his forehead
shining with sweat. He opened his mouth, but no sound of
any particular significance emerged. And so, in the ensuing silence, Tristram Paulet sniffed doubtfully at his glass,
the Bull took a short swig and looked enigmatic, and I
tasted and held the wine long enough in my mouth to be

certain. It was with considerable relief that I realized that
the label on the bottle was an unreliable witness, for the
taste was all too familiar—that of Château Thames Embankment 1985, a particularly brutal year.

'Rumpole's got a pupil.'

'I hope he's an apt pupil.'

'It's not a he. It's a she.'

'A she. Oh, really, Rumpole?' Dodo Mackintosh clicked
her knitting needles and looked at me with deep suspicion.

'A Mizz Liz Probert . . .'

'You call her Liz? The cross-examination continued.

'No. I call her Mizz.'

'Is she a middle-aged person?'

'About twenty-three. Is that middle-aged nowadays?'

'And is Hilda quite happy about that, do you think?'
Dodo asked me, and not my wife, the question.

'Hilda doesn't look for happiness.'

'Oh. What does she look for?'

'The responsibilities of command.' I raised a respectful
glass of Chateau Fleet Street at She Who Must Be Obeyed.
There was a brief silence broken only by the clicking of
needles, and then Dodo said, 'Don't you want to know
what this Liz Probert is like, Hilda?'

'Not particularly.'

It was at this moment that the telephone rang and I
picked it up to hear the voice of a young man called Ken
Eastham, who worked at Vanberry's. He wanted, it
seemed, to ask my legal advice. I spoke to him whilst
Hilda and her old friend, Dodo Mackintosh, speculated on
the subject of my new pupil. When the call was over, I put
down the telephone after thanking Mr Eastham from the

bottom of my heart. It's rare, in any experience, for anyone
to care enormously for justice.

'Well, Rumpole, you look extremely full of yourself,'
Hilda said as I dialled Mr Bernard's number to warn him
that we might be calling another witness.

'No doubt he is full of himself'—Dodo put in her two
penn'orth—'having a young pupil to trot around with.'

'Dodo's coming down to the Old Bailey tomorrow,
Rumpole,' Hilda warned me. 'She's tremendously keen to
see you in action.'

In fact Dodo Mackintosh's view of Rumpole in action was
fairly short-lived. She arrived early at my Chambers, extremely early, and Henry told her that I was still breakfast-
ing at the Taste-Ee-Bite in Fleet Street. Indeed I was then
tucking into the full British with Mizz Probert, to whom I
was explaining the position of the vagal nerve in the neck,
which can be so pressed during a domestic fracas that death
may ensue unintentionally. (I secured an acquittal for Gimlett, a Kilburn grocer, armed with this knowledge—the
matter is described later in this very volume.) At any rate I
had one hand placed casually about Mizz Probert's neck
explaining the medical aspect of the matter when Dodo
Mackintosh entered the Taste-Ee-Bite, took in the scene,
put the worst possible construction on the events, uttered
the words 'Rumpole in action! Poor Hilda' in a tragic and
piercing whisper and made a hasty exit. This was, of
course, a matter which would be referred to later.

I did not, as I think wisely, put Snakelegs Timson in the
witness-box, but I had told Mr Bernard to get a witness
summons delivered to the wine correspondent of the *Sunday Mercury* and took the considerable risk of calling her.

When she was in the box I got the Bull's permission to allow her to taste a glass of the wine which the Prosecution claimed was stolen Château Cheval Blanc, although I had it presented to her in an anonymous tumbler. She held it up to the light, squinted at it through her monocle and then took a mouthful, which I told her she would have to swallow, however painful she found it, as we had no 'expectoration corner'. At which point Tristram Paulet muttered a warning not to lead the witness.

'Certainly not! In your own words, would you describe the wine you have just tasted?'

'Is it worth describing?' Miss Bird asked, having swallowed with distaste.

'My client's liberty may depend on it,' I looked meaningfully at the Jury.

'It's a rough and, I would say, crude Bordeaux-type of mixed origins. It may well contain some product of North Africa. It's too young and drinking it would amount to infanticide had its quality not made such considerations irrelevant.'

'Have you met such a wine before?'

'I believe it is served in certain bars in this part of London to the more poorly paid members of the legal profession.'

'Would you price it at fifty pounds a bottle?' this poorly paid member asked.

'You're joking!'

'It is not I that made the joke, Miss Bird.'

I could see Vanberry, who was looking even more depressed and anxious than he had the day before, pass a note to the prosecuting solicitor. Meanwhile, Birdie gave me her answer. 'It would be daylight robbery to charge more than two pounds.'

'Yes. Thank you, Miss Bird. Just wait there, will you?' I sat down and Tristram Paulet rose to cross-examine, armed with Vanberry's note.

'Miss Bird. The wine you have tasted came from a bottle labelled Cheval Blanc 1971. I take it you don't think that is its correct description.'

'Certainly not!' The admirable Birdie would have none of it.

'At a blind tasting which took place at Mr Vanberry's shop, did you not identify a Cheval Blanc 1971?' There was a considerable pause after this question, during which Miss Bird looked understandably uncomfortable.

'I had my doubts about it,' she explained at last.

'But did you not identify it?'

'Yes. I did.' The witness was reluctant, but Paulet had got all he wanted. He sat down with a 'thank you, Miss Bird', and I climbed to my hindlegs to repair the damage in re-examination.

'Miss Bird, on that occasion, were you competing against a Mr Monty Mantis, a garage owner of Luton, in the blind-tasting contest?

'Yes. I was.'

'Did he express a poor opinion of the alleged Cheval Blanc?'

'He did.'

'But were you encouraged by Mr Martyn Vanberry to identify it as a fine claret by a number of hints and clues?'

'Yes. He was trying to help me a little.' Miss Bird looked doubtfully at the anxious wine merchant sitting in the well of the Court.

'To help you to call it Cheval Blanc?' I suggested.

'I suppose so. Yes.'

'Miss Bird. What was your opinion of Mr Monty Mantis?'

'I thought him a very vulgar little man who probably had no real knowledge of wine.' She had no doubt about it.

'And, thinking that about him, were you particularly anxious to disagree with his opinion?'

'There was a pause while the lady faced up to the question and then said with some candour, 'I suppose I may have been.'

'And you were anxious to win the contest?' Paulet rose to make an objection, but I ploughed on before the Bull could interrupt. 'As Mr Vanberry was clearly helping you to do?'

'I may have wanted to win. Yes,' Miss Bird admitted, and Paulet subsided, discouraged by her answer.

'Looking back on that occasion, do you think you were tasting genuine Cheval Blanc?' It was the only important question in the case and Bullingham and Martyn Vanberry were both staring at the expert, waiting for her answer. When it came it was entirely honest.

'Looking back on it, my Lord, I don't think I was.'

'And today you have told us the truth?'

'Yes.'

'Thank you, Miss Honoria Bird.' And I sat down, with considerable relief.

With Honoria Bird's evidence we had turned the corner. Young Ken Eastham, who had rung me at home, went into the witness-box. He told the Court that Vanberry had a few dozen of the Cheval Blanc, and then a large new consignment arrived from a source he had not heard of before. Martyn Vanberry asked him to set the new bottles apart from the old, but he had already unpacked some of the later consignment, and put a few bottles with the wine already there. Later, almost all the recently delivered 'Chevel Blanc' was stolen, and Martyn Vanberry seemed quite unconcerned at the loss. Subsequently, and by mistake he thought, one of the new bottles of 'Cheval Blanc' must have been used for the blind tasting. When I asked Mr Eastham why he had agreed to give this evidence he said, 'I've done a long training in wine, and I suppose I love the subject. Well, there's not much point in that is there, if there's going to be lies told on the labels.'

'Mr Rumpole'—his Honour Judge Bullingham was now interested, but somewhat puzzled—'I'm not absolutely sure I follow the effect of this evidence. If Mr Vanberry were in the business of selling the inferior stuff we have tasted, and Miss Honoria Bird has tasted, as highly expensive claret surely the deceit would be obvious to anyone drinking...?'

'I'm not suggesting that the wine was in Mr Vanberry's possession for drinking, my Lord.' I was doing my best to help the Bull grasp the situation.

'Well, what on earth did he have it for?'

Of course Vanberry had fixed the burglary at his wine shop just as he had fixed the stealing of his alleged Victorian watercolours, so that he could claim the insurance money on the value of expensive Cheval Blanc, which he never had. No doubt, whoever was asked to remove the swag was instructed to dispose of it on some rubbish tip. Instead it got sold round the pubs in Bromley, where Snakelegs bought it, and was tricked, without his knowledge, into a completely honest transaction, because it was never, in any real sense of the word, stolen property. So I was able to enlighten Bullingham in the presence of the chief prosecution witness, who was soon to become the defendant, in a case of insurance fraud: 'Mr Vanberry didn't ever have this wine for anyone to drink, my Lord. He had it there for someone to steal.'

When the day's work was done I called into the Taste-Ee-Bite again and retired behind the *Standard* with a pot of tea and a toasted bun. At the next table I heard the monotonous tones of Soapy Sam Bollard, Q.C., our Head of Chambers. 'Your daughter's really doing very well. She's with Rumpole, a somewhat elderly member of our Chambers. Perhaps it's mixing with the criminal classes, but Rumpole seems somewhat lacking in a sense of sin. A girl with your daughter's background may well do him some good.'

I could recognize the man he was talking to as Red Ron Probert, Labour Chairman of the South-East London Council. Ballard, who never watches the telly, was apparently unable to recognize Red Ron. Liz's father, it seemed, had come to inquire as to his daughter's progress and our Head of Chambers had invited him to tea.

'I didn't realize who you were at first,' Ballard droned on. 'Of course, you're in mufti!'

'What?' Red Ron seemed surprised.

'Your collar.'

'What's wrong with my collar?'

'Nothing at all,' Ballard hastened to reassure him. 'I'm sure it's very comfortable. I expect you want to look just like an ordinary bloke.'

'Well, I am an ordinary bloke. And I represent thousands of ordinary blokes . . .' Ron was about to deliver one of his well-loved speeches.

'Of course you do! I must say, I'm a tremendous admirer of your work.'

'Are you?' Ron was surprised. 'I thought you lawyers were always Right . . .'

'Not always. Some of them are entirely wrong. But there are a few of us prepared to fight the good fight!'

'On with the revolution!' Ron slightly raised a clenched fist.

'You think it needs *that*'—Ballard was thoughtful—'to awaken a real sense of morality . . . ?'

'Don't you?'

'A revolution in our whole way of thinking? I fear so. I greatly fear so.' Ballard shook his head wisely.

'Fear not, Brother Ballard! We're in this together!' Red Ron rallied our Head of Chambers.

'Of course.' Ballard was puzzled. 'Yes. Brother. Were you in some Anglican Monastic Order?'

'Only the Clerical Workers' Union.' Red Ron laughed at what he took to be a Ballard witticism.

'Clerical Workers? Yes, that, of course.' Ballard joined in the joke. 'Amusing way of putting it.'

'And most of them weren't exactly monastic!'

'Oh dear, yes. There's been a falling off, even among the clergy. I really must tell you . . .'

'Yes, Brother.' Red Ron was prepared to listen.

'Brother! I can't really . . . I should prefer to call you Father. It might be more appropriate.'

'Have it your own way.' Ron seemed to find the mode of address acceptable.

'Father Probert,' Ballard said, very sincerely, 'you have been, for me at any rate, a source of great inspiration!'

I folded my *Standard* then and crept away unnoticed. I felt no need to correct a misunderstanding which seemed to

be so gratifying to both of them, and had had such a bene-
ficial effect on Mizz Probert's legal career.

That night I carried home to Froxbury Court a not unusual treat, that is to say, a bottle of Pommeroy's Château
Thames Embankment. I was opening it with a feeling of
modified satisfaction when Hilda said, 'You look very full
of yourself! I suppose you've won another case.'

'I'm afraid so.' I had the bottle open and was filling a
couple of glasses: '"Oh, for a draught of vintage! that hath
been Cool'd a long age in the deep-delved earth, . . ."' And
then I tasted the wine and didn't spit. 'A crude Bordeaux-
type of mixed origins. On sale to the more poorly paid
members of the legal profession.' I couldn't help laughing.

'What've you got to laugh about, Rumpole?'

'Bollard!'

'Your Head of Chambers.'

'He met Mizz Probert's father. Red Ron. And he still
thought he was some Anglican Divine. He went entirely by
the name on the label . . .' I lowered my nose once more to
the glass. '"Tasting of Flora and the country green . . ."'
Isn't it remarkably quiet around here? I don't seem to hear
the fluting tones of your old childhood chum, Dodo Mackintosh.'

'Dodo's gone home.'

'Dance, and Provençal song, and sunburnt mirth.'

'She's disgusted with you, Rumpole. As a matter of fact,
I told her she'd better go.'

'You told Dodo that?' She Who Must Be Obeyed was
usually clay in Miss Mackintosh's hands.

'She said she'd seen you making up to some girl, in a
tea-room.'

'That's what she said?'

'I told her it was absolutely ridiculous. I really couldn't

imagine a young girl wanting to be made up to by you,
Rumpole!'

'Well. Thank you very much.' I refilled the glass which
had mysteriously emptied:

> 'O for a beaker full of the warm South,
>   Full of the true, the blushful Hippocrene,
>   With beaded bubbles winking at the brim,
>   And purple-stained mouth . . .'

'She said you were in some sort of embrace. I told her
she was seeing things.'

> 'That I might drink, and leave the world unseen,
>   And with thee fade away into the forest dim:
>
> Fade far away, dissolve, and quite forget
>   What thou among the leaves hast never known,
>   The weariness, the fever and the fret . . .'

I must say the words struck me as somewhat comical. At
the idea of my good self and She dancing away into the
mysterious recesses of some wood, the mind, as they say,
boggled.

```
          W A L D E N B O O K S


SALE          1209    103   7379   2/17/92
              REL    2.5    27   10:37:03


PREF NO.       528453673
01 0140126953                      4.50
PREF DISC     4.50 10% OFF         0.45-
              SUBTOTAL             4.05
NEVADA  7.0% TAX                    .28
              TOTAL                4.33
              CASH                 5.03
              CHANGE                .70-
              FV# 0037379



   PREFERRED READERS SAVE EVERY DAY
```

Rumpole and the Old, Old Story

Those of you who may have followed these memoirs which I have scribbled down from time to time (in the privacy of my Chambers during temporary lulls in business—I would not wish She Who Must Be Obeyed to have a sight of them and she studiously avoids any knowledge of their publication) will know that from time to time there is a bit of an East wind blowing around our homestead in Froxbury Court. Sometimes, in fact, the icy winds of Hilda's discontent could best be described as a blizzard, and then, if I can't organize a case in a distant town, I leave almost at dawn to breakfast in the Taste-Ee-Bite in Fleet Street and return as late as possible after a spot of bottled courage in Jack Pommeroy's Wine Bar, although this last expedient never seems to do much to warm up the domestic hearth.

Usually these moments of high drama subside. She Who Must Be Obeyed gives a few brief words of command, all hands snap to it, and the Rumpole marriage sails for a while into somewhat calmer waters. There was a time, however, and not too long ago at that, when the old tramp-steamer, with its heavy load of memories of my various delinquencies and its salt-stained smokestack, seemed to be heading for the rocks. My wife Hilda and I actually came, on one occasion, to the parting of the ways. I cannot decide whether to look back at that dramatic period of my life with nostalgia or regret. I can tell you that it came when I was most intellectually stretched, grappling as I was with one of my most important cases: the curious affair of the alleged attempted murder of Captain Arnold Gleason at the Woodland Folk Garden Centre. And, lest the readers should suspect the presence of some 'other' woman in the case, let me say at once that I have no reputation as a Lothario, that Mizz Liz Probert, about whom my wife's best friend, Dodo Mackintosh, nursed some unworthy suspicions, had not yet appeared at our Chambers, and neither of the two ladies for whom I have in the past entertained some tender feelings, that is to say, Bobby O'Keefe, once of the Women's Auxiliary Air Force, and a young woman named Kathy Trelawny, whom I defended on a drugs charge, had anything to do with the case.* Hilda and I, in fact, severed relations as the direct result of a joke.

We are not great diners-out. By the time I get home from Pommeroy's and remove the winged collar and put on the carpet slippers, preparatory to an evening's work on robbery or sudden death, a scrambled egg or, at best, a grilled

---

*See 'Rumpole and the Alternative Society' in *Rumpole of the Bailey*, Penguin Books, 1978.

chop, is about all we run to. On the night in question, however, Marigold Featherstone, wife of our old Head of Chambers, Sir Guthrie Featherstone, now translated to the Bench—an ermine- and scarlet-clad figure who had everything it takes to be a justice of the Queen's Bench Division except for the slightest talent for making up his mind—had given us a couple of tickets they couldn't use for the Scales of Justice annual dinner at the Savoy. Gatherings of lawyers at the trough are usually to be avoided like the plague, but Hilda was dead set on being among those present on this occasion and, in view of the opportunity offered of hacking away at the Savoy Hotel claret, I didn't oppose her wishes too strenuously. So she got my old soup and fish out of mothballs, cleaned the stains off the jacket with some pungent chemical, renewed a few essential buttons on the dress trousers, and we found ourselves ensconced at a table presided over by another scarlet judge, this time of a somewhat malign and Welsh variety, known as Mr Justice Huw Gwent-Evans, together with his spouse, Lady Gwent-Evans; Claude Erskine-Brown and his better half, Phillida Erskine-Brown, née Trant, the Portia of our Chambers; mixed with an assortment of younger barristers with their wives or live-in companions.

As dinner drew to an end, I discovered that my glass had been refilled at such regular intervals that I was seeing the whole proceedings lit by a kind of golden glow. I also saw, somewhat to my surprise, that She Who Must Be Obeyed was in animated conversation with the Welsh Judge who was regarding her with admiration, his small eyes bright with enjoyment at her lengthy reminiscences of life in the distant days when her Daddy, C. H. Wystan, ruled our Chambers at Equity Court. At long last the proceedings wound to an end and Mr Justice Gwent-Evans pulled out his gold repeater and said, with every appearance of disappointment, 'Good heavens, is that the time? I hate to break up such an extraordinarily enjoyable evening but...'

'The learned Judge is looking at the time.' My voice sounded, from where I sat, pleasantly resonant. I had the cue for one of my best stories, one which has never failed, in my long experience, to set the table on a roar.

'I well remember when old Judge Quentin Starkie at Inner-London Sessions looked at the time. It was during an indecent assault, sort of thing that always went on in the cinemas round Bethnal Green. This girl was giving evidence...' I was conscious of not playing to a particularly good audience. Indeed, Lady Gwent-Evens appeared to dread the outcome of the anecdote. Erskine-Brown stifled a yawn. Phillida looked at me tolerantly, although I knew that the outcome of the story would be no surprise to her. Hilda was stony-faced and the Judge cleared his throat in a warning manner. In spite of all discouragement I carried on, giving my well-known imitation of the witness's fluting tones: '"So he put his hand up my skirt, my Lord. This bloke sitting beside me in the one and nines." Now I mimicked old Judge Starkie's low growl: '"Put his hand up your skirt, did he?"' And then his Honour looks at the clock and finds it's dead on lunchtime. '"Put his hand up your skirt? Well, I suggest we leave it there until ten past two!"'

One of the wives laughed loudly, the other young barristers seemed more moderately amused. Phillida did her best, and there was a weary titter from Claude, but no smiles from the Judge's wife or Hilda. The Welsh wizard looked as though he had just witnessed an act of adultery in Chapel. Erskine-Brown broke the ensuing silence with a

somewhat pointless remark: 'They don't have them nowadays.'

'Indecent assaults in flick houses? Of course they do.
Why, only the other day at Uxbridge...'

'No. I mean one and ninepennies...'

'Perhaps you're right. Let's say it's a joke from my distant past. Not a bad story, though, whenever it happened.'

The Judge rose to his feet in determined manner and
asked his wife if she were ready to go; she told him that
she'd been ready for some time. 'Delighted to meet *you*,
Mrs Rumpole. Quite delightful,' the Judge said before he
left us. 'I do hope we meet you again soon.' I noticed that I
was not included in his eager anticipation of any future
get-together.

'Telling that disgusting story about the girl in the Odeon!'
Hilda sat in the taxi travelling down the Mall, leaving as
much unoccupied seat between us as possible. The temperature had dropped to a point at which your fingers would
fall off if you stayed out in it too long.

'It wasn't the Odeon,' I ventured to correct her. 'It was
the Regal Cinema, Bethnal Green.'

'And you told it for the hundredth time! You must be
getting senile.'

'Old jokes are always welcome. Like old poetry, old
wine, old...' But she interrupted my speech. 'The Judge
didn't know where to look.'

'Mr Justice Gwent-Evans bores for Wales,' I told her. 'A
man with about as many laughs in him as a post-mortem.'

'He was a perfect gentleman, which is more than can be
said for you, Rumpole. Fancy telling a blue joke with the
Judge's wife sitting right beside you!'

'It was the Savoy Hotel, Hilda, not the Chapel in the valley.' At this point our taxi rattled to a halt by a traffic light.

'Wherever it was you made a fine fool of yourself tonight, Rumpole!'

And then, I suppose, something snapped, and the habit of years was broken. I knew it as I opened the taxi door and felt, as I stepped out into the night, like the Count of Monte Cristo when he made his final and perilous escape from the Château D'If. I had at last found freedom. The world was in front of me; behind was Hilda's voice saying, 'What on *earth* are you doing, Rumpole?'

'Saying goodbye,' I told her, as I walked on across St James's Park and never, for one moment, turned back.

The reader will be no doubt relieved to turn from the painful and somewhat sordid world of married life to the more salubrious atmosphere of crime and criminals. Captain Arnold Gleason, ex-soldier and ex-golf club secretary, had become a partner in the Woodland Folk Garden Centre, just outside the large country town of Worsfield, some fifty miles to the West of London. Although he was a man in his sixties, with a prominent stomach and little hair, Captain Gleason must have had some charm for he had married Amanda Gleason, a red-haired beauty some thirty years his junior. He also had a partner, a handsome and youngish member of the Council for the Preservation of Rural England, the Friends of the Earth and such-like organizations dedicated to the saving of hedgerows and the protection of the badger, with a name like the hero of a Victorian novelette, Hugo Lutterworth. When I tell you that, from time to time, Mr Lutterworth and Mrs Gleason were seen kissing in the greenhouses, you will readily understand that the

scene at Woodland Folk Garden Centre was set for a trian-
gular drama and a nasty accident.

The accident came about when Captain Gleason got into
his Volvo Estate car to leave the Garden Centre. He drove
carefully, as was apparently his practice, out of the Garden
gates and started down a steepish hill which led to a junc-
tion with the main road to Worsfield. As the car descended,
it became out of control as the braking system had clearly
failed. With considerable presence of mind, the Captain
steered into an area half-way down the hill used by the
Garden Centre for assorted statues. He crashed into a sun-
dial, ricocheted off a couple of heavy cherubs and finally
came to rest among the gnomes. Captain Gleason mercifully escaped with nothing more than a mild concussion, a
cut forehead, a number of bruises and a considerably battered Volvo Estate. Subsequent inquiries by the industrious
Detective Inspector Rolph of the Worsfield force led to the
arrest of young Hugo Lutterworth on a charge of attempted
murder.

Lutterworth had one small piece of luck. His solicitor, a
grey-haired and generally harmless Mr Dennis Driscoll,
knew absolutely nothing about crime. He had however met
Mr Bernard, one of my regular customers, and the long-
time representative of the Timson family, over a matter of
conveyancing. They struck up a friendship, and when Mr
Driscoll happened to mention that he had an attempted
murder on his hands, Bernard wisely replied, 'Then Rumpole's your man,' or uttered words to the like effect. I
suppose if Captain Gleason had crashed into a lorry on the
main road and thereby met his end, there would have been
talk of taking in some querulous Q.C., some artificial silk
to lead me (and this, despite the success I scored, some
years ago now, in the Penge Bungalow Murders, alone and

without a leader). As it was such a peculiarly unsuccessful attempt, I was allowed to handle the matter on my own.

The first time I saw Hugo Lutterworth was in a cell in Worsfield Gaol, a small Victorian prison with no proper interviewing facilities. He was a fine-featured young man with an aureole of fair hair, so that he looked like Sir Galahad, or Lancelot or any of the rather over-sensitive chaps from the Table Round in a Pre-Raphaelite painting. Mr Driscoll asked me what I thought the chances of a conviction were, bearing in mind that the evidence clearly showed that the brakes in Captain Gleason's Volvo Estate had been tampered with. What I thought was that, even if the Prosecution were conducted by a first-year law student with a serious speech impediment, we were likely to be defeated. What I said was, 'I think we face ... certain difficulties. You and Captain Gleason,' I asked Lutterworth, 'were partners in the Garden Centre business?'

'I drew up the partnership agreement'—Driscoll was fumbling among his papers, happy to be back in a branch of the law he understood—'I think I've got it here.'

'Never mind about that now, Mr Driscoll.' I turned to Hugo to ask him the four-thousand-dollar question: 'And you were clearly having a bit of a walk-out with Gleason's wife?'

'I don't want Amanda's name mentioned.' The man was clearly keen on a place in a stained-glass window.

'You may not, old darling, but the Prosecution are going to mention it every ten minutes. Listen! Someone surely drained the fluid from the brakes in Gleason's car. There's no dispute about that.'

'No dispute at all,' Driscoll agreed.

'Well, what we want to know is, was that someone

you?' It was clearly a tactless question. Hugo turned from
me to ask Mr Driscoll if Amanda Gleason was all right.

'No one tampered with *her* brakes,' I was able to reassure him.

'She hasn't been questioned, has she? Not...not arrested?'

'There's no statement from Mrs Gleason among the
prosecution documents.'

'They're not going to arrest her?'

'Not...as far as we know.'

'Can't we find out?'

'I suppose Mr Driscoll could have a word with the prosecution solicitor,' I suggested. 'Just in an idle chat on the
phone, couldn't you, Driscoll? See if there's any intention
of proceeding against Mrs Gleason for any offence...'

'I can't decide anything until I know about Amanda,'
Hugo Lutterworth told us, and I wondered, idly but aloud,
what offence he thought she might be charged with.

'I'd rather not say anything'—my client looked nobly
resolute—'not till I'm sure Amanda's safe. Do you understand?'

'No, Mr Lutterworth'—I was beginning to lose patience
with all this nobility—'I'm not at all sure that I do understand. This isn't *Gardeners' Question Time,* you know. I
didn't come all this way for a nice chat about the herba-
ceous border. We're here to discuss matters of life and
death.'

And then he gave me an answer which struck a kind of
chill into the air of the over-centrally-heated cell. 'Gardening is really a matter of life and death,' he told us. 'Things
either do well, or you just have to pull them up and throw
them on the bonfire. There's no room for mercy in garden-

ing.' When we left our client he was going to consider
taking us into his confidence once he had established that
his precious Amanda Gleason was in the clear; but I
thought that if he talked as ruthlessly about Captain Gleason's 'accident' as he had about gardening I might be saying goodbye to Sir Lancelot for about five years.

While we were in Worsfield I asked Mr Driscoll to show
me the scene of the crime. The Garden Centre was surprisingly large and seemed well cared for. The slope in front of
the gates was fairly steep, and led down to the busy junc-
tion where heavy lorries were frequently passing. My instructing solicitor took in all these facts and said, 'It's so
out of Lutterworth's character.'

'Know him well, do you?'

'Oh, for years. And his father too. You know I always
thought Hugo was almost painfully honest. That's why he
needed a bit of protection in the partnership agreement.'

'Old Sir Lancelot was probably pretty honest,' I told
him, 'until he started messing around with Queen Guinevere.'

'I suppose if Hugo gets sent away, Gleason'll have to
sell this place.' We had wandered into the gates of the
Garden Centre and were standing in the Cheap and Cheerful Shrub Department. 'One of those horrible great supermarkets has been after this site for years. Hugo was dead
against selling. He'd built up the business, really. And he
lived for his flowers. I say, we had better go, this is rather
embarrassing.'

Mr Driscoll was looking out towards the hardy peren-
nials. I saw an elderly, ill-tempered-looking man, walking
with a stick. Beside him was a red-haired beauty, pale and
with that rather self-conscious air of spirituality, which
makes Pre-Raphaelite pictures so irritating. She walked

with her arm in his; Queen Guinevere was making a fuss of King Arnold. Domestic harmony seemed to have been restored.

I am running ahead of myself. My pre-trial visit to Worsfield Gaol occurred after my separation from Mrs Horace Rumpole. I had walked away from the taxi across the park with a lightness of step and a curious feeling of elation which I hadn't felt, perhaps, since the Jury brought in their not guilty verdict in the Penge Bungalow Murders. As I walked past the sleeping pelicans and towards Big Ben and shivered slightly in the night air, I began to consider the question of lodgings for the night. At first, in my enthusiasm, I considered the Savoy, but I soon remembered that very few people are able to stay at that inn on legal aid. So I turned my footsteps towards what I now regarded as my real home, Equity Court in the Temple, London E.C.4.

I had no doubt that my separation from Hilda was then permanent. What is a man, after all, but his old jokes, and to be matched with a wife who spurned them seemed to me a fate considerably worse than death. As I walked I repeated some lines by Percy Bysshe Shelley not, for some reason, known to Sir Arthur Quiller-Couch or included in my old India-paper edition of *The Oxford Book of English Verse*. Rather an irritating young man in many ways, Percy Bysshe, and unable to hold a candle to the Great Wordsworth, but he had some telling phrases on the subject of marriage, the 'beaten road' he called it:

> Which those poor slaves with weary footsteps
> tread,
> Who travel to their home among the dead
> By the broad highway of the world, and so

With one chained friend, perhaps a jealous foe,
The dreariest and the longest journey go.

My own journey was to freedom and Equity Court, and
then I remembered a few minor drawbacks about the place.
Our Head of Chambers, Soapy Sam Ballard, Q.C., was
intent on declaring the place a smoke-free zone, banning
all cheroots, panatellas, whiffs and fags, so that our
Chambers might, as he put it, stand shoulder to shoulder
with the Clean Air Brigade. He was also constantly re-
minding us that the lease specified that our home from
home should be used 'for business purposes only', and not
for any form of domestic life. A fellow named Jeffrey
Mungo had recently been evicted from his Chambers in
Lincoln's Inn for using them as a bedsitter. Despite this
terrible warning, I thought I could probably settle fairly
comfortably into my room at Equity Court, and Ballard
would be none the wiser.

It cannot be said, however, that the suspicions of our
Head of Chambers were not aroused. At our next
Chambers meeting when we assembled to discuss the vital
questions of the hour (Dianne's request for a rise in salary
to keep up with the increased cost of nail varnish and
women's magazines, or the escalating consumption of
Nescafé), Ballard's desk was littered with a number of exhibits: Item One, a yellowish shaving-brush, still damp;
Item Two, one tub of shaving soap; Item Three, one
safety-razor (Gillette) and a slightly rusted blade. As those
present gazed upon these articles in some bewilderment,
Ballard opened the proceedings on a solemn note.

'Standards in Chambers,' he told us, 'must be kept up.
We must give the impression of a tight and happy ship to
the solicitors who visit us . . .'

'Aye, aye, Cap'n!' I felt it was appropriate to mutter.

'I was hearing of a set in Lincoln's Inn, where they had trouble with a tenant *cooking* in his room.' Ballard ignored my interruption and then Uncle Tom (T. C. Rowley, our oldest and briefless inhabitant) gave us a passage from his memoirs: 'Old Maurice MacKay had a pupil from Persia, I recollect. This fellow gave a birthday party and roasted half a sheep in the middle of Maurice's Turkey carpet.' Whereupon Ballard, feeling perhaps, that the case might be diverted into other channels, called our attention to the exhibits. 'These things'—he glanced at them with distaste— 'were found in the upstairs lavatory when the cleaning lady arrived this morning. The discovery was immediately reported to our clerk, Henry, who took them into his custody. Does anyone lay claim to them? They seem to be articles of antique shaving-tackle.'

'Well, they're certainly not mine,' Portia assured us.

'Of course they didn't have takeaway dinners in those days . . .' Uncle Tom rambled on. 'He ended up as a Prime Minister somewhere.'

'Who did?' Erskine-Brown asked.

'Old Maurice Mackay's pupil. The one who cooked the sheep . . .'

'Rumpole'—Ballard reasserted his command—'do you know anything about these objects?'

'Oh, I never plead guilty, my Lord. Sorry I can't join in the fun, got to get down to a little place in the country.' I rose to leave the meeting.

'Your weekend cottage, Rumpole?' Uncle Tom asked.

'No. Worsfield Gaol.'

I had been summoned to a second conference with Hugo Lutterworth, who had, it seemed, something to impart. Mr Driscoll had been assured there was no prosecution of Mrs

Amanda Gleason intended, but she had, a fact we didn't know at the time, visited Lutterworth in prison. When I called on him, he immediately told me that he had no further need of my services. As you can see, it was not a period of unmitigated success in the Rumpole career.

'You're giving me the sack?' I couldn't help it, my spirits were a little dashed.

'It's just I don't see what you can do for me. It was my fault, you see. Entirely my fault. I know that perfectly well.'

'Couldn't you think of me as an endangered species?'

'What?' Lutterworth was puzzled.

'Avocatus minimus volubilis, the lesser-booming barrister.' I lit a comforting small cigar. 'We're being flushed out of our natural habitats in Crown Courts and before the Magistrates. Batty bureaucrats are going to take away our right to juries and shift the burden of proof and leave us defenceless. Soon we'll be replaced by a couple of chartered accountants and a good computer. If you care for conservation at all, Mr Lutterworth, help save the barrister.' My client looked seriously concerned—not much of a sense of humour in Sir Lancelot. 'Do one thing for me. Let me cross-examine the prosecution witnesses. Let's just see if they've got a case.'

'No harm in that, Hugo.' Mr Driscoll advised him.

'All right.' Hugo Lutterworth thought it over and appeared to be prepared to do something to save the Rumpole from extinction. 'But I can't go into the witness-box and give evidence. I can't say anything that might implicate Amanda.'

So I would be fighting a hopeless battle with one hand tied behind my back. Things did not go entirely smoothly either, in my stay at Equity Court. I had settled down moderately comfortably, and, much to my surprise, there was no message or telephone call from Mrs Hilda Rumpole, and I certainly did not lift the telephone to her. Well, I had little enough time on my hands, what with visits to Worsfield and fending off the unwelcome attentions of our Head of Chambers.

Soapy Sam Ballard, strolling down Fetter Lane, happened to glance into the window of Sam Firkin's barbershop, where he saw Rumpole well-lathered, reclining in a chair and receiving the attention of Sam's cut-throat razor, to be followed by a hot towel and a dash of astringent lotion. From this glimpse he deduced, as Erskine-Brown told me much later, that I must either be in funds to enjoy the luxury of having myself shaved, or, and this seemed to him the more likely explanation, I had lost my shaving-tackle when our cleaning lady, Mrs Slammery, found it apparently abandoned in Chambers' upstairs lavatory.

Resolved to make further inquiries, Ballard called late at Chambers and was rewarded, again my informant is my learned friend, Claude Erskine-Brown, with a glimpse of a bedroom slipper and, above it, a portion of flannel-pyjama'd leg disappearing up a darkened stairway. He went in hot pursuit and beat on Rumpole's locked door, calling out my name repeatedly but answer came there none. One morning he arrived at Chambers early and asked Mrs Slammery, who was sweeping the doorstep, if she had seen me, but she was unable to help in his inquiries. I then turned up, full of bacon and eggs from the Taste-Ee-Bite.

'Rumpole,' Ballard pounced on me. 'What on earth are you doing?'

'Arriving at work,' I assured him, 'as I have been these last forty years.' Not satisfied with this answer he pursued me up to my room and began a minute examination of the broken-springed couch in the corner under the bookcase.

'I see you make yourself quite at home here, Rumpole.' He did his best to sound sarcastic. 'A person could easily sleep on that old Chesterfield.'

'Of course. Care for forty winks?'

'Filthy ash-tray.' He examined the object in question.

'Mrs Slammery hasn't flipped her magic duster yet.'

'I think I'd better warn you. I'm proposing that Chambers becomes a smoke-free zone, in accordance with present-day medical advice.'

'You're what?' I assumed surprise, although, of course, I had wind of Ballard's great plan from Erskine-Brown.

'It's not enough to abstain oneself. It's the other fellows' poison getting up your nostrils.'

'You want to ban smoking in Chambers?' I had to be sure of the prosecution case.

'That is my intention.'

'You can't do that!'

'I imagine the proposal will command pretty general support.'

'It's entirely illegal . . .' I peered back into the distant days at Keble when I had been up on *Constitutional Law in a Nutshell*.

'*What?*' Ballard appeared somewhat taken aback.

'It would be against our ancient rights of freedom, those great principles of justice our fathers fought and bled for. It would be clean contrary to Magna Carta.'

'I bow to your superior knowledge of history, Rumpole. Could you just remind me which clause in Magna Carta deals with smoking?'

'No freeman shall be taken or imprisoned, or destrained

on or exiled or denied the comfort of the occasional cheroot . . . unless by the lawful judgement of his peers!' I gave him the sonorous quotation he asked for. 'I know you're remarkably ignorant of the common law of England, Bollard . . . however encyclopedic your knowledge of the Rent Laws and the Factory Acts.'

'Ah! Talking of which . . .'

'Of what?'

'The Factory Acts.'

'Do we have to?'

'I think we do. These Chambers, Rumpole . . .'

'To which you are a comparative newcomer,' I was at pains to remind him.

'. . . are designated as a place of work. This is not a dosshouse. As your Head, I'm not in the business of running a hotel or some sort of Salvation Army hostel!'

'*What* are you suggesting?' I appeared not to follow his drift.

'I'm simply suggesting that you've been living in here, Rumpole. Sleeping rough.' He darted to a cupboard and pulled the door open, finding nothing but a few books and an umbrella. 'Last night I saw a pyjama leg!'

'I expect you did—on retiring for the night.'

'When I came in here. Late. After dining in Hall with Mr Justice Gwent-Evans. I called into Chambers and I distinctly saw a leg in pyjamas . . . beating a hasty retreat towards *your* room, Rumpole!'

He ended triumphantly, but I only looked at him in a sorrowful and pitying fashion. 'Lay off it, Bollard,' I said.

'It's a matter I intend to pursue, for the benefit of the other tenants.'

'Please! Lay off the booze. That's what I mean. Keep

off the sauce. Cut down on the quaffing! I know what you Benchers get up to at the High Table in Hall. No wonder you've started seeing things!'

'*Things?*' Now he was struggling to follow *my* drift.

'Pyjama legs now'—I ostentatiously lit a small cigar —'in a little while it will be elephants. And pink mice crawling up the curtains. Look, why don't you lie down quietly, sleep it off before you go blundering across the road and make a complete pig's breakfast of a Planning Appeal?'

At this Ballard coughed, equally ostentatiously, and moved towards the door.

'I'm absolutely firm on my principles,' he said. 'This is not the end of the inquiry. Remember Mungo.'

'Mungo?' I pretended ignorance of the Lincoln's Inn squatter.

'He tried to save money by moving into his Chambers. He was found heating tins of Spaghetti Bolognese on the electric fire. Jeffrey Mungo has been given three months' notice to quit!'

'Cut down on the port, Bollard.' I looked at him sadly. 'May you find the strength to kick the habit. I shall pray for you.'

So the first attack by our Head of Chambers was repelled. Some nights later I was seated at my desk by the roaring electric fire as usual of a evening, dining on Château Fleet Street and a takeaway curry, tastefully served on a silver-paper dish from the Star of India, half-way up Chancery Lane. I was reading *The Oxford Book of English Verse,* and had reached what to my mind is one of the old sheep of the Lake District's finest, a sonnet I really had no need to read, as I had its inspiring lines by heart.

It is not to be thought of that the Flood
Of Rumpole's freedom, which, to the open sea
Of the world's praise, from dark antiquity
Hath flowed, 'with pomp of waters unwith-
    stood' . . .
should perish.

Then there was a knock on the door; I hastily covered
my oriental dinner and *The Oxford Book* with a brief, and
Mrs Phillida Erskine-Brown marched in. She had been
working late and was wearing her glasses. 'Ballard knows
all about it,' she said, coming to the point at once.

'Ballard knows all about what?'

Phillida lifted the statement of evidence and exposed my
half-eaten dinner. 'You. Eating these takeaway curries in
chambers.'

'How on earth? . . .'

'Really, Rumpole. After nearly half a century of mixing
with criminals you might have picked up a few tips. At
least don't leave the evidence scattered around your waste-
paper basket. Mrs Slamery's been finding Star of India
placky bags around the place for days.'

'I don't see that it proves a thing. Is there anything
wrong with a fellow, exhausted after a long case, taking a
mouthful of Chicken Bindaloo on his way home?'

'But you're not.'

'Not what?'

'Not on your way home.'

'Perhaps . . . not exactly.' There was no doubt she had hit
upon a weak spot in my defence, and our Portia was now
staring at me over the top of her glasses, barking questions

in the way I had, long ago, taught her to deal with a hostile witness. My lessons had clearly been well learnt.

'What do you mean, *not exactly?* You're either on your way home or you're not. Or do you make a vague shot at Froxbury Court and sometimes miss?'

'Not exactly...'

'Rumpole, do *try* and answer the question.' She sighed with that weary patience I often adopt in Court. 'I put it to you, you're living in Chambers!'

'Not exactly living...'

'*The Oxford Book of English Verse*—isn't it your regular bedside reading?' And when I merely shrugged my shoulders, she pressed the point home. 'Why don't you answer? Are you afraid you might be incriminated?'

'I like a spot of Wordsworth before dropping off. Nothing wrong with that, is there, Portia?'

'Nothing at all. So *The Oxford Book of English Verse* is to be found on your bedside table. In the Gloucester Road?'

'Of course.' At which she pulled another mean Courtroom trick, rolled back the brief on my desk further and revealed my favourite anthology.

'Then what's it doing here? Rubbing shoulders with *Bloodstains I Have Known* by Professor Ackerman and an out-of-date *Archbold on Crime?*'

'I brought it here ... to prepare a final speech in a case.' Quick thinking you'll agree, but she was on to me like a terrier.

'Which case?'

'Which what?'

'Case! Am I not speaking clearly?'

'An attempted murder. My client's an excellent gardener

and a remarkably unsuccessful murderer. I have to address the Jury...'

'No, you haven't! That case doesn't start until next week.'

'How do you know?'

'Because I'm prosecuting. The game's up, Rumpole!'

'All right, guv.' I was, I confess it, beaten. 'You've got me bang to rights.'

'Oh, Rumpole. You know perfectly well criminals don't *say* that any more.' At that, she sat down, exhausted by her forensic brilliance, in my client's chair.

'A fellow is entitled to his own anecdotes for God's sake,' I started to explain. 'I mean, where would I be without my anecdotes?'

'Hilda took exception to one of them?' She guessed the terrible truth.

'An excellent story. You remember I told it at the Scales of Justice dinner. Went down rather well, I thought.'

'Did you? And what did Hilda have to say about it?'

'I prefer not to remember. I believe the word "senile" featured in her address to the Court. I opened the cab door and found freedom.'

'You'll have to go back sometime.' And she added thoughtfully, 'Anyway, you can't stay here. After the Jeffrey Mungo case, Ballard'll have you evicted for breaking the terms of the lease!'

'Mungo cooked Spaghetti Bolognese.'

'And you import curry; I'd say the offence is a great deal worse. They're on to you, Rumpole. Stay here another night and you'll lose your tenancy.' She looked at me with a sort of amused desperation. 'What *are* we going to do about you?' She sighed and made up her mind. 'Oh well. I

suppose there's nothing else for it. Just till you find somewhere else, you understand . . .'

So it came about that I took up residence in a spare
bedroom in the Erskine-Browns' agreeable house in Can-
onbury Square. I was, although I say it myself, no trouble
at all to Claude and Phillida. For instance, I always did my
own breakfast, manning the cooker to produce my own
bacon, eggs and fried slice, whilst the family gloomily di-
gested muesli (stuff which looked as though it were manu-
factured to line birdcages) and fat-free yoghurt. In the
evenings I entertained my hosts with an anthology of my
best anecdotes, together with a complete account of my
cross examination of the pathologist in the Penge Bungalow Murders, a triumph of which I have almost total recall.
I must say that the Erskine-Browns were kind and generous
hosts; the same could not be said of their issue, children
operatically named Tristan and Isolde. This couple of mere
infants, no more than nine and seven years old respectively, were amazingly puritanical, and on the whole as
censorious of Rumpole as Soapy Sam Ballard at his most
disapproving.

One morning I was at the cooker in a dressing gown,
smoking a small cigar, and blowing out a slight fire caused
by some leaping bacon fat on the grill. Portia was deep in a
brief and Erskine-Brown had just had *Opera* magazine hot
from the press, and the children were dressed for school
when Tristan said, 'I can't understand why people have to
smoke.'

'I can't understand why people have to chew gob-stoppers!' I was quick with my reply.

'I never chew gob-stoppers. They're bad for your teeth.'

'For one so young, you seem remarkably careful of your
health. Let me tell you, Tristan, and you too, Isolde, if

you'd care to listen, there's no pleasure on earth that's worth sacrificing for the sake of an extra five years in the geriatric ward of the Sunset Old People's Home, Weston-Super-Mare.'

'My teacher says they're going to make all smoking illegal,' young Isolde announced. 'They're going to send you to prison for it.' I wondered if Portia had given birth to a couple of prosecuting counsel when the child continued, 'My teacher says you shouldn't be allowed to smoke, even if you're all by yourself, sitting in a field in *the open air.*'

'Why ever not?'

'You might set yourself on fire with the matches; they'd have to cure your burns on the National Health.' Tristan supplied the answer with considerable satisfaction. Then Erskine-Brown rose to take his infants off to school. As they left the room, Isolde make a remark to her father which caused the fried slice to turn somewhat sour in my mouth and make me feel but a temporary visitor to Islington. 'Daddy,' I heard her piping up, 'how long is that man going to live here?'

In search of an answer to the same question, I heard much later, Phillida visited She Who Must Be Obeyed in Froxbury Court. She found Hilda with her feet up in an unusually tidy flat, listening to *The Archers* (a programme which used to cause some controversy between us) and tried to effect a reconciliation. It seems she told Hilda that I was missing her greatly, whereupon my wife said that she was hardly missing me at all, and thanked Phillida for her courage in putting up with me. So much for the gratitude of a woman to whom I had continually returned home at a more or less regular hour from Pommeroy's Wine Bar for the last forty years. No wonder I had chosen freedom.

A few nights before *R.* v. *Lutterworth* started, I came

home late from Chambers and let myself in quietly, thinking Tristan and Isolde might have been mercifully asleep.
The kitchen door was open a crack and I thought I heard
the sound of voices. Phillida and Claude were no doubt
sampling a rather cheeky little Bergerac he had got in a
job-lot from an old school-friend in the wine trade. I
paused by the door and heard Phillida say, 'You've got to
talk to him, Claude. She doesn't want him back! He might
be with us for ever.'

'You invited him to stay. You ought to talk to him.'
Claude Erskine-Brown was showing his usual courage.
'Go on, Philly. Be a man!'

'I'm not a man,' Phillida said, and there was clearly
force in her argument. 'You're the man, remember?'

A fellow can't help feeling a bit of a pang, when he
hears he's not a welcome guest in the house of a lady to
whom he's taught all she ever knew of the subject of cross-
examination, and I trod the cold stairway up to bed a little
sadly.

So I was still a wanderer, with a temporary billet *à côté
de chez* Erskine-Brown, when our Portia rose to open the
case of *R.* v. *Lutterworth* to the Jury.

'It's the old, old story,' she told them. 'A young and
attractive wife, married to an elderly husband who had,
perhaps, lost some of his charm for her over the years. So
she allowed herself to drift into a love affair with her husband's partner, that no doubt physically more attractive
young man, Hugo Lutterworth, the defendant in this case.
Lutterworth is here today because he was not content with
mere sex! He wanted his partner, Captain Gleason, out of
the way so that he could enjoy his business *and* his wife,
without having to share them with anybody. Members of

the Jury, it's difficult for us, who no doubt have stable homes and contented marriages, to understand the lengths to which some unhappy people will go in inflicting pain and suffering on others.'

Mrs Erskine-Brown, Q.C., was no doubt at her most eloquent, but I wasn't listening to her. I was gazing in fascinated horror at the Bench above me. There, chosen to preside over the Court, was the Welsh wizard, Mr Justice Huw Gwent-Evans, the Chapel guru who had failed to laugh at my joke in the Savoy Hotel, and there beside him, equally unamused, sat She Who Must Be Obeyed, my wife, Hilda, staring down at me apparently prepared to judge Rumpole, come to an unfavourable verdict and impose the severest penalty known to the law.

Among Phillida Erskine-Brown's early witnesses was a Garden Centre worker named Daphne Hapgood, a chunky, red-headed young daughter of the soil, whose nails were broken with much potting up. She testified to having seen Hugo Lutterworth bestowing a passionate kiss on Mrs Gleason in a greenhouse (people who live in glasshouses shouldn't kiss their employers' wives), evidence which shocked the Judge and She Who Must Be Obeyed equally. She also described seeing Lutterworth doing some work on the Volvo Estate, bending over it with the bonnet open, on the day before it crashed. She added that it was not unusual for Hugo to work on the cars, being apparently as handy with sparking plugs as he was with seedlings. Through all this evidence I noticed Amanda Gleason couldn't resist looking distressed and lovingly at Hugo in the dock, bestowing upon him long glances which he, unfortunately, returned in a way which was doing us no good at all with the Jury.

'Did you ever hear Captain Gleason ask Hugo Lutter-worth to look at his car for him?' I asked Daphne when I rose to cross-examine.

'I can't remember. He may have done.'

'May have on this particular occasion?'

'I suppose it's possible.'

'Thank you.'

'Is that all, Mr Rumpole?' The Judge seemed surprised. 'You're not challenging the evidence about the intimate conduct between your client and his partner's wife?'

'Oh, no, my Lord. That's admitted.'

'So this man'—the Welsh wizard was working himself up to a denunciation from the pulpit—'admits kissing Mrs Gleason in full view of the Garden Centre workforce. He seems to have had a very tenuous grasp on morality.'

'This judge,' I whispered to Mr Driscoll, 'is suffering from a bad case of premature adjudication.'

'Did you say something, Mr Rumpole?' His Lordship was looking at me suspiciously, and I could see that my lady wife was not too pleased either. 'In due course there will be a full explanation,' I told him.

I hoped there would, but at the minute I had no particular idea what it was going to be. Happily the moment for luncheon had arrived and the Judge, showing that he had remembered more of my well-known anecdote than he cared to admit, said, 'Very well, Members of the Jury, we'll leave it there until . . .'

'Ten past two, my Lord?' I suggested. At which Sir Huw Gwent-Evans rose without another word and, ignoring my signals, She Who Must Be Obeyed swept out after him.

Later, after I had hung about for a while in the marble-paved hallway of the Worsfield Court, I saw Hilda advancing upon me in the company of Posnett, the Judge's clerk.

'Hilda!' I found myself, for once in my life, almost at a loss for words. 'What on earth...?'

'The Judge invited me down to luncheon and to hear a bit of your case, Rumpole. You may remember how well *I* got on with Mr Justice Gwent-Evans at the Savoy.'

Of course judges did ask distinguished visitors down to lunch in their lodgings, and they did ask such people—sheriffs, lords-lieutenant of the county and their good ladies, persons of that ilk—to sit beside them on the Bench during particularly fascinating cases. But persons of the ilk of She Who Must Be Obeyed? I suppose I found it hard to believe that the Judge had taken *such* a shine to her.

'Well, you might have let me know. It came as something of a shock to me, seeing you in the seat of judgement.'

'How could I let you know, Rumpole? I keep looking round the flat and you're nowhere to be found.'

'The Judge is just coming, Mrs Rumpole,' the Clerk said and started to withdraw from the presence.

'Oh, thank you, Posnett. I'll be waiting here. That's Posnett, the Judge's clerk. Quite a sweetie,' she explained to me, as though I were a child in matters concerning the legal profession. Then she said, 'Oh, by the way. That case of yours. Have you noticed the way Mrs Gleason keeps looking at your client? Quite an exhibition, isn't it? Don't you think she's really making it *too* obvious?'

The scarlet judge appeared with his clerk, Posnett, in attendance, and She was spirited off with them into the municipal Daimler to lunch in his lodgings. But what had happened was something of a miracle, a bit of a turn up for the book. What She had said had given me an entirely new view of the case; in fact She had come up with some sort of a legal inspiration. I went off in search of Driscoll and asked to see the original partnership agreement which came into existence when Gleason and Lutterworth got together to buy the Woodland Folk Garden Centre.

Hilda did not return to Court in the afternoon, and took no further part in the case. We heard evidence about the brakes on the Volvo Estate car having been cut, and when I suggested that it was a strange criminal who left such clear evidence of his crime, the Judge went so far as to suggest that the criminal clearly expected the runaway car to be mashed up by a passing lorry on the main road, so that the damage might have been obscured in the resulting mess. Whatever friends I had in the world, they clearly did not include Mr Justice Gwent-Evans. An officer then gave evidence that Hugo's fingerprints had been found near the area of the braking system. I managed to slip in a request for further investigations to see if the prints of anyone else who was connected with the Garden Centre could be found, and counsel for the Prosecution agreed readily. No doubt she wanted to propitiate me so that I would move out of her matrimonial home.

When I got back to Chambers I found a small handbill on my tray, which was the only message I had, and went to my room to bone up on the laws of partnership. Before I got down to work I read the handbill, which ran, as I remember, somewhat as follows:

LAWYERS AS CHRISTIANS:
THE SUFFRAGEN BISHOP OF SIDCUP
WILL GIVE AN ADDRESS ON
'THE CHRISTIAN APPROACH TO THE RENT ACTS'.
EVERYONE INTERESTED CORDIALLY INVITED.

**SHERRY AND SANDWICHES WILL BE SERVED
AFTER THE DISCUSSION.
SAMUEL BALLARD, Q.C., PRESIDENT.**

Something about the connection between Soapy Sam Bollard and sherry had put a thought in my head, and then the door opened and Erskine-Brown was upon me.

'I wanted to have a word with you'—he perched uncomfortably on the arm of my client's chair—'Philly's idea really.'

'A short word. I'm studying the law of partnership, in depth.'

'Of course, it has been tremendous *fun* having you to stay with us, for a short while. Just till you get fixed up.'

'Enjoyed some of the old stories, eh?' I lit a small cigar. 'Better than watching television. I've got plenty of them, for the long winter evenings.'

'Good.' Erskine-Brown sounded unenthusiastic. 'Philly and I would love that.'

'Well then. Does that solve your problem?'

'*Our* problem, yes . . . But not Hilda's.'

'Hilda's?'

'Philly went to see her. She's most terribly upset.'

'Your wife's upset?' I was puzzled. 'She seemed quite bobbish in Court.'

'No. Hilda's, well, terribly down and lonely. She wants you back desperately, Rumpole. We were both, well, rather sad about it.'

I looked pityingly at Erskine-Brown. Then I got up and slapped him heartily on the back. 'Claude. I have good news for you!'

'You're going back to Hilda?' The man appeared to have some hope.

'No. Set your mind at rest. Hilda's bright as a button.
Happy as the day is long. She's chummed up with a peculiarly nauseating brand of Welsh judge and she's having an
exotic social life round the Worsfield Assizes. She wanted
me to tell you that she's enormously grateful to you and
Portia for having me and long may the arrangement continue. Now, is that good news for you?' Erskine-Brown
didn't answer. 'It isn't, is it?' Erskine-Brown still didn't
answer. 'In fact, it's somewhat dashed your hopes? You
really want to give me the order of the Imperial Elbow,
don't you? Say no more! I can take a hint, Erskine-Brown.
I can tell, when your children simulate terminal bronchitis
every time I walk into a room, that it's time I was moving
on. Only one thing. You'll have to help me to another
billet.'

'How am I expected to do that?' the poor fellow asked
weakly.

'Let me tell you, old cock. It's perfectly simple. All you
have to do is go to this shindig.' I let him have the handbill
for nothing. 'The Bishop of Sidcup on "The Christian Approach to the Rent Acts".'

'But that night I've got tickets for *Rigoletto*,' he protested.

'*Rigoletto* will still be around in a hundred years' time,'
I assured him. 'This is your one opportunity to hear the
Bishop of Sidcup on this fascinating subject. Roll up,
Claude! Be among those present on the night! Join Soapy
Sam Bollard, our slithery Head of Chambers, and partake
liberally of the sherry and sandwiches. Particularly the
sherry...'

'Why on earth should I?'

'Because if you do this properly, old darling, I can fold
my tent, take the Golden Road back to Chambers and stay

here undisturbed. Now, this is all I'm asking you to do . . .'
And I began to fill him in with the details of my plan.

The next day Captain Gleason went into the witness box, a
bulky figure in a double-breasted blue suit and a regimental
tie; he seemed such an unlikely consort for the beautiful
red-head in the well of the Court that it came as no surprise
when she hardly looked at him. Phillida was winding to the
end of her examination-in-chief when she asked the Captain when he became doubtful about his wife's relationship
with Hugo Lutterworth.

'I had been suspicious of my wife and Hugo for some
time. About a year ago I came back from a regimental dinner in London and discovered them in a . . .
compromising position.' Gleason spoke quietly, sounding
the most forbearing husband. 'I decided to forgive them
both. Of course, I had no idea that my partner would . . .
try to get rid of me.'

'We have heard evidence that your wife visited Lutterworth in prison.'

'I heard that. Yes.' The Captain shook his head sadly.

'In spite of that, what is your present attitude towards
your marriage?'

'I'm still prepared to give it another chance.'

'In spite of an attempt that may have been made on your
life?'

'Yes. In spite of that.'

You could almost hear the purr of approval from the Jury
as Phillida thanked him and sat down. The Judge added his
thanks and then the Captain asked if he might sit during my
questions as he had a little heart trouble.

'Of course, Captain Gleason,' the Welsh judge cooed at
him. 'A glass of water? Usher, bring Captain Gleason a

glass of water. Are you sure you feel quite well, Captain Gleason? You just sit there and take it quite easily. You won't be long, will you, Mr Rumpole?'

'Not very long, my Lord. And I'll try and adopt my best bedside manner.' I turned to Gleason and started quietly, 'Captain Gleason. Did my client, Hugo Lutterworth, look after the cars from time to time?'

'He did. Yes.'

'If they needed a service, or some adjustment, used he to do it?'

'He said he didn't trust garages.'

'The day before, let us use a neutral expression and call it the "accident", had you told him your estate car wasn't running very smoothly and asked him to have a look at it?'

'I can't remember.'

'Can you not?' I spoke more crisply, with a little vinegar in the honey. 'Did Mr. Lutterworth tell you he'd adjusted the points, or the plugs? Something of that nature?'

'He may have done.' The answer came after a pause.

'So you *may* have asked him to look at your car?'

'It's possible. I haven't got much of a talent with mechanical objects.' Captain Gleason smiled at the Judge, who smiled back in a thoroughly understanding manner. Clearly they were both useless when it came to carburettors.

'You weren't in army transport?'

'No.'

'You were in the Catering Corps?'

'What about it?' The witness sounded defensive.

'Nothing at all. I'm sure you were a very gallant caterer. So you never attended to your car yourself?'

'Never.' The evidence was, happily, quite positive.

'Never even opened the bonnet?'

'Never. I got it filled up at the garage.'

'Hugo Lutterworth did the rest?'

'Did rather too much, on that particular occasion.' There was an unsettling rattle of sympathetic laughter from the Jury, in which his Lordship was pleased to join. I wiped the smile off his face when I asked, 'You say that, Captain Gleason. But looking back on it, wouldn't you agree that my client has done you a simply enormous favour?'

'I have no idea what you mean!' Gleason appeared startled and looked to the Judge for help.

'Neither have I, Mr Rumpole.' The Judge seemed all too willing to come to the witness's aid.

'You know exactly what I mean, Captain! Had you not had a very tempting offer for the Garden Centre site from a chain of immense supermarkets? Might not your greenhouses have become promenades for the purchase of everything from butterscotch to bedsteads...?'

'My Lord, I can't see how my business affairs can possibly be relevant.'

'Neither can I at the moment. Mrs Erskine-Brown, do you object to the question?'

'No, my Lord. Not at this stage.'

'Thank you, Portia. I'll be moving out soon,' I rewarded her with a whisper. 'Well, Captain Gleason?'

'We have had an offer for the site. Yes,' he answered with the utmost caution.

'And Mr Lutterworth was determined not to sell?'

'That's what he said.'

'Because he believes in flowers and badgers and butterflies and woodland folk. All that sort of thing. But you wanted to sell and make a thumping great profit?'

'I was in favour of the Arcadia Stores offer. Yes.' The Captain was still being very cautious.

'Captain Gleason. I would like the Court to see the partnership agreement between yourself and my client...'
Driscoll handed copies of the agreement to the Usher, who
started distributing them to the Judge, Jury and the witness.
'Mr Rumpole. How can that possibly be relevant to this
charge?' His Lordship was displeased, and I started to
launch into a legal argument which I had prepared with the
aid of Mr Driscoll, who knew about partnership agreements. 'It goes right to the heart of the matter! It is the
simple solution to what your Lordship and the Jury may
have found an extremely puzzling case.'

'I can't speak for the Jury, of course. But I haven't
found it in the least puzzling.'

'Not puzzling?' I did my best to sound extremely surprised. 'An alleged criminal who does everything in the
presence of witnesses. A case of attempted murder which
is so bungled that the victim suffers nothing but a few
minor cuts and bruises? I should have thought that might
have caused a certain amount of bewilderment, even to
your Lordship.'

The Judge struggled with his irritation and suppressed it.
Then he asked, *'Why* do you say I should look at this document?'

'Because I understand my learned friend has no objection.' Once again I whispered my bribe to Phillida, 'I'll be
out of your place by Thursday!'

'My Lord. We wouldn't wish to shut out any document
which might possibly have some relevance.' She rose, I
must say, splendidly to the occasion.

'Look at it, will you?' I asked the witness before the
Judge could draw another breath. 'The Jury have their
copies. "Whereas..." Skip all the waffle. Just look at
Paragraph 12. Read it out, will you?'

'"If either of the said partners shall perform an act which is prejudicial to the interests of the partnership or shall be convicted of a criminal offence..."' Gleason started to read as quietly as possible.

' *"Or shall be convicted of a criminal offence,"* ' I gave the Court the sentence at full volume. '"All his rights in the partnership property and income and all other benefits due to him from the said partnership shall revert immediately to the other partner who shall, from the date of the said act or offence, be solely entitled to all the partnership assets."' I lowered the agreement and looked at the witness, smiling. 'Congratulations. You've done extremely well out of this little case, haven't you, Captain Gleason?'

'I take the greatest exception to that!' The Captain rose to attention and almost shouted. He seemed to have momentarily recovered his health.

'Do you?' I hope I sounded mildly surprised. 'All you had to do was crash your car into the bird baths. Get a few superficial cuts and bruises, and you became solely entitled to the Woodland Folk Garden Centre, which you could then flog to the supermarket and make yourself a fortune.'

'Mr Rumpole. That *isn't* all he had to do.' A remarkable display of judicial bad temper was brewing up on the Bench.

'Oh, I'm grateful to your Lordship.' I tried to pour oil on the troubled judge. 'Your Lordship has got my point, of course. There was one other thing you had to do, wasn't there, Captain Gleason? You had to get the unfortunate Hugo Lutterworth convicted of a crime. But after that little formality—once the Jury came back and found my client guilty of attempted murder—you'd be laughing all your way to your newly bought holiday home on the Costa del Sol.'

There was a decided change in the atmosphere in Court. The Jury was looking with interest and some suspicion at Captain Gleason. Even the Judge was silent. Mrs Gleason was now looking at her husband, with some anxiety, and my client was beginning to look less blissfully unconcerned.

'I haven't got a house on the Costa del Sol,' was the only answer the Captain could manage.

'Oh, I'm sorry. Formentera? No matter. I still congratulate you. You've come into a fortune.'

Captain Gleason looked helplessly down at the partnership agreement. 'I don't know how that clause got in there...'

'Let me tell you. My client's solicitor, Mr Driscoll here, drew up the agreement. He didn't altogether trust you, did he? I don't know what it was. Some rumours about how you came to leave the Army? A story about the accounts when you were secretary of a golf club in Surrey? He put that in to protect Mr Lutterworth, and you remembered it when you wanted to get rid of him. Isn't that the truth *Captain* Gleason?'

'My Lord. Mr Rumpole is attacking my client's character!' Phillida threw self-interest to the winds and objected at last.

'Attack his character?' I protested. 'God forbid. I'm sure the Captain is as honest a man as ever perverted the course of justice.'

'Mr Rumpole! Will you please make your suggestion against this witness absolutely clear.' The Judge was still no Rumpole fan.

'With the greatest of pleasure.' I turned to the witness. 'You needed a way to get Lutterworth out of the partnership. I suspect your wife also wanted to get rid of him.

They'd had a brief affair, but that was all over, at least so far as she was concerned.' There was a sound behind me, my client calling out some sort of protest, but I was doing too well to bother about Sir Lancelot's romantic susceptibilities. 'And you knew the terms of the partnership agreement. All you had to do was to stage the attempted murder of yourself and make it look as though Mr Lutterworth had done it. So you asked him to look at the points in your car. He'd done that often enough before, hadn't he, without trying to kill you?'

'I told you he'd done it before, yes.' Captain Gleason was swaying slightly and his speech was less clear.

'Mr Rumpole. Aren't you forgetting something?' It was his Lordship's last stand on behalf of the witness.

'Am I, my Lord? Remind me.'

'*Someone* cut this gentleman's brake cables.'

'Of course. You did that, Captain Gleason, didn't you?'

'Oh yes? And risk killing myself . . .' The Captain was trying to laugh; it was a somewhat grisly sound.

'Not much of a risk, was it? A short run down the drive and a crash into the statuary. No real risk—for a driver who knew exactly what had happened to his brakes?'

There was a long silence, but answer came there none. At last Captain Gleason swayed and fell crumpled at the side of the witness box. Amanda cried out and ran to kneel beside him: Queen Guinevere was showing her unaccountable love for the crotchety and dishonest old King Arnold. The Court Clerk and a police officer were opening Gleason's collar.

'We'll adjourn now.' The Judge decided to leave the field of battle. Mr Driscoll, a kindly fellow, was looking across at the fallen witness. 'Is he all right?'

'Oh, I think the Captain will survive,' I reassured him. 'He's survived most things.'

After that cross-examination the case was downhill all the way. Further investigation revealed Captain Gleason's prints on the brake cables. He was an incompetent crook, but then the ones with any talent rarely come our way. Hugo Lutterworth would clearly never forgive me for my revelations, but he agreed to give evidence and was finally acquitted. There was still one other matter which I had to bring to a successful conclusion.

Claude Erskine-Brown, no doubt driven by a longing to clear Rumpole from his domestic hearth, did his work well. At the Lawyers As Christians meeting, he saw Ballard was suitably plied with sherry; indeed after the first two or three, Soapy Sam appeared to be cooperating with enthusiasm. When they finally emerged into the Temple car park, the Bollard walk was not altogether steady, nor his speech entirely clear. I have done my best to reconstruct their dialogue from what Claude told me later, but it seems to have gone somewhat as follows.

'The thing about the Bishop of Sidcup,' Ballard spoke with resonant emphasis, 'is that he knows *exactly* where he stands.' Already our Head of Chambers was fumbling for his car keys, preparing to motor home.

'Yes. But do *you?*' Claude asked.

'What?'

'Know where you stand? A bit unsteadily, if you ask my opinion. I mean'—he looked suspiciously at Ballard's sleek black Granada—'you're not going to drive that thing, are you?'

'Of course I am. Back to Waltham Cross.'

'How many sherries did you have, Ballard?'

'Three. No more than three, Erskine-Brown.'

'Half a dozen at least. Way over the limit! I mean, do get in and drive! But if you ever want to be a judge . . .'

'What?' A Bollard nerve had been touched. Of course he wanted to be a judge.

'Drunk driving! The Lord Chancellor's going to cross you off his list of possibles. And in front of the Waltham Cross Magistrates, fellow in Arbuthnot's Chambers was telling me, it's automatic prison on a breathalyzer, a month inside! "Stamp out this menace!" You know the sort of thing you get from a bench of teetotallers.'

'But I've missed the eleven fifteen'—Ballard looked at his watch—'I don't think there's another. Erskine-Brown, what am I going to do?'

'It's entirely up to you. Waltham Cross, eh? I'm afraid it's not on my route . . .' Erskine-Brown moved towards his own motor. 'Good-night, Ballard.'

Fate, for once, was on my side. Ballard consulted his wallet and found he had forgotten to go to the Bank and had indeed left his cheque book at home. He called out to Claude for a loan to pay a minicab, but my trusty ally had switched on his engine and was roaring out of the car park. Ballard put his car keys in his pocket and walked sadly off in the general direction of Chambers.

And there I found him the next morning. In fact I took him up a cup of tea as he awoke shivering slightly under an overcoat on a sofa in a corner of his room.

'Morning, Bollard,' I greeted him. 'Been sleeping rough?' I sat down on a chair which also contained his trousers. 'Kipping on the couch reserved for the clientele? What do you think this place is, the Sally Ann? I mean, what would the chaps think if they knew you were using our Chambers as a common boardinghouse?' Ballard sat up, took the teacup and raised it to his lips. Then he said, 'You're not going to tell them?'

'It's my clear and definite professional duty to do so.' I can be remorseless on occasions. 'This is not living accommodation; you're in breach of the terms of our lease. What happened, old darling? Mrs Bollard had enough of you?'

'There is no Mrs Ballard.'

'No. I don't suppose there is.'

Silence reigned while Ballard took another sip of tea. 'Rumpole,' he said, 'I've been thinking.'

'Don't overdo it.'

'I've been thinking'—he sounded judicial—'it might be better if we approached the question of smoking in Chambers on a purely voluntary basis.'

'Well, now you're talking.'

'I mean, you were able to point out to me the provisions of the Magna Carta!'

'And the European Convention on Human Rights.'

'What's that got to say about it?' He frowned.

'No citizen shall be persecuted on the grounds of race, creed or colour or because he lights up occasionally.'

'Oh well. You may be right. So, having given the matter my mature consideration . . .'

'And I'm sure no consideration could be more mature than yours . . .'

'We needn't put smoking on the Agenda for our next meeting. In view of that, it may not be necessary for you to mention the question of any person . . .'

'Dossing down in Chambers?'

'Exactly! I'm sure we understand each other.'

I got up and moved to the door. 'Of course. That's what

I admire about you, Bollard. You're absolutely firm on your principles. I hear the Bishop of Sidcup was a most tremendous hit.'

So I left him, still sipping thoughtfully. All that day I pondered on the simple observation by She Who Must Be Obeyed, which had put me on to the truth of *R.* v. *Lutterworth*. In the evening, believing that Dianne, our tireless typist, had really no further use for the geranium I had brought her from the Woodland Folk Garden Centre, I took it home to Froxbury Court, where I found Hilda comfortably ensconced and listening to *The Archers*.

'We won the case, you know,' I told her, after a pause, during which She looked not at all overjoyed by my return.

'So you should have.'

'I said *we* won it. You gave me the idea. I mean, you found the bull point. The way the girl looked at him.'

'I'm not Daddy's daughter for nothing! Daddy had forty-five years at the Bar.'

'Dear old C. H. Wystan. Knew nothing about bloodstains, but let that pass.'

'Daddy knew a good deal about human nature.'

'Yes. Well. All the same, I've got to give you the credit for our victory.'

'What are you doing here, Rumpole?' She looked at me doubtfully.

'Doing here? I came to give you a geranium. Hope you like it.' It was then I presented the plant. I can't say it was received with undiminished rapture.

'It looks as though it's seen better days.'

'Well. It happens to all of us. Anyway. I live here, don't I?'

'Do you? I haven't noticed you living here lately.'

'I expect you've been busy. Sweeping under beds. Listening to everyday stories of country folk. That's what I've been doing too, come to think of it.'

'Well, you can't just come and go as you please.'

'Do you think I'm running a hotel?' I suggested a thought for her speech.

'How did you know I was going to say that?'

'Most people do. Let me pour you a G and T. Celebrate your great victory in Court. Not every day you win a case, Hilda.' I found the bottles and mixed a drink for her, taking the liberty of opening a bottle of Pommeroy's Ordinary for myself.

'Daddy once won a case,' Hilda said thoughtfully, as she raised her glass.

'Extraordinary!'

'What did you say?'

'Well, that was nothing out of the ordinary.'

'When C. H. Wystan, when Daddy was a young man at the Bar, he did a dock brief. He defended a pickpocket for nothing. Fellow who was accused of stealing a watch . . .'

'Oh, really?' Hilda was embarking on an anecdote, one of her few.

'Anyway, Daddy got the fellow off! His first real success and he was pleased as Punch. And as he was leaving the old London Sessions, this pickpocket came up to him and said, "I'm so grateful to you, Mr Wystan. You've saved me from prison and I've got no money to pay you. But I can give you this." So what do you think the pickpocket did?'

'I've no idea!' Well, I can occasionally lie in a good cause.

'Offered Daddy the watch!' She laughed and then stopped laughing, and looked at me with deep suspicion. 'You've heard it before?'

'No, Hilda. I promise you, never!'

'Do take that poor plant out to the kitchen and offer it some water. It looks exhausted.'

Of course, as ever, I obeyed her command.

Rumpole and the
Official Secret

Lawyers and priests deal largely in secrets, being privy to matters which are not meant for the public ear. I don't know how it is in the religious life, or whether, when two or three prelates are gathered together, they regale each other with snatches from the Confessional, but barristers are mostly indiscreet. Go into Pommeroy's Wine Bar any evening when the Château Fleet Street is flowing and you may quickly discover who's getting a divorce or being libelled, which judge has got which lady pupil in the club or which Member of Parliament relaxes in female apparel. I don't join much in such conversations; my own clients' activities are, in the main, simple and uncomplicated transactions, and 'Who turned over Safeways?' or 'Which bloke supplies logbooks for stolen Cortinas?' are rarely questions which get much airing in the Mr Chatterbox column in the *Sunday Fortress*.

Of course, often the most closely guarded secrets turn

out to be matters of such stunning triviality that you wonder why anyone ever bothered to keep quiet about them. Such, it seemed, was the closely guarded matter of the Ministry of Defence Elevenses which formed the basis for the strange prosecution of Miss Rosemary Tuttle. This was a case which, although it began with a laugh, and laughter was, as always, a weapon for the defence, certainly ended in what I will always think of as a tragedy.

But let me begin at the beginning, which was roughly Sunday lunchtime at 25b Froxbury Court, our alleged 'mansion' flat off the Gloucester Road. I was relaxing with the *Sunday Fortress* propped up against the Pommeroy's plonk bottle, and Hilda was removing what was left of the roast beef and two veg, when the following item met my eye under an alluring headline:

BISCUIT WAR IN THE MINISTRY OF DEFENCE

Government extravagance has been highlighted by the astonishing sums spent subsidizing tea and biscuits consumed by civil servants at the Ministry of Defence. The cost of elevenses plus the money spent on entertaining a long list of foreign visitors would, it is calculated, have paid for the Crimean War three times over.

Such was the item of what passes for news nowadays, leading the Mr Chatterbox column. Although I usually have a keen eye for crime, I can't say that I realized that this apparently harmless story was in itself, a breach of the Official Secrets Act.

And then Hilda was calling me from the kitchen to ask if I wanted 'afters'. 'Of course I want "afters",' I called back. 'Didn't I hear a rumour of baked jam-roll?'

'We need a hatch, Rumpole,' the voice from without called, and then She entered with the tray of pudding. 'If we had a hatch I shouldn't have to walk all the way round by the hall to get your "afters.".'

Hilda had touched and reopened an old and sometimes bitter controversy. Personally, I am against hatches. We had one when I was a boy in the vicarage, a horrible thing that came trundling up from the bowels of the earth and smelled of stale cabbage. Besides which, hatches aren't things that are given away. The construction and the necessary excavation of the wall might run away with an alarming sum in legal fees. Hilda's argument, delivered with increasing volume as she went out again for the custard, was that the hatch wouldn't entail anything trundling up from anywhere, as it would go straight into the kitchen.

'If we hadn't spent all that money on biscuits at the Ministry of Defence, we might have had three Crimean Wars,' I called out to her as I thought she might have cared to know. 'Who do you imagine finds out these things?'

'I can't hear you, Rumpole,' Hilda called back. 'And that's because we haven't got a hatch.'

I should now go back to the start of the story of Miss Rosemary Tuttle and the great elevenses' leak at the Ministry of Defence. Miss Tuttle herself was a spinster lady in her fifties of vaguely central European extraction, whose parents had settled in Swiss Cottage shortly before the war. She lived alone, took her lunch in all weathers on a bench in St James's Park, being especially fond of fresh air and bright peasant-style knitted clothes, so that it was never difficult to spot Miss Tuttle in a crowd.

One night, a certain Thorogood, Private Secretary to the Minister of State, was working late and he heard the sound of a copying-machine from down the corridor. He went to investigate, but by the time he got there the room was empty, although he found one bright green, embroidered glove, later identified as the property of Miss Tuttle, by the still warm machine.

'Mr Chatterbox' masks the identity of a youngish, untidy, slightly dissolute old Etonian named Tim Warboys. At his office in the *Sunday Fortress,* Warboys received an anonymous typewritten message telling him that at 2 p.m. the next day he would, if he were to be in view of a certain bench in St James's Park, see a fifty-year-old lady in bright clothing arise from her seat. She would leave behind her a copy of the *Daily Telegraph* into which would be folded certain documents. Having done as he was instructed, Warboys discovered the newspaper in the appointed place and so came into the possession of figures concerning certain entertaining expenses in the Ministry of Defence, including the amount spent on coffee and biscuits. The biscuits alone, it seems, would have gone some way to financing the Navy. He was able to include this story in his next Sunday's column.

In due course Miss Tuttle was accused of the crime and a decision had to be taken as to her prosecution. Her immediate superior was the Assistant Under-Secretary, Oliver Bowling, an old Wykehamist, who, from time to time, went to the Opera with the Erskine-Browns. Bowling, when I came to meet him, appeared to be a thoroughly sensible sort of chap who was fond of Miss Tuttle and regarded her as a harmless eccentric. He took the reasonable view that to prosecute her for what was undoubtedly —so asinine can the law be on State Occasions—a breach of Section 2 of the Official Secrets Act would merely serve to bring the Civil Service in general, and the Ministry of

Defence in particular, into ridicule and contempt. This view was not shared by Basil Thorogood who thought that whether the Secrets concerned biscuits or bombs, the safety of our Kingdom depended on the rigid application of the law and the consequent hounding of Miss Tuttle. Higher authority in the shape of Sir Frank Fawcett, K.C.B., the Permanent Under-Secretary, sent the papers to the Attorney-General who, somewhat to everyone's surprise, decided to prosecute.

When this decision was given to Oliver Bowling, he was apparently outraged at the crassness of our bureaucracy. Having prophesied that any prosecution would make the Ministry look absurd, he was secretly anxious to be proved right. He asked his old school-friend, Erskine-Brown, if he happened to know a barrister whose particular skill was getting cases laughed out of Court, and Claude, who felt he owed me a debt of gratitude for having returned to my matrimonial home, recommended the very one. The consequence was that I found myself briefed by the upmarket City firm of Farmilow, Pounsford & James for the defence of Miss Rosemary Tuttle on the sinister and mole-like activity of betraying our biscuits to the enemy.

The brief in this *cause célèbre* arrived in a peculiarly impressive manner. One day I entered our clerk's room to see Henry, Dianne and Uncle Tom staring respectfully at a heavy green safe.

'A present,' Uncle Tom explained, 'from Her Majesty the Queen.'

'No, Uncle Tom. A loan from the Ministry of Defence,' Henry corrected him with some pride.

'What's it got in it?' I asked. 'The Crown Jewels?'

'It's your brief, Mr Rumpole, in the Secrets trial. Gov-

ernment-issue safes are supplied to defence counsel when
the matter is highly confidential. So that the papers don't
fall into the wrong hands.' Henry's voice sank in awe.

'All right. How do we open it?'

'There's a number, for the combination. But'—Henry
looked round nervously as the grey figure of Hoskins, the
barrister, came into the room—'it doesn't do, Mr Rumpole, to mention these things in public.'

'Well, just whisper it into the lock, Henry. There's a
brief in there, a money brief with any sort of luck.'

'Four . . . five . . . three, eight, one,' Henry muttered, as
he turned the dial on the safe. Then he pulled the handle,
but it didn't open. Dianne almost shouted, 'Four, five, *two*,
eight, *two* wasn't it, Henry?' Henry said, 'Dianne, *please*,'
and tried again, but the safe still refused to divulge its
contents.

'Open Sesame!' I thumped the green top with my fist.
The door swung open and I collected a slender brief and
went upstairs to meet the clientele.

'The number of gingernuts consumed in the Ministry of
Defence! The amount spent on cups of tea in the Department of Arms Procurement! The free holidays charged up
as entertaining foreign visitors!' I stood smoking a small
cigar in Chambers in the company of Mr Jasper James, the
instructing solicitor, a well-nourished fifty-year-old in an
expensive city suiting; Miss Rosemary Tuttle, dressed apparently for the Hungarian gypsy encampment scene in
Balalaika; and my faithful amanuensis, Liz Probert, who
was trying hard to find the dread hand of the C.I.A. somewhere behind the biscuits.

'Miss Tuttle *is* bound by Section 2 of the Official Secrets

Act. And it's alleged that she copied confidential documents and gave them to the Press. If that's a true bill, then . . .' Mr. James, the solicitor, made a regretful clucking sound, apparently indicating that he wouldn't put 5p on our chances.

'Look, James, my dear old sweetheart'—I tried to cheer up the eminent solicitor—'it's a well-known fact that Section 2 of the Official Secrets Act is the raving of governmental paranoia.'

'But if she's broken the law . . .'

'If Miss Tuttle's broken the law, the Jury are entitled to acquit her! It's their ancient and inalienable privilege, I shall tell them. It's the light that shows the lamp of freedom burns.' I gave them a foretaste of my speech to the Jury: 'If you think it a sign of bureaucracy run mad, Members of the Jury, that this unfortunate lady, whom I represent, should be hounded through the Courts just because our masters in Whitehall can't restrain their revolting greed for Bath Olivers and Dundee shortbread, then you are fully entitled to return a resounding verdict of not guilty. She did what she did so that the tax-payer, that is you and I, Members of the Jury, should not be stung with an escalating bill for Maryland cookies and chocolate-covered digestives, and God save us all, macaroons. She has been the guardian of our democracy and saved the waistlines of Whitehall!'

'Look, I'm awfully sorry to butt in . . .' Miss Tuttle butted in, interrupting my flow. 'You can say all that in Court, if you like.'

'I *do* like, Miss Tuttle. I like very much indeed. Strong stuff, perhaps, but I feel entirely justified.'

'But I didn't do it, don't you see? I didn't do anything!'

'Nothing?' I was, I confess, a little dashed to hear it.

'No. I never copied those figures, or sent them to the papers. I'm jolly well innocent, Mr Rumpole.'

'Innocent . . .' It was a disappointment, but then I saw a glimmer of hope. 'But your glove was found that night by the copying-machine!'

'I can't understand how it got there at all. It must have walked!' She smiled round at us, like a child who has just thought of a joke.

'Miss Tuttle. You copied those documents from the Personnel and Logistics Section of the Ministry of Defence and you gave them to Mr Tim Warboys of the *Sunday Fortress*, so he could make his little joke about the Crimean War in his Chatterbox column.' I was doing my best to convince her; if she were not guilty, there could be no hilarious speech.

'Would I do such a thing, Mr Rumpole?'

'It seems completely creditable to me. Why ever not?'

'I was in a position of trust.' Now she looked like a serious child, one who always keeps the school rules.

'Consider this. If you admit this noble act, I can turn you into a heroine, a Joan of Arc, Miss Tuttle, in shining armour doing battle against the forces of bureaucracy.' I made a last appeal to her.

'And if I deny it?'

'Then you're just an ordinary criminal, trying to lie your way out of trouble. Do think, Miss Tuttle. Do please think carefully.'

We sat in a minute's silence while Miss Tuttle thought it over. Then she said quietly, 'I've got to tell the truth.'

'Yes,' I agreed sadly. 'Oh, yes, Miss Tuttle. I suppose you have.' I looked at Jasper James in a resigned manner.

'We'd better check the evidence, Mr James. I suggest we do our own typewriter test . . .'

Whilst I was thus concerned with affairs of State, Claude Erskine-Brown was considering entering into secret negoti-ations of an entirely different nature. He plumped himself down next to Liz Probert, who was enjoying a solitary sandwich in the Taste-Ee-Bite café in Fleet Street, and told her that it was no picnic being married to a busy silk. Phillida was always away doing important cases in Man-chester or Newport, or such far-flung outposts of the Em-pire, and he was left a great deal on his own. He then startled Mizz Probert by saying, as she told me much later, 'To be quite honest with you, Sue, it's a pretty ghastly situation. My wife has absolutely no time for it.' Mizz Probert could think of no suitable reply to this, except to say that her name was Liz.'

'Of course, I think I knew that. On the rare moments Phillida's at home, she's far too tired. I feel I'm missing a vital part of my life. Can you understand that at all?'

When Liz Probert said that she supposed she could, in a way, Claude carried on in a manner she found embarrass-ing, she told me at the time. 'I mean,' he said, 'it's not the sort of thing a fellow likes to do on his own.'

'No, I suppose not.'

'It'll be eighteen months now. I'm having the most terri-ble withdrawal symptoms.'

At which Liz tried to gobble her sandwich, but Claude was relentless. 'All she could manage, ' he told her, 'was a little bit of Offenbach at Christmas. You must know how it feels.'

'Well, not exactly.'

'To be honest with you,' Claude apparently told her then, 'I can't remember when my wife and I last sat down together to a decent Wagner opera.'

If this was an enigmatic conversation for Miss Liz Probert, it was as nothing compared to the extraordinary encounter I had with Claude as I left Chambers after my work was done a few days later. Bear in mind the situation. I had no idea of the confidences my learned friend had bestowed on Mizz Probert, and he came popping out of his door and waylaid me in an urgent manner.

'Rumpole! A word in confidence!'

'Not another secret?' Secrets, it seemed, were in season around Equity Court.

'I've invited you to the Opera next month.' Erskine-Brown might have been passing on the recipe for Star Wars.

'Not Wagner?'

'Well, it does happen to be *Meistersinger*.'

'An entertainment about the length of a long firm fraud, tried through an interpreter. Who was it who said Wagner's music isn't nearly as bad as it sounds?'

'Don't worry, Rumpole. You won't actually have to *come* to the Opera.'

'You mean you're *not* going to ask me?' I wasn't entirely disappointed.

'Oh, I did ask you.'

'And I refused?'

'Oh no. You accepted. You'd like to get to know a good deal more about music drama.'

'White man speak in riddles.' The fellow was confusing me.

'It's just that if my wife asks you where I was on the

twenty-eighth of next month we went to the Opera together,' Erskine-Brown explained as though to a slow-
witted child.

'But I won't have been there!'

'Ssh!'—Erskine-Brown looked round nervously—'that's
the whole point!'

'Will *you* have been there?' I was doing my best to follow his drift.

'That's . . . something of a secret. I can count on you,
can't I, Rumpole?' He began to move briskly away and out
of Chambers, but I called out and came pounding after
him. 'Why on earth should I assist you in this sordid little
conspiracy?'

'Because I've done you an enormous favour, Rumpole. I
recommended you to Batty Bowling.'

'Your old school-friend,' I remembered.

'Exactly. I was instrumental in getting you the brief in
the Official Secrets case.'

'Civil of you. Claude'—I was considerably molli-
fied—'really remarkably civil. I suppose, if you can't get a
hold of anyone else, I might as well not go to the Opera
with you.'

DO YOU WANT TO HEAR ABOUT TEA AND SCANDAL, THEIR
ANCIENT CUSTOM, IN THE MINISTRY OF DEFENCE? IT'S ALL
HIGHLY SECRET AND MIGHT MAKE A GOOD STORY FOR YOUR
COLUMN. COME INTO ST JAMES'S PARK THURSDAY LUNCH-
TIME, FROM THE MALL. I'LL BE ON THE FIRST BENCH TO
THE RIGHT AFTER YOU'VE CROSSED THE BRIDGE. DON'T
SPEAK TO ME. I'M FIFTY YEARS OLD, BROWNISH HAIR
GOING GREY, AND I WEAR SPECTACLES AND RATHER
BRIGHTLY COLOURED CLOTHES. I'LL GET UP AT 2 P.M.
WHAT YOU WANT WILL BE LEFT ON THE SEAT FOLDED IN-
SIDE A COPY OF THE DAILY TELEGRAPH.

I was sitting by the gas-fire in the living room of 25b Froxbury Court, with the brief *R. v. Tuttle* open on my knees. What I was reading was a photostat of the note, typed in capitals, that my client was alleged to have sent to Mr Chatterbox. One phrase stuck in my mind, 'tea and scandal'. It seemed too literary for Miss Tuttle, and had a sort of period flavour. No doubt it was a point of no importance and I dismissed it from my mind as the telephone rang and Hilda leapt to her feet and went out into the hall to answer it. This was somewhat odd, as there is a perfectly good extension in the living-room.

'Why not take it in here,' I called after her.

'Isn't a person entitled to a little privacy,' she called back, and kicked the door shut. I was left alone to wonder if even She Who Must Be Obeyed had secrets and what on earth those secrets could be. Was our mansion flat sheltering a mole, and could Hilda be selling off the secrets of my defence briefs to the Prosecution? My curiosity got the better of me and I gingerly lifted the sitting-room phone, but I got only an angry buzz and Hilda's voice behind me calling, 'Rumpole!' as she returned to the room. 'What's the matter with our phone?'

'It looks perfectly all right to me.' I surveyed the instrument I had hastily returned to its rest.

'It makes little hiccuping sounds. Have you paid the bill, Rumpole?'

'Perhaps not . . . Pressure of work lately.'

'If you haven't paid the bill it ought to be cut right off. It ought not to hiccup.' She looked at me severely as though any malaise of our telephone was undoubtedly my fault.

'To hear is to obey, O Mistress of the Blue Horizons,' I said, but not out loud.

The next day my journey to work was unusually eventful. I got off the tube, as usual, at Temple station and stopped to buy a *Times*. (They had been sold out at Gloucester Road.) A man in a cap and mackintosh, whom I had noticed on the train, seemed to loiter by the newsagent, and when I had bought my newspaper and set off towards Middle Temple Gardens, Fountain Court, and so to Equity Court, he seemed to be in casual pursuit. When I stopped to do up a shoelace, he stopped also. When I paused to admire the roses, he admired them also. I was wondering what I had done to earn the attention of the man with the cap, when a voice called out 'Rumpole', and Mizz Liz Probert engaged me in conversation. As we ambled on together, my unknown follower put on a sudden spurt, and walked past us.

'I wanted to tell you something.' Liz Probert was clearly in a confiding mood.

'Not a secret?' How many more could I take?

'It's about Claude Erskine-Brown. He's asked me to the Opera.'

'To *Meistersinger?*' I hazarded a guess.

'I think it's at Covent Garden actually.' Mizz Probert was clearly not a Wagnerite. 'What do you think . . .?'

'Well, at your age it's probably all right. For me, well, life's getting a bit short for Wagner.'

'It might be terribly embarrassing.'

'Why? I don't remember that they did much strippingoff at Nuremberg.'

'You don't think he'd use it as an excuse to project some sort of masculine aggression? Might he say I've got extremely nice eyes, or something horrible?'

'Oh, I don't think you need worry about that.' It was kindly meant, but I realize it wasn't exactly well put.

'Don't you?' She smiled.

'I didn't mean . . . they're *not* nice.'

'Rumpole'—she was no longer smiling—'don't you start presenting as a male stereotype!'

'No, of course not. God forbid! Purely functional eyes, yours. Scarcely worth a mention.'

We had reached the door of Chambers and Mizz Probert changed the subject. 'How's your Secrets case?'

'A farce!' I told her. 'Anyone who calls it a Secrets case has had their brains addled by too many spy stories.'

I carried my battered old brief-case into the clerk's room to collect my letters which were mainly buff envelopes and sent to me by Her Majesty. As I filed a couple of them in the waste-paper basket, I noticed some sort of workman, a black man as I remember it, standing on a step-ladder and doing something to the electric light. I also saw Uncle Tom, our oldest inhabitant, who had just arrived with *his* brief-case, which, being dark brown and equally battered, seemed to be the twin of mine. As Uncle Tom had not, to my certain knowledge, received a brief of any sort for the last twenty years, I was prompted to ask what he carried in his brief-case, a question which had long been troubling me. 'Care to have a look?' Uncle Tom was ever obliging. He opened his luggage to reveal a carton of milk, the green muffler his sister always insisted he took with him to Chambers, two golf balls, a packet of cheese and tomato sandwiches, the *Times* and a tin of throat pastilles.

'What are the zubes for?'

'Really, Rumpole! Doesn't *your* voice get tired when you speak in Court?'

'Yes. But you don't speak in Court.'

'One never knows, does one, when one might not get called on?'

As we left the clerk's room Uncle Tom said, 'That chap up the ladder was like you.'

'Well, not very like me.'

'He seemed extraordinarily interested in my brief-case.'

Events continued their unusual course when I got up to my room. I was hanging up the hat and mac when our Head of Chambers, Soapy Sam Ballard, slid in at the door and almost whispered, 'Thought I'd call in on you up here. Walls have ears you know, especially in the clerk's room. I'm prosecuting you in the Secrets case.'

'Oh, you mean the Biscuits case?'

'No, the Secrets.'

'The secret biscuits.' Entering into the spirit of the thing, I stabbed at the curtains with my umbrella and a cry of 'Dead for a ducat, dead!'

'What *are* you doing, Rumpole?'

'I thought there might be a couple of Russians behind the arras.'

'It's a particularly serious case.' Ballard looked pained; well he usually does. 'What's at stake isn't merely biscuits.'

'I know that. It's lavatory paper too.'

'Rumpole!'

'And cups of tea, naturally, and free holidays. And entertaining named persons.'

'It's a question of loyalty to the Crown. I'm sorry to have to tell you this but the Attorney-General himself takes a serious view.'

'Is the old darling keen on biscuits?' I suppose I shouldn't have said that, but as I did so Ballard became unexpectedly friendly. 'Look here, Rumpole, Horace...' he said. 'I don't know whether you know, I've just been elected to the Sheridan Club.'

'Great news, Bollard. Was it on telly?'

'I just wondered whether you'd care to join me there for a spot of luncheon.'

Usually I fear prosecuting counsel when they come offering lunch, but Ballard was extremely insistent and even paid for the taxi to the Sheridan, a rambling, grey building in the hinterland behind Trafalgar Square in need of a spring-clean, decorated with portraits of old actors and judges (the Judges looked more theatrical and the actors considerably more judicial), where that small, stage army of persons most closely engaged in running the nation's affairs meet to get mildly sloshed at lunchtime. In the small and crowded bar Sir Frank Fawcett from the M.O.D. was having a gin and tonic with Oliver Bowling, the Assistant Under-Secretary; an ex-Cabinet Minister was trying to persuade a publisher to buy his unreadable memoirs; Mr Chatterbox of the *Sunday Fortress* was giggling with a little group of journalists in the corner; and Ballard became almost unbearably excited when a sleepy-eyed, longish-haired man in a double-breasted suit and striped shirt—a middle-aged debs' delight—came wafting over to us. 'Mr Attorney!' Ballard greeted him loudly. 'This is Horace Rumpole. He's defending Tuttle.'

'Pink gin, thanks Sam. Lots of ice.' And when Ballard had gone about his business, Sir Lambert Syme, Her Majesty's Attorney-General, said, 'I imagine Tuttle's a plea of guilty.'

'Absolutely no harm in imagining.'

'It's only the tip of the iceberg, you know.'

'Of course. There's something far more serious at stake. Swiss Roll.'

'Molesworth!' The Attorney shook his head. He wasn't smiling.

'My name's Rumpole.'

'No. *Molesworth*.'

'No, really.'

'The American Air Force Base,' he explained carefully, 'where alleged protesters camp out with their thermoses, or is it "thermi"? I must say, if they're all genuine C.N.D. protesters, my name's Gorbachev. No point in going into Molesworth. I imagine Sam would take a plea on the biscuits. If she confesses to that, Lord Chief'll probably keep the old bat out of chokey.'

'The Lord Chief!' I was amazed at the compliment paid to me and Miss Tuttle. 'He's coming down to try it?'

'Oh, yes. Question of loyalty in the Civil Service. The Government's pretty concerned about it. It'll be quite a party.' And as Ballard returned to us with the drinks, the Attorney asked, 'Wouldn't you, Sam? Take a plea on the biscuits?'

'I'd be guided, of course, by the Law Officers of the Crown.' Ballard meant that he'd do as he was told.

Before we left him and went down to lunch, I had one other question to ask the Attorney-General: 'It's about my telephone at home,' I said. 'It's started to hiccup.'

'Perhaps it's had rather too much claret.' He looked down at the glass in my hand.

'What's more, I got a red notice at least a month ago and they haven't cut it off yet.'

'Well, you're in luck's way, aren't you, Rumpole?' The Attorney-General smiled and moved away from us. Ballard then bought me a perfectly good luncheon during which he continued to tell me how extremely grateful the Government of the day would be if Miss Tuttle put her hands up, and thus saved herself and all of us from further embarrassing revelations. I ploughed through the boiled beef, carrots

and a suet dumpling, topped up with treacle tart, and offered the Government of the day no sort of comfort at all.

Miss Rosemary Tuttle used to keep her own portable Olivetti Lettera 22 typewriter in her office at the Ministry of
Defence, and used it to do her own letters and reports when
the typing pool was busy. This machine, a prosecution exhibit, was now incarcerated in New Scotland Yard, to
which Jasper James and I took our client so that we might
conduct our own typewriting test. While she sat typing
placidly in her peasant attire, Detective Inspector Fallowes,
the Officer-in-Charge of the case, started up a new mystery, drawing me a little apart from the clatter of the Olivetti.

'By the way, Mr Rumpole,' he muttered confidentially.
'A word of warning, sir. A gentleman of your stamp has to
be careful of his position when he's on a sensitive case like
this.'

'Has he?' I was perplexed.

'Oh, yes, sir. Does the name of O'Rourke mean anything to you? Seamus O'Rourke? Suspected I.R.A. sym-
pathizer.'

'Absolutely nothing,' I said truthfully, whilst Miss Tuttle
was resolutely typing I'LL BE ON THE FIRST BENCH TO THE
RIGHT AFTER YOU'VE CROSSED THE BRIDGE.

'Perhaps it means something to your wife then.' Detective Inspector Fallowes smiled in a friendly fashion. 'We'd
just like you to be extremely careful. There now'—he
picked up Miss Tuttle's finished sheet and gave it to
me—"look at it all ways up, Mr Rumpole; no doubt it
comes from the same machine as the note to the *Fortress*.
So glad to have been able to help you.'

'Tea and scandal.' The words bothered me again, as I

read them in the note Miss Tuttle had just typed. Back in Froxbury Court I looked up tea in the Index of my old *Oxford Dictionary of Quotations:* 'is there honey still for t.?' no, 'sometimes counsel take—and sometimes t.,' not that; and then I saw it: 't. and scandal'. Rather an obscure phrase in fact from Congreve's dedication to his play *The Double Dealer:* 'Retired to their tea and scandal, according to their ancient custom'. Well, there it was, but I couldn't see, for the moment, how it helped Miss Tuttle. So I called for my wife's assistance on another mystery. 'Hilda. It just crossed my mind. Have you by any chance an Irish friend called Seamus O'Rourke?'

'What sort of friend?'

'Any sort of friend.'

'Why do you ask that, Rumpole?' We were seated in the kitchen of our mansion flat, and She was dishing out stew.

'God knows.'

'What?'

'God knows why I ask. It's some sort of Official Secret.'

'What's that meant to mean?'

'That no one knows what the hell it's about except the Government and probably it's not of the slightest importance anyway.' Hilda sat down to her steaming plateful and looked at me, doubtfully.

'They haven't heard about the hatch, have they?' She wondered.

'What?'

'The Government haven't heard about my idea for a new kitchen hatch?'

'Oh, I expect so, Hilda. I expect your idea for a kitchen hatch ranks high in the list of classified information. Along with biscuits and the next American attack on somewhere or another!'

'I wish you'd stop talking nonsense, Rumpole.' Hilda then attacked her dinner and I could get no more out of her.

When I bought the next morning's *Times* and sat reading it on my journey to Temple station, I discovered that Whitehall was buzzing with rumours of a serious new leak from the Ministry of Defence. An article in the American magazine *Newsweek* had suggested that information concerning the sensitive N.A.T.O. 'Operation Blueberry' was already in the hands of the Russians. The matter was expected to be raised in Parliament during Prime Minister's Question Time . . . So one mystery was solved at least; I thought I knew why the Lord Chief Justice of England was descending on the Old Bailey in person to try Miss Rosemary Tuttle.

Perhaps I had absorbed some of the general air of mystery surrounding the case, but I decided to carry my brief in *R. v. Tuttle* enclosed in my old brief-case, which I left for a while in the clerk's room whilst I went to refresh my memory of Section 2 of the Official Secrets Act. So I arrived at the door of the Court, with Liz Probert, who was to take a note for me, fully robed and carrying my brief-case, and there I met for the first time, Oliver Bowling, the pleasing and cultivated head of Miss Tuttle's department, who had the good sense of having me briefed in the case. Although he had apparently borne the nickname Batty Bowling when at school with Claude, I could see no basis for any suggestion of insanity.

'This is a most ridiculous business,' Bowling told me. 'It's not going to do anyone the slightest good.' He was a quietly spoken man in a tweed suit which must have cost a good deal in its day, and he had wrinkles of amusement at the corners of his eyes; I thought Miss Tuttle was lucky to have him on her side. 'If there's anything I can do to help?' he said. 'Character witness. That sort of thing...?'

'There *is* something you can tell me. Miss Tuttle was eating her sandwiches in St James's Park. Is that where she always took her lunch?'

'Oh, I believe so. She was very regular in her habits.'

'By regular, you mean she always left the park at the same time?'

'Back in the office by ten past two. You could set your watch by her. Pretty rare nowadays...'

'Outdoor sandwich-eaters?'

'I really mean someone you can depend on. Utterly.' And then he excused himself saying he had to get back to the Ministry. Nearer the door of the Court I had a far less pleasant encounter. A pale and deeply disturbed Sam Ballard, Q.C., waylaid me.

'A word in your ear.' He took my arm and steered me apart.

'Bollard! I sighed. 'We're not going into secret session again?' He was looking across at Liz, who was chattering to Jasper James, our solicitor, and he almost hissed, 'That girl Probert, she can't possibly come into Court!'

'She's taking a note for me.'

'Impossible!'

'She's a member of the Bar, Bollard. You can't keep her out.'

'We were grossly deceived.' Ballard's voice sank to a note of low tragedy. 'She's not a clergyman's daughter!'

'Oh? Is the Court only open to clergymen's daughters today? You and I'd better clear off home.'

'Detective Inspector Fallowes has just told me who she is.'

'Is it any of the Detective Inspector's business?'

'She's the daughter of Red Ron Probert!' The news came from him in an appalled whisper. 'Socialist Chairman of South-East London Council. Well, you do see? We can't have a girl like that in Court on a sensitive case.'

'You mean a case about sensitive biscuits?'

'It may not just be biscuits any more.' He sounded most grave. 'We may have to apply to add new charges!'

'Why don't you? And make this prosecution look even more fatuous.'

'Look, Rumpole. I would advise you to take this matter seriously. In the national interest!'

Then I used a phrase which I had planned for some time, and this seemed an ideal moment to trot it out: 'And I'd advise you, Bollard, if you can find a taxidermist willing to take on the work, to get stuffed.' I then called loudly to Miss Liz Probert to follow me, and swept into Court.

We were only just in time. Ballard and his team followed us in, and then, at exactly twenty-nine minutes past ten, Lord Wantage took his seat on the Bench. I knew the Lord Chief Justice was a healthy-looking fellow who spent most of his spare time on the golf course, and who dispatched his business with a great reliance on short judgements and long sentences. His bluff and cheerful manner concealed an extremely conventional and sometimes brutal lawyer. He was also not noted for his criticisms of the Government's legislation, and I suspected that I would have to get the Jury, and not his Lordship, to laugh the case out of Court.

So, as Ballard rose to apply for certain parts of the evidence to be heard behind closed doors, I settled in my seat and opened the battered brief-case I had brought in with me, and as I did I gave what must have been an audible gasp of horror. My brief was notably absent, and all I had

was a green muffler, a carton of milk, a *Times,* a packet of
cheese and tomato sandwiches, two golf balls and some
throat pastilles. Uncle Tom's brief-case had, at long last,
got into Court.

Those who know me best around the Bailey will know
that, when in full flood, I rarely consult my brief, and I did
have most of the simple facts in *R.* v. *Tuttle* at my fingers'
ends. However, it is somewhat unnerving to be in a Court
crowded with reporters, appearing before the Lord Chief
Justice of England, with nothing much to consult except a
green muffler and a cheese sandwich. I sent Liz Probert off
to phone Henry and get my effects sorted out, and then sat
through an uneasy half-hour. Before the Jury was sworn in,
the Lord Chief, who clearly knew more about the case then
he let on, asked Ballard if he were applying to add more
charges. Ballard answered that he wasn't going to do so for
the moment, and although I reared up to protest, the Chief
allowed the Prosecution to keep this threat of unknown and
mysteriously serious allegations dangling.

The Jury assembled and Ballard opened his case. His
first witness was Tim Warboys of the *Sunday Fortress,* and
by the time I rose to cross-examine this star of journalism,
Henry had come down from Chambers in a taxi, and I had
my brief and Uncle Tom had his sandwiches.

'Mr Warboys...or should I call you Mr Chatterbox?' I
began and Ballard rose to protest, 'There's no need for my
learned friend to be offensive to the witness.'

'Oh, keep still, Bollard!' I growled at him. 'It's his
name in the paper.'

'It would probably be better if you simply used the witness's name, Mr Rumpole.' The Chief started his interrup-

tions politely and Ballard sat down, smiling with gratifica-
tion.

'Oh, much obliged, my Lord. I'll try to remember.' I
was also starting politely. 'Mr Warboys. You make your
living by divulging secrets, don't you?'

'I don't know what you mean.' The investigative jour-
nalist clearly didn't like being investigated; he sounded
narked.

'Who's sleeping with whom is one of your subjects. You
keep your eye perpetually to the keyhole?'

'I write a gossip column, yes,' Mr Chatterbox admitted.

'And you know that some gossip is strictly protected by
our Lords and Masters?'

'Some information is classified, yes.'

'Classified gossip. Exactly! And you are familiar with
Section 2 of the Official Secrets Act?'

'I know something about it.' A very cautious chap, I
thought, the dashing old Etonian, Warboys.

'You know that it's an offence to receive secret information?'

'I believe it is.'

'For which you can get two years in the nick.'

'Two years' imprisonment, Mr Rumpole,' the Chief Justice corrected me, still with smiling courtesy.

'Oh, I beg its pardon, my Lord. Imprisonment.'

'For a story about biscuits?' Warboys sounded incredulous.

'Oh, they're very protective of their biscuits in the Ministry of Defence.' I scored my first hit with that; there was
some laughter from the Jury. The Chief turned to them and
showed intense disapproval.

'Members of the Jury,' he said. 'You may hear a good

deal from the Defence about biscuits in this case, and I suggest that, after Mr Rumpole has got his laugh, we take this matter seriously. This is a case about whether or not a servant of the Crown was loyal to the interests of the Government. Very well...'

'Your Lordship doesn't wish me to call a biscuit a biscuit?' I asked politely. 'Should we settle for *une petite pièce de pâtisserie?*' I got a suppressed titter for that from the twelve good citizens, and a cold 'What's your next question, Mr. Rumpole?' from the Bench.

'Ah. Yes. I was so fascinated by your Lordship's address to the Jury that I have forgotten my next question. No! Now I remember it! Do you expect to be prosecuted for receiving secret information, Mr Warboys?'

'No. Not really.' Mr Chatterbox was hesitant.

'The police have set your mind at rest?'

'I've been told I have nothing to worry about.' He smiled modestly.

'In return for shopping Miss Tuttle?' At which the Lord Chief uttered a warning 'Mister Rumpole!' 'Oh, I do beg your Lordship's pardon. In return for giving evidence against the middle-aged spinster lady whom I represent, you're saving your own skin, Mr Warboys?' I suggested.

'I have agreed to cooperate with the police, yes.'

'Thus upholding the finest traditions of British journalism.'

'Mr Rumpole!' The Lord Chief's patience was in short supply. 'Have you any relevant questions to ask this witness?'

'Of course. About your alleged meeting with Miss Tuttle in St James's Park. On that occasion you didn't speak to her at all. In fact, by the time you reached her bench, she had gone?'

'That's what happened . . .'

'From the moment you saw her get up and go until you reached the bench and collected the envelope . . .'—I picked up the envelope containing the copied documents—'. . . was the newspaper folded round it always in your view?'

'I can't be sure,' he had to admit.

'There may have been other people passing in front of the bench!'

'There may have been.'

I gave the Jury one of my most meaningful looks. 'So you never really met Miss Tuttle at all?'

'Not if you put it like that. No.'

'And you have no doubt that it was Miss Tuttle, the defendant, you saw.'

'No doubt at all. She . . .' He looked at the figure in the dock.

'What were you going to say?'

'I was going to say that she wears rather distinctive clothing.'

'So she could be easily identified?'

'Yes.'

'Rather a foolish thing to do, I suppose, if she was in the business of leaking secrets?'

Ballard rose to protest, and the Judge smiled wearily at him, as though they were both reasonable adults watching the antics of an extremely tiresome child. 'I know, Mr Ballard,' he spoke soothingly, 'but perhaps we should both possess our souls in patience. No doubt the truth will finally emerge in this case, despite Mr Rumpole's suppositions.'

'The truth! Yes. I'm so much obliged to your Lordship.' I acted deep and humble gratitude. 'Let's see if we can discover the truth. Remember, Mr Warboys, you're on your oath; you had never seen Miss Rosemary Tuttle before?'

'No. I had had her letter, of course.'

'You say *her* letter. It wasn't signed by her?'

'No.'

'It didn't even have her name on it.'

'No.'

'So when you say it was her letter, it is a pure guess.'

'The letter said she would be sitting on the park bench, and would leave at two o'clock. And there she was!'

'But to say that the note was written by her is a pure guess!'

'I suppose Mr Ballard will say to the Jury that it's a reasonable deduction, Mr Rumpole.' The Lord Chief sounded the embodiment of common sense.

'My Lord! I really can't be held responsible for what my learned friend Mr Ballard may say to the Jury. Thank you, Mr Ch—Mr Warboys.'

I sat down then, fairly well satisfied, although I still had no clear idea which way the case was going. I wondered idly what you have to do to become Lord Chief Justice of England, and wear a golden lavatory chain on State occasions. Play remarkable golf? Shoot with the Lord Chancellor? Manners can't have anything to do with it. That means there might be a chance for Rumpole! Lord Rumpole of the Gloucester Road, Baron Rumpole of the Temple Station ...I came down to earth to hear Warboys tell Lord Wantage, in answer to a flagrantly leading question, that he had no doubt at all that it was Miss Tuttle he had seen in St James's Park.

Before we had started to quarrel I had persuaded the Lord Chief to give Miss Tuttle bail during the lunch hour, and when I came out of Court there she was waiting patiently for instructions. I tried to cheer her up, told her that the case was going as well as possible and that, in any event, she had a good friend in old Batty Bowling.

'Oh, he is the most super boss,' she agreed, in her quaint English schoolgirl's lingo. 'Always listens to your problems, but never spares himself. Burns the midnight oil. Well, so do I. Often when I'm working late at the Ministry, he's still there. Sometimes I hear him singing to himself. He seems very happy.'

'Well . . .' I began to move off to the robing room. 'Care for a Guinness and a steak pie at the pub?'

'Oh, no. I brought sandwiches and there's a dear little churchyard across the road.'

'I'm sure there is. Oh. There was one thing I did mean to ask you. About Congreve.'

'Congreve?' Miss Tuttle looked blank. 'Is he at the Ministry?' There was clearly a gap in her English schoolgirl education.

'William Congreve, Miss Tuttle, and English dramatist of genius, born in Good King Charles's golden days, carried on rather shockingly with the Duchess of Marlborough. The name doesn't ring any kind of bell?'

'Sorry. I was an economist, actually.' I absorbed the information, and then asked, 'One other little matter. The bomb.'

'The what?'

'More politely known as the nuclear deterrent. Have you got any affection for it?'

'Oh golly yes!, Mr Rumpole.' She smiled enthusiastically. 'Like all the chaps at the Ministry. We're a hundred per cent behind the bomb.'

'Thank you, Miss Tuttle. That was all I wanted to

know.' I moved away from her then, leaving her standing
alone in the middle of the hall. I would do almost anything
for a client, except share her sandwiches in the courtyard.

There was one part of R. v. Tuttle which I was looking
forward to keenly. I may be a child when it comes to partnership agreements, a dolt about Real Property, and I may
even have some difficulty construing the more opaque provisions of the Obscene Publications Act. But I do know
about bloodstains, gunfire wounds and typewriters. The
analysis of typewriting is a fascinating subject and one I
have discussed with great enjoyment across many a
crowded Court with Peter Royce-Williams, the uncrowned
King of the questioned documents. Royce-Williams is no
longer young; did he not, when we were both Juveniles,
give evidence about the questioned suicide note in the
Penge Bungalow Murders? But he is unrivalled in his field.
He is a short, stout man with the pale face and strong,
tinted spectacles of a man who spends his life with micro-
scopes and darkrooms, pursuing forgeries.

That afternoon, Royce-Williams stood in the witness-
box with his enlarged pictures of the two documents: the
note sent to Mr Chatterbox and that typed by Miss Tuttle in
New Scotland Yard. His conclusion was that both documents were typed on the sort of paper used in government
departments on the Olivetti Lettera 22 portable, which, according to the evidence, belonged to my client, the defendant Tuttle.

When I got up to cross-examine, I knew that there would
be no point whatever in a head-on clash with the witness.
Peter Royce-Williams must be led gently and with the
greatest respect to the point where we might, with any
luck, agree. And having thought the matter over carefully,

with the aid of a pint of Guinness during the luncheon adjournment, I now felt clear about what that point might be.

'Mr. Royce-Williams,' I began. 'As an acknowledged expert, would you agree that a typewriter doesn't work itself, a human being is involved in the operation . . .?'

'Yes, of course, Mr. Rumpole.' It was delightful to chat to old friends.

'And human operators have varying degrees of skill?'

'I should have thought that was obvious.'

'Bear with me if I have a very simple mind, Mr Royce-Williams.' The old boy smiled at that, although the Judge didn't. 'A highly experienced typist will, on the whole, type smoothly, hitting all the keys with equal force. A person not so used to the machine may hit harder, perhaps after a hesitation, or more faintly because their fingers are less skilled?'

'That's certainly possible.'

'Have you considered that, in relation to these documents?'

'No. I must confess I haven't.' Like all good experts he was completely candid about the limits of his research.

'Just look at the word "scandal" in the note to Mr Warboys, and in that typed by Miss Tuttle in Scotland Yard. In the one sent to the newspaper, aren't the 's' and 'c' heavier and the other letters lighter?'

Royce-Williams held the documents very close and raised his dark glasses, the better to peer at them with his naked and watery eyes.

'That would seem to be so,' he agreed at last.

'And in that typed in the Detective Inspector's office they all have the same clarity?'

'Yes. I think they have.'

'Might that not lead you to the same conclusion that they were typed by different people using the *same machine and paper?*'

There was a pause that seemed to me to go on for ever, as Royce-Williams carefully put down his papers and polished his glasses. But he was too good at his job to exclude the possibility I had mentioned. 'I suppose it might,' he said.

'You suppose it might,' I repeated with suitable emphasis for the benefit to the Jury.

'Mr Rumpole. Where is this evidence leading us?' The Lord Chief clearly seemed to feel that the case was wandering out of his control.

'Your Lordship asks me that?' I would, if I'd been as honest as Royce-Williams, have gone on: 'Believe me, old darling, I wish I knew.' What I actually said was: 'To the truth, my Lord. Or isn't that what we want to discover?'

Furiously making a note, Lord Wantage then broke the point of his pencil. He whispered to the wigged Court Clerk below him, and when the man stood up to get him another, I thought I could hear him whisper, 'Is Rumpole always as outrageous as this?'

'I'm afraid so, my Lord,' I know the Clerk whispered back. 'Absolutely always.'

'Thank you, Mr Rumpole. I enjoyed that.' Oliver Bowling was waiting for me when I got out of Court that evening, having apparently taken an afternoon off from the defence of the Nation to sample some of the free entertainment the Old Bailey alone provides. Grateful of his support, I took him for a cup of tea in the unglamorous surroundings of the Old Bailey canteen, where the cheese rolls were just being stored away for the night.

'You had another leak from your Ministry? Anything

important?' He smiled at me over his cup of strong Indian tea, made not, I imagined, how he really liked it.

'Sometimes I wonder what *is* important.' Bowling smiled at me. 'Wouldn't the world be a healthier, more peaceful place if we told everyone exactly what we'd got and stopped trying to frighten each other with a lot of spurious secrets? Mustn't say that in the Department, of course.'

'No. Of course not.' I crunched a chocolate biscuit; it's hungry work cross-examining experts in questioned documents. 'I've got to have a go at your big cheese tomorrow. The Permanent Under-Secretary. What sort of chap is he?'

'Comes from "a branch of one of your ante-diluvian families, fellows that the flood couldn't wash away." That sort of thing. He'll be immensely fair,' Bowling reassured me. 'Give me a ring if there's anything I can do.'

'I might call you at home, when Court's over.'

'Oh, right. Here's the number.' He took a card from his wallet and gave it to me. 'I'll be leaving the Ministry fairly early. Chap at the Foreign Office's got the use of the Royal Box at Covent Garden. You can dine there, you know. Rather fun.'

'Is it really?' I was prepared to take his word for it. When we parted I looked at the visiting card he had given me, then I turned it over and wrote, on the back, a sentence from our conversation. At home I paid another visit to *The Oxford Dictionary of Quotations*.

Sir Frank Fawcett, the Permanent Under-Secretary, walked solemnly into the witness-box the following afternoon in a Court from which the public had been excluded at Ballard's request. Could all this pomp and circumstance possibly be about so many thousand mid-morning snacks, or was it entirely occasioned by the activities of Miss Rosemary Tuttle, who sat, a small and somewhat garish figure, in the dock? I asked Sir Frank about her when I climbed to my feet and started to cross-examine.

'You know something about my client, Miss Tuttle?'

'Yes. I have the reports on her.'

'You have no reason to suppose that she would constitute any sort of danger to the State, have you?'

'May I refresh my memory, my Lord?' His Lordship gave permission and a file was handed up to the witness.

'Rosemary Alice Tuttle,' he read out. 'Born of Austrian parents, Franz and Maria Toller, who emigrated to this country when she was two years old and changed their name. Educated at Hampstead High School for Girls and the London School of Economics.'

'No mystery about that—except that they chose the name Tuttle.'

The Jury smiled at that and the Lord Chief was displeased. 'She was, of course, thoroughly vetted when she took up her post with us,' Sir Frank told them.

'Nothing else known against her?'

'Do you really want all this evidence in?' I had a whispered warning from Liz Probert, sitting beside me, who was rapidly turning into quite a conventional form of barrister. 'Keep your head, Mizz Probert, when all about you are losing theirs and blaming it on you,' I whispered back, and challenged the witness to tell us the worst.

'Unconfirmed reports that she was seen at Molesworth American Air Force Base in January 1986...' Sir Frank sifted through the file.

'Taking part in an entirely peaceful demonstration?' I asked him.

'She was questioned about the matter and denied it. She suggested it might have been someone else similarly dressed.'

'Did that seem to you rather improbable?' The Lord Chief smiled understandingly at the witness.

'It did, my Lord, yes. After that she was not recommended for further promotion and kept under special surveillance.'

'Surveillance which in this case seems to have been somewhat ineffective?' His Lordship was telling Sir Frank that men of their stamp always had problems with incompetent underlings.

'I'm afraid so, my Lord.'

'She got at the biscuits . . .' I understood the full horror of the position and the Chief uttered a warning 'Mr Rumpole!'

'All right. Let's try to take this little scandal seriously. Have you been able to check whether the information leaked to the Press about money spent on refreshments and entertaining, and so on, is accurate?'

'It's not entirely accurate.' Sir Frank had blinked at an unexpected question and taken a while to answer. Now he seemed embarrassed.

'The report is exaggerated?'

'I'm afraid my inquiries have led me to believe that we spend a good deal more than has been suggested, my Lord.'

'So the secrets she's supposed to have leaked aren't accurate Official Secrets at all?' I went on, before My Lord could interrupt.

'Not . . . entirely accurate. No.'

'Sir Frank Fawcett'—I paused and looked seriously at

the witness—'there's something a good deal more significant than biscuits at the bottom of this case, isn't there?'

'I'm not sure what you mean exactly.'

'Neither am I, Mr Rumpole.' The Lord Chief wasn't
going to be left out.

'We're not all assembled here—you, the Permanent
Under-Secretary and my learned friend and the Lord Chief
Justice of England—to sit in secret session in a Court
which has now been closed to the public . . .'

'Mr Rumpole. It was I who decided that Sir Frank's
evidence should be taken in camera,' the Judge reminded
me, but I soldiered on: 'Denying the principle that justice
should be seen to be done, just to discuss a few little white
lies about the number of bikkies you took with your
elevenses! Far more sensitive information than that has
recently been leaked from the Ministry of Defence,
hasn't it?'

'Mr Rumpole. Do you really think that question is in the
interests of your client?' The Judge wanted the Jury to
know that, in his view, I was about to land Miss Tuttle in
the soup.

'That's why I asked it. Now will you answer it, Sir
Frank?'

'My Lord . . .' The witness turned to the Lord Chief for
guidance but he merely sighed heavily and said, 'You'd
better answer Mr Rumpole's question. We *are* in camera.'

'The answer'—again it came after a long pause—'is
yes.'

'You don't know the source of that leak?'

'No . . .'

'And no application has been made to add further
charges against my client, Miss Tuttle?'

'Not as yet, my Lord,' Ballard interjected in a vaguely

threatening manner, which was echoed by the Judge. 'No, Mr Rumpole, not as yet.'

'And when those charges are brought against whoever it is, these little leaks about Civil Service extravagance will seem even more paltry and insignificant.'

'Isn't that going to be a matter for the Jury?' The Lord Chief had had enough of Rumpole and wanted his tea.

'Oh, I entirely agree, my Lord.' I was at my most servile. 'It will be a matter for the Jury. If this petty prosecution lasts until the end.'

The Court rose then, not in the best of tempers, and the Usher intoned his usual rigmarole that marks the ending of another day: 'All persons who have anything further to do before my Lords, the Queen's Justices at the Central Criminal Court may depart hence and give their attendance here again tomorrow at ten thirty o'clock in the forenoon. God Save the Queen.' 'And protect her'—I joined silently in the prayer—'from her civil servants.'

Back in Chambers, I sat at my desk with the curiously elated feeling of having solved the mystery and learned something, at least, of the secrets of *R*. v. *Tuttle*. I lifted the telephone and asked Dianne to ring Oliver Bowling's number for me.

In the long interval which took place before she called me back, Claude Erskine-Brown came into my room with the haunted and hangdog look of a man who has spent the past few nights being pursued by the Valkyries. 'I have to tell you, Rumpole,' he announced. 'We didn't go to the Opera together.'

'Pity. I was looking forward to it.'

'I mean, if you see my wife, if Phillida should happen to bump into you around Chambers, don't bother to tell her how much you enjoyed *Meistersinger*.'

'Snoozed off in it, did I?'

'She knows I didn't take you.'

'Been rumbled, Erskine-Brown?' I couldn't help looking at the man with pity.

'As I suppose you might say "grassed".' He gave a small and quite mirthless laugh. 'Well, I may as well tell you the horrible truth. Liz Probert rang up Phillida and said that I'd invited *her* to Covent Garden.'

'But hadn't you?'

'Of course I had.'

'And Mrs Phillida Erskine-Brown, the Portia of our Chambers, hasn't shown much of the quality of mercy?'

'She doesn't speak, Rumpole.' The fellow was clearly in distress. 'Breakfast passes by in utter silence. And I did nothing, you understand! Absolutely nothing.'

'Not even compliment Mizz Probert on her eyes?'

'How do you know?' He looked at me as though I had the gift of second sight.

'That was your mistake, Claude. Girls don't care for that sort of thing nowadays.'

'To go and blurt out the truth like that, to a chap's wife! It was totally uncalled for!'

'Perhaps Mizz Liz Probert doesn't believe in Official Secrets. Talking of which . . .'

'What?'

'Your friend Bowling,' I wondered. 'Why did you call him Batty?'

'No reason, really. He never minded what he said, questioned everything in class, that sort of thing. And he was a bit of a show-off.'

'Show-off? What about?

'Oh, his literary knowledge. Something like you, Rumpole.' He looked up at me and finally asked in a tragic way, 'Do you think Philly will ever speak to me again?'

'Oh yes. I imagine so. If only to say goodbye.' And then the phone rang on my desk, and I was able to tell Batty Bowling that I wanted an urgent word with him about Miss Tuttle. He said he was about to leave home, but he would come out of *Tosca* quarter of an hour before the end of the first Act, and we could have a quiet word in the room behind the Royal Box. I told him that I would go anywhere for a client, and he rang off with every expression of goodwill.

So, after a few thoughtful glassfuls at Pommeroy's Wine Bar, I strolled through the gift shops and boutiques and bistros of Covent Garden (lamenting the days of ever-open pubs and old cabbage stalks) to the small Floral Street entrance to the Royal Box. At the mention of Bowling's name an ornately uniformed attendant pointed me up a back staircase, which led to a small dining-room. There, under a chandelier, the remnants of an excellent light dinner still littered the table, and whiffs of excited music came from a curtained doorway. At exactly the appointed time, Oliver Bowling emerged from the doorway wearing a black velvet dinner-jacket that might have seen some service. 'I can give you ten minutes.' He looked at his watch and I thought there was a certain irritation beneath the habitual charm. '*Tosca* doesn't really get going until the second Act, does it?'

'Until she kills him?'

'Well, exactly,' he smiled. 'How can I help you?'

'I wanted to defend Miss Tuttle on the basis that what she did was entirely public-spirited and honourable...' I began at the beginning.

'I'm inclined to agree.'

'But she's always maintained she did nothing'—I was looking at her Head of Department—'and I believe her.'

'But my dear chap.' Bowling smiled tolerantly. 'The evidence!'

'What evidence exactly?' I asked him. 'Someone left her glove beside a copying-machine. Someone used her typewriter, someone who wasn't a trained typist. She went to the park as she always did, to feed the ducks. Perhaps she had no idea that Mr Chatterbox from the *Sunday Fortress* was there watching her. She got up as the clock struck two. Someone else could have passed the bench and dropped an envelope wrapped in the *Daily Telegraph*.'

'Why should anyone . . . ?'

'Want to frame Miss Tuttle on a silly charge about biscuits?'

'Yes. Why?'

'Someone wanted to make her look ridiculous and dishonest, and total unreliable,' I told him. 'Someone wanted her to appear in public as a gossiping little busybody who couldn't even get her facts right. So that, if she ever gave evidence about anything really important, no one would take a blind bit of notice!'

'Really important?' He was still smiling. Somehow I longed to dislodge his smile. 'The big leak . . . The great hole in the system. Whatever it was. Weapons. Submarine bases. Engines of death. Perhaps, after all, it was no more important than biscuits. Would the world be any more dangerous if we did without secrets all together? You don't think so, do you, Mr Bowling?'

'Did I say that to you?'

'Oh yes. I'm prepared to believe your intentions were

honourable. The end of the arms race perhaps. The beginning of peace . . .'

A burst of music penetrated the curtain. Bowling looked
at his watch; the smile had gone now. 'I really ought to get
back to the Opera.'

'I don't know exactly when it was, but I'm sure it was
some time when you ought to have been away on leave and
out of the office. It was late at night and she heard you
singing, whistling or whatever. So she came in and saw
you with . . . perhaps she never realized what she saw you
doing. But you couldn't be sure of her, could you? Bank
robbers shoot witnesses. It's a great deal more subtle to
make fools of them. Perhaps that's the sort of thing they
teach you at Winchester.' I poured the remains of a bottle
of wine into an empty glass. 'You want to go back to the
Opera? Try and remember not to sing the tunes around the
office. Opera appears to be the downfall of Englishmen
who want to keep secrets.' I held up the glass to the chandelier. 'Perfectly decent bit of claret. It seems a pity to
waste it.' I didn't.

'What are you going to do?' Bowling asked after a long
silence.

'I suppose, recall Sir Frank and put the whole business
to him. Remember Sir Frank whose family survived the
flood. That was your quotation from Congreve. *Love for
Love.*'

'Congreve . . . ?'

'Who was also quoted in your note to Mr Chatterbox.
That was what Erskine-Brown told me about you. You
couldn't resist showing off your literary knowledge, even
when engaged on forgery. Poor old Miss Tuttle; she's extremely conventional at heart and does her best to be an

English spinster lady. She'd never dream of demonstrating at Molesworth; you should never have started that rumour. And I'm afraid she's never even heard of Congreve...'

Bowling said nothing. He turned back to the curtain. He seemed about to go and then said, almost pleading with me. 'Rumpole...'

'I'm sorry, I can't help you. It's a question of loyalty to my client. She has my allegiance; I can't worry about yours.' Far away from us, on the stage, the *Te Deum* was swelling from the Cathedral on the stage. The curtain was about to fall. 'You'd better get back to *Tosca*,' I told him. 'Isn't this where the melodrama begins?'

There was a small item in the next morning's *Times*. A man, later identified as Mr Oliver Bowling, O.B.E., Assistant Under-Secretary at the Ministry of Defence, had apparently slipped while waiting on the platform at Covent Garden underground station and fallen under a passing train. Mr Bowling had been quite alone at the time and foul play was not suspected. He was dead on his admission to hospital.

When I arrived, robed, that morning outside the Court, Sam Ballard came up to me. 'Rumpole'—he looked almost apologetic—'there's been a development.'

'I know. A small accident at Covent Garden underground station. It was unnecessary,' I told him. 'Like everything else about this case.'

'I've been in touch with the Attorney-General.'

'Really? What did he feel like?'

'We're offering no further evidence. In view of the fact that the information leaked to the Press was apparently inaccurate.'

'Oh, that gives you the out, does it? Lucky for you, Ballard. And my client's discharged without a stain on her character?'

Ballard was silent and then forced himself to say, 'Yes.'

'Bowling finally told the truth, did he?'

'I'm not prepared to divulge that.'

'Old Batty Bowling. Bit of a literary show-off. But not a bad fellow, all the same. What did he do? Telephone Sir Frank from the Opera?'

'I told you. I'm not prepared to divulge . . .'

'Secrets! My God, Bollard. I wonder what we'd do without them. But they lead to death, don't they? Stupid, unnecessary secrets lead to death?'

So Miss Tuttle and the rest of us were released by the Judge and I went home to Froxbury Court. Hilda was not there, no doubt out on some shopping spree, and I felt unusually tired. I pulled out my old India-paper edition of *The Oxford Book of English Verse*, and started to read by way of consolation: 'The clouds that gather round the setting sun/Do take a sober colouring from an eye/That hath kept watch o'er man's mortality;'—My thoughts were interrupted by the sound of hammering—'Another race hath been, and other palms are won./Thanks to the human heart by which we live,/Thanks to its tenderness, its joys, and fears, . . .' By now the hammering was building to a crescendo. I put down the book, and went to the window, opened it and looked out into the street where I thought the din must be coming from. But as I did so, there was a final crash from behind me, and I turned to see, to my horror, the end of a chisel appear through my living-room wall. Was the Secret Service getting its revenge? In a matter of moments I had doubled into the hall and flung open the kitchen door. There I was greeted with the spectacle of a small gnome-like person of undoubtedly Irish extraction, who, armed with a bag of tools, was tunnelling through my wall.

'A fair cop!'

'Mr Rumpole?' The man apparently recognized me.

'There's one thing to be said for a practice at the criminal Bar,' I told him. 'You don't expect to be burgled . . .'

'Burgled, Mr Rumpole?' He seemed shocked at the suggestion.

'You know the meaning of the word. Breaking and entering! Except you seem to have entered my kitchen and you're breaking out. Do you mind me telling you, that's an inside wall you're attacking. I suggest you give up your life of crime, old darling, you've clearly got very little talent for it.'

'Crime! I don't know what you're talking about, Mr Rumpole.'

'House-breaking instruments!' I was looking at his bag of tools. But at this moment we heard the front door open and the voice of Hilda calling 'Rumpole!'

'I might have sent you on your way with a promise of future good behaviour,' I told the intruder, 'but one is coming in whom the quality of mercy is considerably strained.'

'I thought you were in Court all day.' She came into the kitchen and viewed me with every sign of disfavour.

'Hilda! There is a man here.'

'Of course there's a man in here. He's come to do that hatch. How are you getting on, Mr O'Rourke?'

'O'Rourke? Not Seamus O'Rourke by any chance?' The name rang a pretty enormous bell. Then the man pulled out a smudged card and offered it to me. SEAMUS O'ROURKE, I

read, ALL REPAIRS AND CONVERSIONS CHEERFULLY UNDER-
TAKEN. 'They've been listening to you on the telephone,
Hilda.'

'Speaking of telephones, Rumpole . . .'

'Listening to you! On the subject of a kitchen hatch.' At
which point, She moved to the wall, took down the telephone and held it out to me.

'The instrument has died on us at last! Listen to that!
Silent as the tomb! I told you to pay the bill.'

'The bill? It must have slipped my mind. Pressure of
business . . .'

'And now they've cut it off.'

I listened for a moment to the silent telephone, and then
restored it to its place on the wall. 'They've cut it off at
last,' I agreed with Hilda. 'No one's listening to us any
more. No one wants to look in my brief-case. No one's
following me from the tube station. The Secrets case is
over. Old Batty Bowling is dead, and normal service will
be resumed shortly.'

Rumpole and the
Judge's Elbow

Up to now in these accounts of my most famous or infamous cases I have acted as a faithful historian, doing my best to tell the truth, the whole truth, about the events that occurred, and not glossing over the defeats and humiliations which are part of the daily life of an Old Bailey hack, nor being ridiculously modest about my undoubted triumphs. When it comes to the matter of the Judge's elbow, however, different considerations arise. Many of the vital incidents in the history of the tennis injury to Mr Justice Featherstone, its strange consequences and near destruction of his peace of mind, necessarily happened when I was absent from the scene, nor did the Judge ever take me into his confidence over the matter. Indeed as most of his almost frenetic efforts during the trial of Dr Maurice Horridge were devoted to concealing the truth from the world in general, and old Horace Rumpole in particular, it is a truth which may never be fully known. I have been, however, able to piece together from the scraps of information at my disposal (a word or two from a retired usher, some conversations Marigold Featherstone had with She Who Must Be Obeyed) a pretty clear picture of what went on in the private and, indeed, sheltered life of one of the Judges of the Queen's Bench. I feel that I now know what led to Guthrie Featherstone's curious behaviour during the Horridge trial, but in reconstructing some of the scenes that led up to this, I have had, as I say for the first time in these accounts, to use the art of the fiction writer and imagine, to a large extent, what Sir Guthrie or Lady Marigold Featherstone, or the other characters involved, may have said at the time. Such scenes are based, however, on a long experience of how Guthrie Featherstone was accustomed to behave in the face of life's little difficulties, that is to say, with anxiety bordering on panic.

I think it is also important that this story should be told to warn others of the dangers involved in sitting in Judgement on the rest of erring humanity. However, to save embarrassment to anyone concerned, I have left strict instructions that this account should not be published until after the death of the main parties, unless Mr Truscott of the Caring Bank should become particularly insistent over the question of my overdraft.

Guthrie Featherstone, then plain Mr Guthrie Featherstone, Q.C., M.P., became the Head of our Chambers in Equity Court on the retirement of Hilda's Daddy, old C. H. Wystan, a man who could never bring himself to a proper study of bloodstains. I had expected, as the senior member in practice, to take over Chambers from Daddy, but Guthrie Featherstone, a new arrival, popped in betwixt the election and my hopes.

I have forgotten precisely what brand of M.P. old

Guthrie was; he was either right-wing Labour or left-wing
Conservative until, in the end, he gave up politics and
joined the S.D.P. He was dedicated to the middle of the
road, and very keen on our Chambers 'image', which, on
one occasion, he thought was being let down badly by my
old hat. Finally, the Lord Chancellor, who was probably
thinking of something else at the time, made Guthrie a
scarlet judge, and the old darling went into a dreadful state
of panic, fearing that there had been a premature announce-
ment of this Great Event in the History of our Times.*

From that time, Sir Guthrie Featherstone was entitled to
scarlet and ermine and other variously coloured dressing-
gowns, to be worn at different seasons of the year, and sat
regularly in the seat of Judgement, dividing the sheep from
the goats with a good deal of indecision and anxiety. When
his day's work was done, he returned to the block of flats
in Kensington, where he lived with his wife, Marigold.
The flats came equipped with a tennis court, and there the
Judge and his good lady were accustomed to playing mixed
doubles with their neighbours, the Addisons, during the
long summer evenings. Mr Addison, I imagine, was exces-
sively respectful of the sporting Guthrie and frequently
called out 'Nice one, Judge,' or 'Oh, I say, Judge, what
frightfully bad luck,' during the progress of the game.

What I see, doing my best to reconstruct the occasion
which gave rise to the following chapter of accidents, is
Guthrie and Marigold diving for the same ball with cries of
'Leave it, Marigold!' and 'Mine, Guthrie!'. These two rapidly moving bodies were set on a collision course and,

---

*See 'Rumpole and the Genuine Article' in *Rumpole and the Golden
Thread*, Penguin Books, 1983.

when it happened, the Judge fell heavily to the asphalt, his wife stood over his recumbent figure, and the anxious Addisons came round the net with cries of 'Nothing broken I hope and trust?'. From then on, perhaps, it went something like this:

'Nothing broken is there, Guthrie?' from Marigold.

'My elbow.' The Judge sat up nursing the afflicted part.

'Such terrible luck when it was going to be such a super shot!' said the ever-sycophantic Addison.

'Twiddle your fingers, Guthrie, and let's see if anything is broken.' When the Judge obeyed, Marigold was able to tell him: 'There you are, nothing broken at all!'

'There's an extraordinary shooting pain. Ouch!' Guthrie was clearly suffering.

'Oh, you poor man, you are in the wars, aren't you?' Mr Addison was sympathetic. 'It'll wear off.' Lady Featherstone was not.

'It shows absolutely no sign of wearing off.'

'Rub it then, Guthrie! And for heaven's sake don't be such a baby!'

The next day I was at my business at the Old Bailey, making my usual final appeal on the subject of the burden of proof, that great presumption of innocence, which has been rightly called the golden thread which runs through British justice, when Mr Justice Featherstone, presiding over the trial, interrupted my flow to say, 'Just a moment, Mr Rumpole. I am in considerable pain.' He was, in fact, still rubbing his elbow. 'I have suffered a serious accident.'

'Did your Lordship say "pain"?' I couldn't, for the moment, see how his Lordship's accident was relevant to the question of the burden of proof.

'It's not something one likes to comment about,' the

Judge commented nobly, 'in the general course of events. I have, of course, had some experience of pain, even at a comparatively young age.'

'Did you say comparatively *young,* my Lord?' I thought he was knocking on a bit, for a youngster.

'And if I was the only person concerned I should naturally soldier on regardless . . .'

'Terribly brave, my Lord!' Leaving him to soldier on, I turned back to the Jury. 'Members of the Jury. The question you must ask about each one of these charges is "Are you certain sure?"'

'But I mustn't only think of myself,' the Judge interrupted me again. 'The point is, am I in too much pain to give your speech the attention it deserves, Mr Rumpole?'

'I don't know. Are you?' That was all the help I could give him.

'Exercising the best judgement I have, I have come to the conclusion that I am not. I will adjourn now.'

'At three o'clock?' I must confess I was surprised. 'Pain,' his Lordship told me solemnly, 'is no respecter of time. Till tomorrow morning, members of the Jury.'

'Would your Lordship wish us to send for Matron?' I was solicitous.

'I think not, Mr Rumpole. I'm afraid in this particular instance matters have gone rather beyond Matron.' Norman, the tall, bald usher, called on us all to be upstanding. Guthrie rose, and nursing his elbow, and faintly murmuring 'Ouch,' left us.

Norman the Usher was well known to me as a man of the world, well used to judicial foibles and surprisingly accurate in forecasting the results of cases. He was a man who took pleasure in supplying the needs of others, often coming up to me during lulls in cases to say he knew where to lay his hands on some rubber-backed carpeting or a load of bathroom tiles. Although I felt no need of any of Norman's contacts, he was able, on this occasion, to put Mr Justice Featherstone in touch with a cure. Long after his retirement Norman returned to the Bailey to look up a few old friends and over a couple of pints of Guinness in the pub opposite he eventually told me of his part in the affair of the Judge's elbow. 'Muscular is it, your Lordship's affliction?' Norman asked when he had led Guthrie out of Court into the Judge's room, a leather and panelled sanctum furnished with law reports and silver-framed photographs of the children.

'Muscular, Norman,' the Judge admitted. 'One does not complain.'

'Only one thing for muscular pain, my Lord.'

'Aspirins?' The Judge winced as he started to unbutton his Court coat.

'Throw away the aspirins. It's a deep massage. That's what your Lordship needs. Here. Let me slip that off for you.' He removed Guthrie's coat delicately. 'Of course, your Lordship needs a massoose with strong fingers. One who can manipulate the fibres in depth.' At which point the Usher grasped the Judge's elbow with strong fingers, causing another stab of pain, heroically borne. 'I can feel that the fibres are in need of deep, deep manipulation. If your Lordship would allow me. I know just the massoose as'd get to your fibres and release the tension!'

'You know someone, Norman?' The Judge sounded hopeful.

'The wife's sister's daughter, Elsie. Thoroughly respectable, and fingers on her like the grab of a crane...'

'A talented girl?'

'Precisely what the doctor ordered. Our Elsie has brought relief to thousands of sufferers.'

'Where . . . does she carry on her practice?' The Judge started tentative inquiries, rather as some fellow in classical times might have said 'Who's got the key to Pandora's Box?'

'In a very hygienic health centre, my Lord. Only a stone's throw down the Tottenham Court Road, your Lordship.'

'Tottenham Court Road?' Guthrie was, at first, fearful. 'Not oriental in any way, this place, is it?'

'Bless you, no, my Lord. They're thoroughly reliable girls. Mostly drawn from the Croydon area. All medically trained, of course.' Norman had hung up the Court coat and was restoring the Judge to mufti.

'Medically trained? That's reassuring.'

'They have made a thorough study, my Lord, of the human anatomy. In all its aspects. Seeing as you've got no relief through the usual channels . . .'

'My doctor's absolutely useless!' The Chelsea G.P. had merely referred the Judge to time, the great healer. Guthrie lifted a brush and comb to his hair, and was again reminded of his plight. 'You're right, Norman. Why not try a little alternative medicine?'

'You wait, my Lord,' Norman told him. 'Just let our Elsie get her fingers on you.'

The address which Norman gave the Judge was situated in a small street running eastward from Tottenham Court Road. After a few days' more pain, Guthrie took a taxi there, got out and paid off the driver, wincing as he felt for his money. 'Had a bit of trouble with my elbow,' he said, as though to explain his visit to the Good Life Health Centre, Sauna and Massage. At which point, the cabby drove away, no doubt thinking it was none of his business, and Guthrie entered the establishment in some trepidation. He was reassured to some extent by the cleanliness of the interior. There was a good deal of light and panelling, photographs of fit-looking young blond persons of both sexes, and a kindly receptionist behind a desk, filing her nails.

'I rang for an appointment,' Guthrie told her. 'The name's Featherstone.' 'Elsie,' the receptionist called out, 'your gentleman's here. You can go right in, dear'—she nodded towards a bead curtain—'and take off your things.' Later, after a brief spell in an airless and apparently red-hot wooden cupboard, the Judge was stretched out on a table, clad in nothing but a towel, whilst Elsie, a muscular, but personable, young lady, who might have captained a hockey team, manipulated his elbow, and asked him if he was going anywhere nice for his holiday.

'Hope so. I'm tired out with sitting,' Guthrie told her.

'Are you really?' Elsie, no doubt, had heard all sorts of complaints in her time.

'In fact I've been sitting almost continuously this year.'

'Fancy!'

'It gets tiring.'

'I'm sure it does.'

'Not how I did my elbow in, though. Tennis. When I'm not sitting, my wife and I play a bit of tennis.'

'Well, it makes a change, dear. Doesn't it?'

When Elsie had finished her manipulations, Guthrie got dressed and came back into the reception area. Being a little short of cash, and seeing the American Express sign on the counter, he decided to pay with his credit card. 'It feels better already,' he told her, as he signed without an 'ouch.' The receptionist banged the paperwork into her machine. 'There you are then.' She tore off his part of the slip and handed it and the credit card back to Guthrie, who thanked her again, and put the card and the slip carefully into his wallet. After he had left, Elsie came out from behind her curtain. 'He says he's tired out, done a lot of sitting,' she told the receptionist, who smiled and said, 'Poor bloke.'

I was not, of course, among those present when Mr Justice Featherstone had his treatment, and I have had to invent, or attempt to reconstruct, the above dialogue. I may have got it wrong, but of one thing I am certain, the Judge's massage was given in strict accordance with the Queensberry rules, and there was nothing below the belt.

Whilst Guthrie had undergone this satisfactory cure and almost forgotten his old tennis injury, much had changed in our old Chambers at 3 Equity Court. I had been away for a week or two, doing a long firm fraud in Cardiff, a case which had absolutely no bloodstains and a great deal of adding up. I returned from exile to find our tattered old clerk's room, with its dusty files, abandoned briefs, out-of-date textbooks and faded photograph of C. H. Wystan over the fireplace, had been greatly smartened up. Someone had had it painted white, given Henry a new desk and Dianne a new typewriter, hung the sort of coloured prints on the walls which they buy by the yard for 'modernized' hotels and introduced a large number of potted plants, at which Dianne was, even as I arrived one morning in my old hat and mac, squirting with a green plastic spray.

'"Through the jungle very softly flits a shadow and a sigh—"': the shadow was Dianne, and the sigh came from

Henry when I asked if this was indeed our old clerk's room or the tropical house at Kew.

'It's Mr Hearthstoke.' Henry pronounced the name as though it were some recently discovered malignant disease.

'Some old gardener?' I asked, clutching three weeks' accumulation of bills.

'The new young gentleman in Chambers. He reckons an office space needs a more contemporary look.'

'And I've been ticked off for putting.' Uncle Tom was in the corner as usual, trickling a golf ball across the carpet.

'Uncle Tom has been ticked off.' Dianne confirmed the seriousness of the situation.

'I've been asked to do it upstairs, but it isn't the same.' Uncle Tom sounded reasonable. 'Down here, you can see the world passing by.'

'Carry on putting, Uncle Tom,' I told him. 'Imagine you're on the fourth green at Kuala Lumpur.'

I forced my way through the undergrowth and went out into the passage; there I found that our clerk had followed me, and was whispering urgently, 'Could I have a word in confidence?'

'In the passage?'

'It's not only my clerk's room Mr Hearthstoke reckons should have a more contemporary look.' Henry started to outline his grievances. 'He says we could do with a smarter typist. Well, as you know, Mr Rumpole, Dianne has always been extremely popular with the legal executives.'

'A fine-looking girl, Dianne. A fine, sturdy girl. I always thought so.' I had the feeling that Henry felt a certain *tendresse* for our tireless typist, although I didn't think it right to inquire into such matters too deeply.

'Worse than that, Mr Rumpole, he wants to privatize the clerking.'

'To *what?*'

'Mr Hearthstoke's not over-enamoured sir, with my ten per cent.'

For the benefit of such of my readers as may never have shared in the splendours and miseries of life at the Bar, I should explain that the senior clerk in a set of Chambers is usually paid ten per cent of the earnings of his stable of legal hacks. This system is frequently criticized by those who wish to modernize our profession, but I do not share their views. 'Good God!' I said, 'if barristers' clerks didn't get their ten per cent we'd have no one left to envy.'

'And he's got his criticism of you too, Mr Rumpole. That's why I thought, sir, we might be in the same boat on this one. Even if we'd had our differences in the past.'

'Of me?' I was surprised, and a little pained to hear it. 'What has this "Johnny Come Lately" got to criticize about me?'

'He's not enamoured of your old Burberry.'

Unreasonable I thought. My mac may not have been hand-tailored in Savile Row, but it has kept out the rain on journeys to some pretty unsympathetic Courts over the years. And then I looked at our clerk and saw a man apparently in the terminal stage of melancholia.

'Henry!' I asked him. 'Why this hang-dog look? What on earth's the need for this stricken whisper? If, whatever his name is, has only been here a few weeks...'

'Voted in when you were in Cardiff, Mr Rumpole...'

'Why does our learned Head of Chambers take a blind bit of notice?'

'Quite frankly, it seems to Dianne and me, Mr Ballard thinks, with great respect, that the sun shines out of Mr Hearthstoke's—' Perhaps it was just as well that he was prevented from finishing this sentence by our learned Head

of Chambers, Soapy Sam Ballard, who popped out of his
door and instructed Henry to rally the chaps for a
Chambers meeting. He didn't seem exactly overjoyed to
see me back.

Charles Hearthstoke turned out to be a young man in his
early thirties, dark, slender and surprisingly goodlooking;
he reminded me at once of Steerforth in the illustrations to
David Copperfield. Despite his appearance of a romantic
hero, he was one of those persons who took the view, one
fashionable with our masters in government, that we were
all set in this world to make money. He might have made
an excellent accountant or merchant banker; he wasn't, in
my view, cut out for work at the Criminal Bar. He had been
at some Chambers where he hadn't hit it off with the Clerk
(a fact which didn't surprise me in the least) and now he sat
at the right hand of Ballard and was clearly the apple of the
eye of our pure-minded Head of Chambers.

'I've asked Hearthstoke to carry out an efficiency study
into the working of Number 3 Equity Court, and I must say
he's done a superb job!' My heart sank as Ballard told us
this. 'Quite superb. Charles, would you speak to this
paper?'

'He may speak to it,' I grumbled, 'but would it answer
back?'

'What's that, Rumpole?'

'Oh, nothing, Ballard. Nothing at all . . .'

But Uncle Tom insisted on telling them. 'That was rather
a good one! You heard what Rumpole said, Hoskins?
Would it answer back?'

'Leave it, Uncle Tom,' I restrained him. Hearthstoke
was now holding up some sort of document.

'In the first section of the report I deal with obvious
reforms to the system. It's quite clear that our fees need to

be computerized and I've made inquiries about the necessary software.'

'Oh, I'm all in favour of that.'

'Yes, Rumpole?' Ballard allowed my interruption with a sigh.'

'Soft wear! Far too many stiff collars in the legal profession. Makes your neck feel it's undergoing a blunt execution.'

'Has Rumpole done another joke . . . ?' Uncle Tom didn't seem to be sure about it.

'Do please carry on, Charles.' Ballard apologized to Hearthstoke for the crasser element in Chambers.

'I'm also doing a feasibility study in putting our clerking out to private tender,' Hearthstoke told the meeting. 'I'm sure we can find a young up-thrusting group of chartered accountants who'd take on the job at considerably less than Henry's ten per cent.'

'Brilliant!' I told him.

'So glad you agree, Rumpole.'

'Wonderful thing, privatization. Why not privatize the Judges while you're about it? I mean, they're grossly inefficient. Only give out about a hundred years' imprisonment a month, on the average. Why not sell them off to the Americans and step up production?'

'That, if I may say so,'—Hearthstoke gave a small, wintry smile—'is the dying voice of what may well become a dying profession.'

'We've got to move with the times, Rumpole, as Charles has pointed out.' Ballard was clearly exercising a great self-control in dealing with the critics.

'As a matter of fact I'm entirely in favour of the privatization of Henry.' This was the colourless barrister, Hoskins. 'Speaking as a chap with daughters, I can ill afford ten per cent.'

'Those of us who have a bit of practice at the Bar, those of us who can't spend all our days doing feasibility studies on the price of paper-clips, know how important it is to keep our clerk's room happy.' That, at any rate, was my considered opinion. 'Besides, I don't want to go in there in the morning and find the place full of up-thrusting young chartered accountants. It'd put me off my breakfast.'

'Is that all you have to say on the subject?' Ballard looked as though he couldn't take much more.

'Absolutely. I'm going to work. Come along, Mizz Probert'—I rose to my feet—'I believe you've got a noting brief.'

'There's a dingy-looking character in a dirty mac hanging about the waiting-room for you, Rumpole,' Erskine-Brown was at pains to tell me. 'And talking of dirty macs'—Hearthstoke looked at me in a meaningful fashion —'There is one other point I have to raise,' he said, but I left him to raise it on his own. I was busy.

The client who was waiting for me was separated from his mac; all the same he cut a somewhat depressing figure. He wore thick, pebble glasses, a drooping bow-tie, and a cardigan which had claimed its fair share of soup. A baggy grey suit completed the get-up of a man who seemed to have benefited not at all from the programme of physical fitness which he sold to the public; neither did he seem to enjoy the prosperity which the Prosecution had suggested. He had a curiously high voice and the pained expression of a man who at least pretended not to understand why he was due to be tried at the Old Bailey.

'Dr Maurice Horridge. Where does the "Doctor" come from, by the way?' I asked him.

'New Bognor. A small seat of learning, Mr Rumpole. In the shadow of the Canadian Rockies . . .'

'You know Canada well?'

'I was never out of England, Mr Rumpole. Alas.'

'So this degree of yours. You wrote up for it?'

'I obtained my diploma by correspondence,' he corrected me. 'None the less valuable for that.'

'And it is a doctorate in . . .?'

'Theology, Mr Rumpole. I trust you find that helpful.' I got up and stood at the window, looking out at some nice, clean rain. 'Oh, very helpful, I'm sure. If you want to be well up in the Book of Job or if you want to carry on an intelligent chat on the subject of Ezekiel. I just don't see how it helps with the massage business.'

'The line of the body, Mr Rumpole, is the line of God.' My client spoke reverently. 'We are all of us created in His image.'

'Yes, I've often thought He must be quite a strange-looking chap.'

'Pardon me, Mr Rumpole?' Dr Horridge looked pained.

'Forget I spoke. But massage . . .'

'Spiritual, Mr Rumpole! Entirely spiritual. I could stretch you flat on the floor, with your head supported by a telephone directory, and lay your limbs out spiritually. All your aches and pains would be relieved at once. I don't know if you'd care to stretch out?'

'The girls in these massage parlours you run . . .' I got to the nub of the case.

'Trained! Mr Rumpole. All fully trained.'

'Medically?'

'In my principles, of course. The principles of the spiritual alignment of the bones.'

'What's alleged is that they so far forgot their spiritual mission as to indulge in a little hanky-panky with the customers.' I explained the nature of the charges to the good doctor; roughly it was alleged that he was living on immoral earnings and keeping a large number of disorderly houses. 'I cannot believe it, Mr Rumpole! I simply cannot believe it of my girls.' He spoke like a priest who has heard of group sex among the vestal virgins.

'So that your defence,' I asked him as patiently as possible, 'is that entirely without your knowledge your girls turned from sacred to profane massage?'

Dr Horridge nodded his head energetically. He seemed to think that I had put his case extremely well.

Now I must try to tell you how the troubles of Dr Maurice Horridge became connected with the painful matter of the Judge's elbow. Meeting his wife at the tennis court one night—he had so far improved in his health, thanks to Elsie, that he felt fit enough to resume mixed doubles with the Addisons—Guthrie found Marigold reading the *Standard*. 'Massage parlours,' she almost spat out the words with disgust.

'Well. Yes. In fact . . .' Guthrie hadn't yet confided the full facts of his visit to the Good Life Health Centre to his wife, who read aloud to him from the paper.

'"Doctor of Theology charged with running massage parlours as disorderly houses". How revolting! What was it you wanted to tell me, Guthrie?'

'Well, nothing really. Just that my elbow seems much better. I can really swing a racket now.'

'Well, just don't dislocate anything else.' She gave him
more of the news. '"Thirty-five massage parlours alleged
to offer immoral services in the Greater London area." Pa-
thetic! Grown men having to go to places like that!'

'I'm quite sure some of them just needed a massage,'
Guthrie tried to persuade her.

'If you'd believe that, Guthrie, you'd believe anything!'
She read on regardless. '"Arab oil millionaires, merchant
bankers and well-known names from television are said to
be among those who used the cheap sex provided at Dr
Horridge's establishment and paid by *credit card"!*'
Guthrie stifled an agonized exclamation of terror. 'What on
earth's the matter? That elbow playing you up again?'

The next thing Guthrie did was to visit the tennis club
Gents, and flush away the American Express slip which he
had retained for the monthly check-up. He didn't want
Marigold, searching for a bit of cash, to find the dreaded
words 'Massage and Sauna' stamped on a bit of blue paper.
The next day, in the privacy of the Judge's room, he made
a telephone call, which I imagine went something like this.

'American Express? The name is Featherstone. Mr Justice Featherstone. No, not Justice-Featherstone with a hy-
phen. My name is Featherstone and I'm a justice. I'm a
judge, that is. Yes. Well, actually I got into a bit of a
muddle and paid someone with a credit card when I should
have paid cash and if I could go and pay them now, could I
get my credit-card slip back and you wouldn't need to have
any record of it at all if it's a purely private matter, just a
question of my own personal accounting? . . . Do I make
myself clear? What's that? Oh. I don't . . .'

It is never easy to recall the past and rectify our mis-
takes. In this case, Guthrie was to find it impossible. Norman, the Usher, who started all the trouble, had suddenly

retired and gone to live in the North of England, and when
Guthrie revisited the address near Tottenham Court Road,
in the hope that his credit-card transaction could be ex-
punged from the records, he found that the Health Centre
had sold up and the premises taken over by Luxifruits Ltd.
He was offered some nice juicy satsumas by the greengrocer now in charge, but all traces of Elsie and the receptionist had vanished away.

Guthrie's cup of anxiety ran over when he bumped into
Claude Erskine-Brown walking up from the Temple tube
station. 'Always so good to see some of the chaps from my
old Chambers,' the Judge was gracious enough to observe
after Claude had removed his hat and then restored it to its
position. 'See your wife was in the Court of Appeal again
the other day. And Rumpole! What's old Horace doing?'

'Something sordid as usual,' Claude told him.

'Distasteful?'

'Downright disgusting. Rumpole's cases do tend to
lower the tone of 3 Equity Court. This time it's massage
parlours! Rumpole's acting for the King of the massage
parlours. Of course, he thinks it's a huge joke.'

'But it's not, Erskine-Brown, is it?' The Judge was serious. 'In fact, it's not a joke at all!'

'I can't pretend my marriage is all champagne and
opera. We've had our difficulties, Philly and I, from time
to time, as I'd be the first to admit. But thank heavens I've
never had to resort to massage parlours! I simply can't
understand it.'

'No. It's a mystery to me, of course.'

'Anyway. That sort of thing simply lets down the tone of
Chambers.'

'Yes. Of course, Claude. Of course it does. The honour
of Equity Court is still extremely important to me, as you

well know. Perhaps I should invite Horace Rumpole to lunch at the Sheridan. Have a word with him on the subject?'

'What subject?' Claude was apparently a little mystified.

'Massage . . . No,' the judge corrected himself, 'I mean Chambers, of course.'

'Oysters for Mr Rumpole . . . and I'll take soup of the day. And Mr Rumpole will be having the grouse and I—I'll settle for the Sheridan Club Hamburger. I thought a Chablis Premier Cru to start with and then, would the Château Talbot '77 appeal to you at all, Horace?' The autumn sunlight filtered through the tall windows that badly needed cleaning and glimmered on the silver and portraits of old judges. Around us, actors hobnobbed with politicians and publishers. I sat in the Sheridan Club, amazed at the Judge's hospitality. As the waitress left us with my substantial order, I asked him if he'd won the pools.

'No. It's just that one gets so few opportunities to entertain the chaps from one's old Chambers. And now Claude Erskine-Brown tells me you're doing this case about what was it . . . beauty parlours?'

'Massage parlours. Or, as I prefer to call them, Health Centres.'

'Oh, yes, of course. Massage parlours.' The Judge seemed to choke on the words and then recovered. 'Well, I suppose some of these places are quite respectable and above-board, aren't they? I mean, people might just drop in because they'd got . . .'

'A touch of housemaid's knee?' I was incredulous.

'That sort of thing, yes.'

'Someone who was as innocent and unsuspecting as that, they shouldn't be let off the lead.'

'Why do you say that?'

The waitress came with the white wine. Guthrie tasted it and she then poured. I tasted a cold and stony Chablis, no doubt at a price that seldom passes my lips. 'Well, to your average British jury, the words massage parlour mean only one thing,' I told Guthrie, without cheering him up.

'What?'

'Hanky-panky!'

'Oh. You think that, do you?'

'Everyone does.'

'Hanky-panky?' The words stuck in the Judge's throat.

'In practically every case.'

'Rumpole! Horace . . . Look, do let me top you up.' He poured more Chablis. 'You're defending in this case, I take it?'

'What else should I be doing?'

'And as such, as defending counsel, I mean, you'll get to see the prosecution evidence . . .'

'Oh, I've seen most of that already,' I assured him cheerfully.

'Have you?' He looked as though I'd already passed sentence on him. 'How extraordinarily interesting.'

'It's funny, really.'

'Funny?'

'Yes. Extremely funny. You know, all sorts of Very Important People visited my client's establishments. Nobs. Bigwigs.'

'Big *wigs,* Horace?' Guthrie seemed to take the expression personally.

'Most respectable citizens. And you know what? They actually paid with their credit cards! Can you imagine anything so totally dotty . . .'

'Dotty? No! Nothing.' The Judge laughed mirthlessly.

'So their names are all . . . in the evidence? Plain for all the world to see?' He broke off as the soup and the oysters were brought by the waitress, and then said thoughtfully, 'I don't suppose that *all* the evidence will necessarily be put before the Jury.'

'Oh no. Only a few little nuggets. The cream of the collection. It should provide an afternoon of harmless fun.'

'Not fun for the . . . big . . . big wigs involved . . .' He looked appalled.

'Well, if they were so idiotic as to use their *credit cards!*' There was a long pause during which my host seemed sunk in the deepest gloom. He then rallied a little, smiled in a somewhat ghastly manner, and addressed me with all his judicial charm and deep concern. 'Horace,' he said, 'don't you find this criminal work rather exhausting?'

'It's a killer!' I admitted. 'Only sometimes a bit of evidence turns up and makes it all worthwhile.'

'Have you ever considered relaxing a little?' He ignored any further reference to big wigs in massage parlours. 'Perhaps on the Circuit Bench?'

'You're joking!' He had amazed me. 'Anyway, I'm far too old.'

'I don't know. I could have a word with the powers that be. They might ask you to sit as a deputy, Rumpole. On a more or less permanent basis. A hundred and fifty quid a day and absolutely no worries.'

'Deputy Circus Judge?' I was still in a state of shock. 'Why should they offer me that?'

'As a little tribute, perhaps, to the tactful way you've always conducted your defences.'

'Tactful? No one's ever called me that before.' I squeezed lemon on an oyster and sent it sliding down.

'I've always found you extremely tactful in Court, Horace. And discreet. Oysters all right, are they?'

'Oh, yes, Judge.' I looked at him with some suspicion. 'Absolutely nothing wrong with the oysters.'

Walking back from the Sheridan Club to Chambers, I thought about Guthrie's strange suggestion and felt even more surprised. Deputy Circuit Judge! Why on earth should I want that? These thoughts flitted through my head. Judging people is not my trade. I defend them. All the same . . . One hundred and fifty smackers a day, the old darling did say a hundred and fifty, and you didn't even have to stand up for it. It could all be earned sitting down. With hacks constantly flattering you and saying 'If your Honour pleases', 'If your Honour would be so kind as to look at the fingerprint evidence.' No one has ever spoken to me like that. But what was the Judge up to exactly? Offering me grouse and oysters and Deputy Circus Judge. What, precisely, was Guthrie's game?

I could find no answer to these questions as I walked along the Strand. Then a voice hailed me and I turned to see a tall, bald man familiar to me from the Bailey. It was Norman, the ex-Usher, who had apparently called down to the old shop to collect his cards. He asked if Mr Justice Featherstone's elbow had improved.

'It seems to be recovered,' I told him.

'In terrible pain, he was,' Norman clucked sympathetically. 'Don't you remember? I was able to put him on to a place where they could give him a bit of relief. Get down to the deep fibres, you know. Have the Judge's bones stretched out properly . . .'

'You recommended a place?' I was suddenly interested.

'The wife's niece worked there. Nice type of establishment, it was really. Very hygienically run.' He looked down the road. 'Here comes a number 11. I'll be seeing you, Mr Rumpole. I don't know if you've got any use for a nice length of garden hose.'

'What place? What place did you recommend exactly?' I tried to ask him, but he skipped lightly on to his number 11 and left me.

The Prosecutor in *R.* v. *Dr Maurice Horridge* was a perfectly decent fellow called Brinsley Lampitt. I called on him at his Chambers and he let me have a large cardboard box of documents, bank statements, accounts and credit-card slips all connected with the questioned massage parlours. My meetings with Guthrie Featherstone and Norman the Usher had given me the idea of a defence which seemed so improbable that at least it had to be tried. I carried the box of exhibits back to Chambers, and set Mizz Liz Probert to sift through them, with particular reference to the credit-card transactions. Then I went down to see Henry.

I found Charles Hearthstoke in the clerk's room asking for P.A.Y.E. forms and petty-cash vouchers for coffee consumed over the last two years. Henry was looking furious and Dianne somewhat flustered. I discovered much later that they had been surprised in a flagrant kiss behind a potted plant when Hearthstoke entered. On my arrival, he turned his unwelcome attentions on me. 'Sorry you had to slip away from the Chambers meeting, Rumpole.' 'What did I miss, Hearthrug?' I asked him. 'Have you replaced me with a reliable computer?'

'Not yet. But we did pass a resolution on the general standards of appearance in Chambers. Old macs are not acceptable now, over a black jacket and striped trousers.'

The Pill then left us, and I looked after him with some irritation and contempt. 'I quite agree with you, Mr Rumpole,' Henry said, and I told him we stood together on the matter. 'Together,' I told him, 'we shall contrive to scupper Hearthrug.'

'It'll need a bit of working out,' Henry said, 'Mr Ballard being so pro . . .'

'Ballard? Leave Bollard to me! Providing, Henry, I can leave something to you.'

'I'll do my best, sir. What exactly?'

'Miss Osgood. The lady who arranges the lists down the Bailey. You know, your co-star from the Bromley amateur dramatics.'

'We're playing opposite each other, Mr Rumpole. In *Brief Encounter.*'

'Encounter her, Henry! Drop a word in her shell-like ear about the massage parlour case. What we need, above all things, is a sympathetic judge . . . "There is a tide in the affairs of barristers," Henry, "Which, taken at the flood, leads on to fortune; Omitted, all the voyage of their life is bound in shallows and in miseries . . ."' On such a full tide were we now afloat, and I took charge of the helm and suggested the name of the Judge whom I thought Miss Osgood would do well to assign to *R.* v. *Horridge.*

So it came about that when Guthrie Featherstone arrived for his next stint of work down at the Bailey, and Harold, the new usher, brought him coffee in his room, he found the Judge staring, transfixed with horror, at the papers in the case he was about to try and muttering the words 'massage parlours' in a voice of deep distress. Not even the offer of a few nice biscuits could cheer him up. And when he entered Court and saw Dr Horridge in the dock, Rumpole smiling up at him benignly and the table of proposed exhibits loaded with credit-card slips, the Judge looked like a man being led to the place of execution.

'Mr Lampitt, Mr Rumpole.' His Lordship addressed us both in deeply serious tones before the Jury was summoned into Court. 'I feel I have a duty to raise a matter of personal nature.' I said I hoped he wasn't in pain.

'No. Not that, Mr Rumpole . . . Not that . . . The fact is, Mr Lampitt . . . Mr Rumpole . . . Gentlemen. I feel very strongly that I should *not* try this case. I should retire and leave the matter to some other judge.'

'Of course, we should be most reluctant to lose your Lordship,' I flattered Guthrie, and Brinsley Lampitt chimed in with 'Most reluctant.'

'Well, there it is. I'll rise now and . . .' Guthrie started to make his escape.

'May we ask . . . why?' I stopped him.

'May you ask what?'

'*Why,* my Lord. I mean, it's nothing about my client, I hope.'

'Oh no, Mr Rumpole. Nothing at all to do with him.' The Judge was back, despondently, in his seat.

'I can't imagine that your Lordship *knows* my client.'

'Know him? Certainly not!' The Judge was positive. 'Not that I'm suggesting I'd have anything against knowing your client. If I did, I mean. Which I most certainly don't!'

'Then, with the greatest respect, my Lord, where's the difficulty?'

'Where's the *what,* Mr Rumpole?' The judge was clearly in some agony of mind.

'The difficulty, my Lord.'

'You wish to know where the difficulty is?'

'If your Lordship pleases!'

'And you, Mr Lampitt. You wish to know where the difficulty is?'

'If your Lordship pleases,' said the old darling for the Crown.

'It's a private matter. As you know, Mr Rumpole,' was the best the Judge could manage after a long pause.

'As I *know,* my Lord? Then it can't be exactly private.'

'Perhaps I should make this clear in open Court. I happened to have lunch at my Club with counsel for the Defence.'

'The oysters were excellent! I'm grateful to your Lordship.'

There was a flutter of laughter and Harold called for silence as the Judge went on: 'And I happened to discuss this case, in purely general terms, with counsel for the Defence.' In the ensuing silence Lampitt was whispering to the police. I asked, 'Is that all, my Lord?'

'Yes. Isn't it enough?' The Judge sounded deeply depressed. Lampitt didn't cheer him up by telling him that he'd spoken to the Officer-in-Charge of the case, who had no objection whatever to the Judge trying Dr Horridge. He was sure that no lunchtime conversation with Mr Rumpole could possibly prejudice his Lordship in any way. 'In fact,' Brinsley Lampitt ended, to the despair of the Judge, 'the Prosecution wish your Lordship to retain this case.'

'And so do the Defence.' I drove in another nail.

'In fact I urge your Lordship to do so,' Lampitt urged.

'So do I, my Lord,' from Rumpole. 'It would be a great waste of public money if we had to fix a new date before a different judge. And in view of the Lord Chancellor's recent warnings about the high cost of legal aid cases . . .'

The Judge clearly felt caught then. He looked with horror at the exhibits and thought with terror of the Lord Chancellor. 'Mr Lampitt, Mr Rumpole,' he asked us without any real hope, 'are you *insisting* I try this case?'

'With great respect, yes,' from Lampitt.

'That's what it comes to, my Lord,' from me.

So the twelve honest citizens were summoned in and one of the strangest trials I have ever known began, because I could not tell who was more fearful of the outcome, the prisoner at the Bar, or the learned judge.

Picture Guthrie after the first day in Court, returning to play a little autumn tennis with his wife. Unfortunately the game was rained off, and he sat with Marigold in the bar of the tennis club and told her, when she asked if he'd had a good day, that he was sorry to say he had not. Then he looked out of the window at the grey sky and asked her if she didn't sometimes long to get away from it all. 'Fellow I was at school with runs a little bar in Ibiza. Wouldn't you like to run a little bar in Ibiza, Marigold?'

'I think I should hate it.'

'But you don't want to hang about around Kensington, in the rain, married to a judge who's away all day, sitting.'

'I like you being a judge, Guthrie,' Marigold explained patiently. 'I like you being away all day, sitting. And what's wrong with Kensington? It's handy for Harrods.'

'Marigold,' he started again after a thoughtful silence.

'Yes, Guthrie.'

'I was just thinking about that Cabinet Minister. You know. The fellow who had to resign. Over some scandal.'

'Did he run a little bar in Ibiza?'

'No. But what I remember about him is his wife stood

by him. Through thick and thin. Would you stand by me, Marigold? Through thick and thin?'

'What's the scandal, Guthrie?' She was curious to know, but he answered, 'Nothing. Oh, no. Just a theoretical question. I just wondered if you'd stand by me. That's all.'

'Don't count on it, Guthrie,' she told him. 'Don't ever count on it.'

Meanwhile, back at 3 Equity Court, Liz Probert was working late, sorting through the prosecution exhibits of which we had not yet made a full list. Hearthstoke saw the light on in my room and, suspecting me of wasting electricity, called in to inspect. He apparently offered to help Liz with her task and, sitting beside her, started to sort out the credit-card slips. She remembered asking him why he was helping her, and hoping it had nothing to do with her eyes. She told him that Claude Erskine-Brown had taken her to the Opera and complimented her on her eyes, a moment she had found particularly embarrassing.

'Erskine-Brown's old-fashioned, like everything else in these Chambers,' he told her.

'Just because I'm a woman! I mean, I bet no one mentions *your* eyes. And Hoskins told me I could only do petty larceny and divorce; quite honestly he thinks that's all women are fit for.'

'Out of the ark, Hoskins. Liz, I know we'd disagree about a lot of things.'

'Do you?' She looked at him; I suppose it was not an entirely hostile gaze.

'I'm standing as a Conservative for Battersea Council,' he told her. 'And your father's Red Ron of South-East London! But we're both young. We both want things changed. When we've finished this, why don't you buy yourself a Chinese at the Golden Gate in Chancery Lane?'

'Why on earth?'

'I could buy one too. And we might even eat them at the same table. Oh, and I do promise you not to mention your eyes.'

'You can if you want to.'

'Mention your eyes?'

'No, you fool! Eat your Chinese at my table.' She was laughing as I came in after a little refreshment at Pommeroy's Wine Bar. I took in the scene with some surprise. 'Hearthrug! What's this, another deputation about my tailoring?'

'I was helping out your Pupil, Rumpole.' He was staring, with some distaste, at my old mac.

'Very considerate of you. I can take over now, after a pit-stop at Pommeroy's for refuelling. Why don't you two young things go home?' Liz Probert went, after Hearthstoke told her to wait for him downstairs. And then he revealed some of the results of his snooping round our Chambers. 'I was just going to ask you about Henry.'

'*What* about Henry?' I lit a small cigar.

'I was looking at his P.A.Y.E. returns. He *is* married, isn't he?'

'To a lady tax inspector in Bromley. That's my belief.'

'So what exactly is his relationship with Dianne, the typist?'

'Friendly, I imagine.'

'Just friendly?'

'That is a question I have never cared to ask.'

'There are lots of questions like that, aren't there, Rumpole?' With that, the appalling Hearthrug left me. I pulled the box of documents toward me and started working on them angrily. In the morning I would have to deal with further snoopers: police officers in plain clothes, or rather, in no clothes at all, as they lay on various massage tables and pretended to be in need of affection.

'Detective Constable Marten,' I asked the solid-looking copper with the moustache, 'that is not a note you made at the time?'

'No, sir.'

'Of course not! At the time this incident occurred, you were deprived of your clothing and no doubt of your note-book also?'

'I made the note on my return to the station.'

'After these exciting events had taken place?'

'After the incident complained of, yes.'

'And your recollection was still clear?'

'Quite clear, Mr Rumpole.'

'It started off with the lady therapist.'

'The masseuse, yes.'

'Passing an entirely innocent remark.'

'She asked me if I was going anywhere nice on holiday.'

'She asked you *that?*' The evidence seemed to have awakened disturbing memories in the Judge.

'Yes, my Lord.'

'Up to that time it appeared to be a perfectly routine, straightforward massage?' I put it to the officer.

'I informed the young lady that I had a certain pain in the knee from playing football.'

'Was that the truth?' I asked severely.

'No, my Lord,' D.C. Marten told the Judge reluctantly.

'So you were lying, Officer?'

'Yes. If you put it that way.'

'What other way is there of putting it? You are an officer who is prepared to lie?'

'In the course of duty, yes.'

'And submit to sexual advances in massage parlours. In the course of duty.' I was rewarded by a ripple of laughter from the Jury, and a shocked sign from the Judge. 'Mr Rumpole,' he said politely, 'can I help?'

'Of course, my Lord.' I was suitably grateful.

'When the massage started, you told the young lady you had a pain in your knee?' The Judge recapped, rubbing in the point.

'Yes, my Lord.'

'From playing tennis?'

'Football, my Lord.'

'Yes. Of course. Football. I'm much obliged.' His Lordship made a careful note. 'So far as the lady masseuse was concerned, that might have been the truth?'

'She might have believed it, my Lord,' the Detective Constable admitted grudgingly.

'And so far as you know, quite a number of perfectly decent, respectable, happily married men may visit these ... health centres simply because they have received injuries in various sporting activities. Football ... tennis and the like!' The Judge was moved to express his indignation.

'Some may, I suppose, my Lord.' D.C. Marten was still grudging.

'Many may!'

'Yes.'

'Very well.' The Judge turned from the officer with distaste. 'Yes, Mr Rumpole. Thank you.'

'Oh, thank *you,* my Lord. If your Lordship pleases.' I stopped smiling then and turned to the witness. 'So at first sight this appeared to be an entirely genuine health centre?'

'At first sight. Yes.'

'An entirely genuine health centre.' The Judge was actually writing it down, paying a quite unusual compliment to the Defence. 'Those were your words, Mr Rumpole?'

'My exact words, your Lordship. No doubt your Lordship is writing them down for the benefit of the Jury.'

'I am, Mr Rumpole. I am indeed.'

I saw Lampitt looking bewildered. Judges who brief themselves for the accused are somewhat rare birds down the Bailey.

'And the whole thing was as pure as the driven snow. In fact it was the normal treatment of a football injury until you made a somewhat distasteful suggestion?'

'Distasteful?' D.C. Marten appeared to resent the adjective.

'Just remind the Jury of what you said, Officer. As you lay on that massage table, clad only in a towel.'

'I said, "Well, my dear,"'—and the officer read carefully from his notebook—'"How about a bit of the other?"'

'The *what*, Officer?' The Judge was puzzled.

'The other, my Lord.'

'The other what?'

'Just. The other . . .'

'I must confess I don't understand.' His Lordship turned to me for assistance.

'You were using an expression taken from the vernacular,' I suggested to the Detective Constable.

'Meaning what, Mr Rumpole?' The Judge was still confused.

'Hanky-panky, my Lord.'

'I'm much obliged. I hope that's clear to the Jury?' Guthrie turned to the twelve honest citizens, who nodded wisely.

'You suggested some form of sexual intimacy might be possible?' The Judge was now master of the facts.

'I did, my Lord. Putting it in terms I felt the young lady would understand.'

'And if you hadn't made this appalling suggestion, the massage might have continued quite inoffensively?'

'It might have done.'

'To the considerable benefit of your knee!'

'There was nothing wrong with my knee, my Lord.'

'No. No, of course not! You were lying about that!' And then, high on his success, Guthrie asked the question that would have been better to leave unsaid. 'When you asked the young lady about "the other", what did she reply?'

'Her answer was, my Lord, "That'll be twenty pounds".'

'Very well, Officer,' Guthrie said hastily. 'No one wants to keep this officer, do they? The witness may be released.'

And as D.C. Marten left the box, Brinsley Lampitt whispered to me, 'Have you any idea why the Judge is batting so strenuously for the Defence?'

'Oh, yes,' I whispered back, 'it must be my irresistible charm.'

Two wives, Marigold Featherstone and Hilda 'She Who Must Be Obeyed' Rumpole, bumped into each other in Harrods, and had tea together, swapping news of their married lives. Hilda said she had been after a hat to wear when Rumpole was sitting. 'I thought I might be up beside him on the Bench occasionally.

'Rumpole sitting?' For some reason Marigold appeared surprised.

'Yes. It was your Guthrie that mentioned it to him actually, when they took a spot of lunch together at the Sheridan Club. Rumpole said that it rather depended on his behaving himself in this case that's going on. But if he's a bit careful... well, Deputy County Court Judge! For all the world to see. It'll be one in the eye for Claude Erskine-Brown. That's what he's always wanted.'

'Guthrie seems to want to give up sitting.' Marigold told Hilda of their mysterious conversation. 'He speaks of going to Ibiza and opening a bar.'

'Ibiza!'

'Terrible place. Full of package tours and Spaniards.'

'Oh dear. I don't think Rumpole and I would like that at all.'

'Tell me, Mrs Rumpole. May I call you Helen?'

'Hilda, Marigold. And you and Guthrie always have.'

'Guthrie's been most peculiar lately. I wonder if I should take him to the doctor.'

'Oh dear. Nothing terribly serious, I hope.'

'He keeps asking me if I'd stand by him. Through thick and thin. Would you do that for Rumpole?'

'Well. Rumpole and I've been together nearly forty years...' she began judicially.

'Yes.'

'And I'd stand by him, of course.'

'Would you?'

'But thick and thin. No, I'm not sure about that.'

'Neither am I, Hilda. I'm not sure at all.'

'Have another scone, dear'—my wife passed the comforting plate—'and let's hope it never comes to that.'

The next morning, Marigold's husband asked Rumpole (for the Defence) and Brinsley Lampitt (for the Prosecution) to see him in his room. 'I thought I'd just ask you fellows in to find out how much longer this case is going to last. Time's money you know. I don't think we should delay matters by going into a lot of unnecessary documents. Will you be producing documents, Lampitt?'

'Just Dr Horridge's bank accounts. Nothing else.' The words clearly brought great comfort to his Lordship. 'I don't think anything else is necessary.'

'Oh no. Absolutely right! I do so agree. I seem to remember hearing something about customers using credit cards. You won't be putting in any of the credit-card slips? Nothing of that nature?'

'No, Judge. I don't think we need bother with that evidence.'

'No. Of course not. That'd just be wasting the Jury's time. I'm sure you agree, don't you, Rumpole?'

'Well, yes.' I was more doubtful. 'That is. Not quite.'

'Not quite?'

'About the credit-card evidence.'

'Yes?' The Judge's spirits seemed to have sunk to a new low.

'I think I'd like to keep my options open.'

'Keep them . . . open?'

'You see, my argument is that no one who wasn't completely insane would pay by credit card in a disorderly house.'

'That's your argument?'

'So the fact that credit cards were used *may* indicate my client's innocence. It's a matter I'll have to consider, Judge. Very carefully.'

'Yes. Oh, yes. I suppose you will.' His Lordship seemed to have resigned himself to certain disaster.

'Was that all you wanted to see us about?' I asked cheerfully.

'How much longer?' was all the Judge could bring himself to say.

'Oh, don't worry, Judge. It'll soon be over!'

After we left, I imagined that Mr Justice Featherstone
got out his Spanish Phrase Book and practised saying,
'*Este vaso no esta limpio.* This glass is not clean.'

It must have been after the prosecution case was closed,
and immediately before I had to put my client in the witness-box, that Guthrie Featherstone's view of life under-
went a dramatic change. He had brought in the envelope
containing his American Express accounts, a document
that he had not dared to open. But, in the privacy of his
room and after a certain amount of sherry and claret at the
Judge's luncheon, he steeled himself to open it. Summing
up a further reserve of courage, he looked and found the
entry, his payment to the Good Life Health Centre. 'Good
Life?' A wild hope rose in an unhappy judge, and he
snatched up the papers in the case he was trying. There
was no doubt about it. Maurice Horridge was charged with
running a number of disorderly houses known as the Good
Line Health Centre. It was clearly a different concern entirely. Guthrie felt like a man given six months to live, who
discovers there's been a bit of a mix-up down the lab and
all he's had is a cold in the head. He had never been to one
of Dr Horridge's establishments, and there was no record
of any judicial payment among the prosecution exhibits. 'I
have no doubt,' he shouted, 'I'm in the clear,' and down
the Bailey they still speak of the little dance of triumph
Guthrie was executing when Harold, the new Usher, came
to take him into Court.

Installed, happy now, on his Bench, Guthrie was treated

to the Rumpole examination-in-chief of my distinctly
shifty-looking client 'Dr Horridge'. I was saying, 'If any of
these young ladies misconducted themselves in your Health
Centres . . .'

'They wouldn't,' the witness protested. 'I'm sure they
wouldn't. They were spiritually trained, Mr Rumpole.'

'All the same, if by any chance they did, was it with
your knowledge and approval?'

'Certainly not, my Lord. Quite certainly not!' Horridge
turned to Guthrie, from whom I expected a look of sympathy. Instead, the Judge uttered a sharpish, 'Come now, Dr
Horridge!'

'Yes, my Lord?' The theological doctor blinked.

'Come, come! We have had the evidence from that
young officer, Detective Constable Marten, that he suggested to one of your masseuses . . . something of "the
other"!'

'Something or other, my Lord?'

'No, Dr Horridge.' The Judge sounded increasingly severe. 'Something *of* the other. I'm sure you know perfectly
well what that means. To which the masseuse replied,
"That will be twenty pounds". A pretty scandalous state of
affairs, I'm sure you'll agree?'

'Yes, my Lord.' What else could the wretched massage
pedlar say?

'Are you honestly telling this jury that you had no idea
whatever that was going on, in your so-called Health
Centre?'

'No idea at all, my Lord.'

'And you didn't make it your business to find out?'
Guthrie was now well and truly briefed for the Prosecution.

'Not specifically, my Lord.' It wasn't a satisfactory answer and the Judge met it with rising outrage. 'Not specifi-

cally! Didn't you realize that decent, law-abiding citizens, husbands and *ratepayers* might be trapped into the most ghastly trouble just by injuring an elbow—I mean, a knee?'

'I suppose so, my Lord,' came the abject reply.

'You suppose so! Well. The Jury will have heard your answer. What *are* you doing, Mr Rumpole?' His Lordship had some reason to look at me. I had wet my forefinger and now held it up in the air.

'Just testing the wind, my Lord.'

'The wind?' The Judge was puzzled.

'Yes. It seems to have completely changed direction.'

When the case was concluded, I returned to Chambers exhausted. Thinking I might try my client's recipe, I lay flat on the floor with my eyes closed. I heard the door open, and the voice of the Hearthrug from far away asking, 'Rumpole! What's the matter? Are you dead or something?'

'Not dead. Just laid out spiritually.' I opened my eyes. 'Losing a case is always a tiring experience.'

'I'm trying to see Ballard,' Hearthstoke alleged.

'Well, look somewhere else.'

'He always seems to be busy. I wanted to tell him about Henry.'

I rose slowly, and with some difficulty, to a sitting position, and thence to my feet. 'What about Henry?'

'Kissing Dianne in the clerk's room.' The appalling Hearthrug did his best to look suitably censorious. 'It's just not on.'

'Oh, I agree.' I was upright by now, but panting slightly.

'Do you?' He seemed surprised. 'I thought you'd say it

was all just part of the freedom of the subject, or whatever it is you're so keen on.'

'Oh, good heavens, no! I really think he should stop rehearsing in his place of work.'

'Rehearsing?' He seemed surprised.

'Didn't you know? Henry's a pillar of the Bromley amateur dramatics. He's playing opposite Dianne in some light comedy or other. Of course, they both work so hard they get hardly any time to rehearse. I'll speak to them about it. By the way, how's the housemaid's knee?'

'The what?' Clearly, my words had no meaning for the man.

'The dicky ankle, dislocated elbow, bad back, tension in the neck. In a lot of pain, are you?'

'Rumpole! What *are* you talking about? I am perfectly fit, thank you!'

'No aches and pains of any sort?' It was my turn to sound surprised.

'None whatever.'

'How very odd! And you've been having such a lot of massage lately.'

'What on *earth* do you mean?' Hearthrug, I was delighted to note, was starting to bluster.

'Unfortunate case. The poor old theologian got two years, once the Judge felt he had a free hand in the matter. But we were looking through the evidence. Of course, you knew that. That was why you came in to give Mizz Probert a helping hand. I was after another name, as it so happens. But I kept finding yours, Charles Hearthstoke. In for a weekly massage at the Battersea Health Depot and Hanky-Panky Centre.'

'It was entirely innocent!' he protested.

'Oh, good. You'll be able to explain that to our learned Head of Chambers. *When* you can find him.'

But Hearthrug looked as though he was no longer eager to find Soapy Sam Ballard, or level his dreadful accusations against Henry and Dianne.

From time to time, and rather too often for my taste, we have Chambers parties, and shortly after the events described previously, Claude Erskine-Brown announced that he was to finance one such shindig; he had some particular, but unknown, cause for celebration. So we were all assembled in Ballard's room, where Pommeroy's most reasonably priced *Méthode Champenoise* was dished out by Henry and Dianne to the members of Chambers with their good ladies and a few important solicitors and such other distinguished guests as Mr Justice Featherstone, now fully restored to health both of mind and elbow. 'Hear you potted Rumpole's old brothel-keeper,' Uncle Tom greeted Sir Guthrie, making a gesture as though playing snooker, 'straight into the pocket!'

'It was a worrying case,' Guthrie admitted.

'It must have been for you, Judge. Extremely worrying.' I saw his point.

'There used to be a rumour about the Temple'—Uncle Tom was wandering down Memory Lane—'that old Helford-Davis's clerk was running a disorderly house over a sweet-shop in High Holborn. Trouble was, no one could ever find it!' At which point, Hilda, in a new hat, came eagerly up to Guthrie and said, 'Oh, Judge. How we're going to envy you all that sunshine!' And she went on in spite of my warning growl. 'Of course, we'd love to retire to a warmer climate. But Rumpole's got all these new re-

sponsibilities. He feels he won't be able to let the Lord
Chancellor down.'

'The Lord Chancellor?' Guthrie didn't seem quite to follow her drift.

'He's expecting great things, apparently, of Rumpole.
Well'—she raised her glass—'happy retirement.'

'Mrs Rumpole. I'm not retiring.'

'But Marigold distinctly told me that it was to be Ibiza.'

'Well. I had toyed with the idea of loafing about all day
in an old pair of shorts and an old straw-hat. Soaking up
the sun. Drinking Sangria. But no. I feel it's my duty to go
on sitting.'

'Ibiza is no longer necessary,' I explained to Hilda, but
she had to say, 'Your duty! Yes, of course. Rumpole is
going to be doing his duty too.' At which point, our Head
of Chambers banged a glass on his desk for silence. 'I
think we are going to hear about Rumpole's future now,'
Hilda said, and Ballard addressed the assembled company.
'Welcome! Welcome everyone. Welcome Judge. It's delightful to have you with us. Well, in the life of every
Chambers, as in every family, changes take place. Some
happy, others not so happy. To get over the sadness first.
Young Charles Hearthstoke has not been with us long, only
three months in fact.' 'Three months too long, if you want
my opinion,' I murmured to Uncle Tom, and Ballard swept
on with his ill-deserved tribute. 'But I'm sure we all came
to respect his energy and drive. Charles has told me that he
found the criminal side of our work here somewhat distasteful, so he is joining a commercial set in the Middle
Temple.' At this news, Henry applauded with enthusiasm.
'I'm sure we're all sorry that Charles had to leave us before
he could put some of his most interesting ideas for the
reform of Chambers into practice...'

At this point, I looked at Mizz Probert. I have no idea what transpired when she and Hearthrug had their Chinese meal together, but I saw Liz's eyes wet with what I took for tears. Could she have been sorry to see the blighter go? I handed her the silk handkerchief from my top pocket, but she shook her head violently and preferred to sniff.

'Now I come to happier news,' Ballard told us. 'From time to time, the Lord Chancellor confers on tried and trusty members of the Bar...'

'Like Rumpole!' This was from Hilda, *sotto voce*.

'The honour of choosing them to sit as Deputy Circuit Judge.'

'We know he does!' Hilda again, somewhat louder.

'So we may find ourselves appearing before one of our colleagues and be able to discover his wisdom and impartiality on the Bench.'

'You may have Ballard before you, Rumpole,' Hilda called out in triumph, to my deep embarrassment.

'This little party, financed I may say,' Ballard smiled roguishly, 'by Claude Erskine-Brown...'

'So kind of Claude to do this for Rumpole,' was my wife's contribution.

'...Is to announce that he will be sitting, from time to time, at Snaresbrook and Inner London, where we wish him every happiness.'

Ballard raised his glass to Erskine-Brown, as did the rest of us, except for Hilda, who adopted a sort of stricken whisper to ask, *'Claude Erskine-Brown* will be sitting? Rumpole, what happened?' 'My sitting,' I tried to explain to her, 'like Guthrie Featherstone's Ibiza, is no longer necessary.' And then I moved over to congratulate the new Deputy Circus Judge.

'Well done, Claude.' And I told him, 'I've only got one word of advice for you.'

'What's that, Rumpole? Let everyone off?'

'Oh, no! Much more important than that. Always pay in cash.'

Rumpole and the Bright Seraphim

I know little of army life. It's true that I was able to serve my country during the last war (sometimes it seems only yesterday, the years rush by with such extraordinary speed) in the R.A.F. at Dungeness (ground staff, they never sent me up in the air). It was there that I met Bobby O'Keefe in the Women's Auxiliary Air Force, and was a little dashed in spirits when she was finally hitched to a pilot officer, 'Three-Fingers Dogherty'—events which I have described elsewhere.* Those years, in turn exciting, boring, alarming and uncomfortable, gave me no insight whatever into life in a 'good' cavalry regiment. I knew nothing of the traditions of the officers' Mess, and I had never even appeared at a court martial until the extraordinary discovery of the body of Sergeant Jumbo Wilson in the 37th and 39th Lancers, clad in women's attire outside the Rosenkavalier bar and discotheque in Badweisheim, West Germany, and the subsequent prosecution of Trooper Boyne for murder. It

*See 'Rumpole and the Alternative Society' in *Rumpole of the Bailey*, Penguin Books, 1978.

is a case which had its points of interest, notably in my cross-examination of an inexpert expert witness as to the time of death and the strange solution at which I arrived by an unaided process of deduction.

When we had any minor cause for celebration, or when the East wind was not blowing and conversation flowed freely between us, it was the practice of myself and She Who Must Be Obeyed to call in at the Old Gloucester pub (Good Food Reasonably Priced, Waitress Service and Bar Snacks), which is but the toss of a glass from our so-called 'mansion' flat at Froxbury Court. It was there we made the acquaintance of a major, recently retired and in his forties, named Johnnie Pageant, who had taken a flat in the Gloucester Road area, and who spent his days writing to various golf clubs, of which he would have liked to become secretary. I found him a most amiable fellow, an excellent listener to my fund of anecdotes concerning life at the Bailey, and never slow to stand his round consisting, invariably, of a large claret for me and jumbo-sized gin and tonics for himself and She.

One evening in the Old Gloucester I was holding forth as usual about the murderers and other friends I had made down the Bailey, explaining that those accused of homicide were usually less tiresome and ruthless customers than parties in divorce cases, and, having often killed the one person they found intolerable, they were mostly grateful for anything you could do for them. 'You've done a lot of murders?' the ex-Major wondered.

'More, perhaps, than you've had hot dinners.'

'Try not to show off, Rumpole,' She Who Must Be Obeyed warned.

'My nephew Sandy Ransom's got a bit of a murder in

his regiment in Germany. Young trooper out there in a spot of bother.'

'Murder, in the Regiment, do you say?'

'Mention the word "murder" and you can see Rumpole pricking up his ears.' My wife, Hilda, of course, knew me of old. 'Murder's mother's milk to Rumpole.'

'Who's this young lad supposed to have murdered?' I wanted further and better particulars.

'His Troop Sergeant, apparently.'

'Murdered his sergeant; isn't that justifiable homicide?' I asked, being ignorant of army law.

'You should know. You've done a court martial or two, I suppose. Perhaps even more than I've had hot dinners,' Johnnie Pageant laughed.

'Court martials?' Of course!' Then I thought it better to qualify the claim. 'Perhaps not more than you've had gin and tonics...'

'Point taken, Horace! Hilda, the other half?'

'Well. Just perhaps the tiniest, weeniest, Johnnie.' So, ex-Major Johnnie wandered off to the bar, and Hilda turned on me. 'What *are* you talking about, Rumpole? You've never done a court martial in your life.'

'Mum's the word, Hilda,' I warned her. 'I thought I could sniff, for a moment, the odour of a distant brief.'

And I was right. A week or so later, when I went into our clerk's room, Henry handed me the brief in a court martial in Germany, the charge being one of murder. I asked if there were any sort of rank attached: Lieutenant-Colonel or Major-General Rumpole? Henry said no, but there was a cheque under the tape and a first-class air ticket to Badweisheim. 'First class?' Well, it seemed only right and proper; an officer and a gent couldn't huddle with other ranks in steerage.

'The solicitors said it was a heavy sort of case and at

first I thought they wanted a silk, Mr Ballard, perhaps, to lead you,' Henry said, as I thought tactlessly.

'Bollard to lead? He'd be following far behind.'

'But then they said no. What they wanted was just an ordinary barrister.'

'An *ordinary* barrister.' I was, I confess, somewhat irked. 'Then they've come to the wrong fellow!'

'Shall I return the brief then, Mr Rumpole?'

'No, Henry. We do not return briefs. When we are called to the colours, we do not hesitate. And if the Army needs me. Company... Atten-shun! *Present Arms!*' So I marched out of the clerk's room with my umbrella over my shoulder, chanting, 'Boots, boots, boots, boots movin' up and down again. There's no discharge in the war!' much to the consternation of Bollard and that grey barrister, Hoskins, who had just come in and no doubt thought that 'Old Rumpole' had taken leave of his senses.

The 37th and 39th Lancers, the Duke of Clarence's Own, familiarly known as the Bright Seraphim because of the sky-blue plumes they still wore, in a somewhat diminished version, in their headgear, had been a crack cavalry regiment with a list of battle honours stretching back to the Restoration. Even now, when they were encased in rattling sardine tins and not mounted on horses, the Regiment was hugely proud of its reputation. Its officers ran to hunters, country estates and private incomes, its Mess silver and portraits were some of the most valuable, and its soldiers the best looked-after in the British forces stationed in Germany. Should one of the Bright Seraphim stray from the paths of righteousness, I learnt early in my preparation for the court martial, the whole regiment would close ranks to protect the boy in trouble and the high reputation of the Duke of Clarence's Own.

The scandalous circumstances surrounding the death of Sergeant James 'Jumbo' Wilson were therefore particularly unwelcome. Military police touring the streets of Badweisheim, the German town close to the Bright Seraphim's barracks, searched, as a result of a telephone call received at 3.45 a.m., an alleyway which ran by the side of the Rosenkavalier disco-bar. It was at 4 a.m. that they then found Sergeant Wilson's body. His short haircut, florid face and moustache indicated his military occupation; the scarlet, low-cut frock he wore did not. He had received a stab wound in the stomach which had penetrated the aorta, but the time of his death was a matter which would become the subject of some controversy. One other matter—the Sergeant was an extremely unpopular N.C.O. and few of those who came under his immediate command seemed to have much reason to love him.

One wing of the barracks at Badweisheim consisted of married quarters for the non-commissioned officers and men; on the whole the officers lived in various houses in the town. Sergeant Wilson and his wife—they were a childless couple—occupied a flat up a short, iron staircase at one end of the wing. Next door, but on a lower level, lived Danny Boyne, a goodlooking Glasgow Irish trooper in his early twenties, with his wife and baby son.

Trooper Boyne had, unusually for anyone in the Regiment, married a German girl, and he was noted for his quick temper and his deep hatred of Sergeant Wilson, who, so many witnesses had noticed, lost no opportunity of picking on Danny and putting him on charges for a number of offences, many trivial but some more serious. Witnesses had also been found who had heard Danny threaten to cut the Sergeant up. He was, undoubtedly, present at the disco on the night the Sergeant died; and when the shirt he wore on that occasion was examined, a bloodstain of Sergeant Wilson's group was found on the cuff. For these cogent reasons, he was put under arrest and now had to face a general court martial with Horace Rumpole called to the colours to undertake his defence.

When I came out into the glass and concrete concourse of Badweisheim airport, a crisp, cheerful and thoroughly English voice called out to me, 'Horace Rumpole? Consider yourself under arrest, sir. The charge is smuggling an old wig through customs.'

The jokester concerned turned out to be a youngish, fair-haired captain, with a sky-blue cockade of the Seraphim in his beret and a lurcher at his heels. 'Very funny!' I hadn't smiled.

'Oh, do you think so? I can do much better than that. Sandy Ransom. I think you know my old uncle Johnnie?'

'Captain Ransom.' I didn't know if I should attempt a salute.

'I'm the Defending Officer.'

'Oh, really? I thought I was doing the defending.'

'Of course, you are. You're O/C Defence. I'm just your fag. Anything you want I'll run and get it. I'm the prisoner's friend. We are all the friends of any trooper in trouble. It's a question of regimental honour.'

'I see,' I said, although I didn't entirely, at the time.

'You'll need a porter, won't you?' He whistled to a man and said in what was, as far as I could tell, an impeccable German accent, '*Träger! Bitte nehmen sie das Gepäck.*' He also whistled to his obedient lurcher and led me to the jeep in which he was to drive me to the barracks. 'I told my Uncle Johnnie we were looking for an ordinary sort of barrister,' he told me when we were *en route*.

'Ordinary!' Again it seemed a most inadequate description of Rumpole's talents.

'The court-martial officers will be from other regiments,' Sandy Ransom explained. 'Pay Corps. That sort of rubbish. Very downmarket. They're all highly suspicious of the Cavalry. Think we're all far too well-off, which is luckily quite true. Parade a flashy Q.C. and they'd convict Danny Boy before he got his hat off. Just to teach the Cavalry a lesson. Anyway, old Uncle Johnnie said you'd done loads of court martials.'

'Oh, yes, loads.' Well, we were far from home and no one, I hoped, would know any different.

At last we drew in at a gate house manned by a sergeant who saluted Sandy and got a brief acknowledgement, and then we were in a huge square surrounded by brick buildings erected, I learned, for the *Wehrmacht*. In the square there was a large collection of military vehicles—cars, jeeps, lorries and even tanks—and we passed various groups of the Duke of Clarence's Own, all of whom saluted us smartly. Some lines from the *Ancient Mariner* floated into my mind:

> This seraph-band, each waved his hand:
> It was a heavenly sight!
> They stood as signals to the land,
> Each one a lovely night.

> This seraph-band, each waved his hand,
> No voice did they impart—

No voice; but oh! the silence sank
Like music on my heart.

And I felt my own hand rising, irresistibly, to the brim of
my hat.

'Steady on, sir,' Sandy told me. 'There's no need for
you to return their salutes.'

That evening the candlelight gleamed on the silver and the
paintings of long-gone generals and colonels wearing wigs
and scarlet coats, three-cornered hats, swords and sashes,
posed against gunmetal skies or on rearing horses. The few
officers dining with us in the Mess that night wore elderly
tweed suits as though they were guests in some rather
grand country house, with the exception of a young lieutenant in uniform. Sandy Ransom introduced me to a
shortish, quietly spoken, amused and intelligent-looking
man—considerably younger than me—as the Colonel of
the Regiment, Lieutenant-Colonel Hugh Undershaft, a
high-flier at Military College from whom even greater
things were apparently expected. The Colonel performed
the other introductions.

'Sandy you know, of course. And this is Major Graham
Sykes.' A greying, rather sad-looking man who, I had been
told, wouldn't rise higher in the service, nodded a greeting.
'And Lieutenants Tony Ross and Alan Hammick. Alan's
Duty Officer, which is why he's all togged up. Is that all
of us?'

'All we could rustle up, sir,' Sandy told him. The lurcher
was also among those present, and was lapping up a bowl
of water before going to sleep under the table.

'Can't lure many people into the Mess nowadays,' the

Colonel admitted. 'They prefer to be at home with their wives or girlfriends. We felt we'd better turn out.'

'Very decent of you, Colonel.'

'I told Borrow to bring up some of the regimental Bollinger in honour of your visit. That suit you?' The elderly white-coated Mess Attendant handed round the champagne, which suited me admirably. I raised my glass and said, 'Well, here's to crime!'

'I think we'd prefer to drink to the Regiment...' the Colonel said quietly and the other officers muttered 'the Regiment', as they raised their glasses. 'The boy had to go to a court martial, of course. But we rely on you to get him off, Rumpole. It's a question of the honour of the Regiment.' It was not the first time I had been told this, and I looked at a gilded coat of arms and list of battle honours hanging on the wall: Malplaquet, Blenheim, Waterloo, Balaclava, Mons, El Alamein, I read and the Regiment's motto 'For the the sake of honour'.

'Well, we can't have it said that we had a murderer in our ranks, can we?' the Colonel asked.

'Certainly not!' I found the courage to say. 'Not after you've killed so many people.' There was an uncomfortable silence, and then Sandy laughed. 'I say, you know. That was rather funny!'

'Was it really?' I asked him to reassure me.

'Oh yes. Distinctly humorous. Bit of a joker aren't you, sir, in your quiet way?' The Colonel looked at me and emptied his glass. 'Shall we start dinner,' he said. 'We heard you were a claret man, Rumpole.'

There was absolutely nothing wrong with the 1971 Margaux, and when the Cockburn 1960 was circulating, I was able to tell the assembled officers that I had done the

State some service under battle conditions in the R.A.F.,
Dungeness. 'Ground staff merely,' I admitted, 'but
that's not to say that we didn't have some pretty hairy
nights.'

'Don't tell me—Sandy was laughing—'a bomb fell on
the N.A.A.F.I.?'

'Well, as a matter of fact it did.' I was a little put out.
'Not a very laughable experience.'

'Of course not,' the Colonel rebuked Sandy mildly. 'The
port seems to have stuck to the table . . .'

'I don't know exactly how many of you gentlemen
served through the Second World War?' I was still a little
stung by Sandy's joke.

'Too young for it, I'm afraid,' even Major Sykes admitted.

'I wasn't even a glint in my father's eye,' this from
young Captain Sandy Ransom.

'My father was in Burma,' Lieutenant Ross boasted.
'He's inclined to be a terrible bore about it.'

'I suppose I was about one when it ended. Hardly in a
position to join the Regiment,' the Colonel told me. 'And
somehow we never even got invited to the Falklands . . .'

'Soldiers of the Queen,' I discovered. 'Born too late for
a war.'

'Do you honestly think it's too late?' The Colonel looked
at me; he was smiling gently.

'Too late for your sort of war, anyway,' I told him. 'Too
late for Blenheim and Balaclava and the Thin Red Line,
and hats off to you fuzzy-wuzzies 'cos you broke a British
square. Even too late for Passchendaele and Tobruk . . .
Next time some boffin will press a button, and good-night
all. "Farewell the plumed troop and the big wars/That
make ambition virtue!"' I was getting into my stride:

> 'O, farewell!
> Farewell the neighing steed and the shrill trump,
> The spirit-stirring drum, the ear-piercing fife,
> The royal banner, and all quality,
> Pride, pomp, and circumstance of glorious war!...
> Farewell! The Colonel's occupation's gone.'

I looked round at their slightly puzzled faces and said, 'Nowadays, let's face it, you're only playing at soldiers, aren't you?'

'Perhaps you're right,' the Colonel admitted. 'But while we're here, we may as well play the game as well as possible; it would be exceedingly boring if we didn't. And we have to do our best for the Regiment.'

'Oh, yes. Yes, of course.' I raised my glass. 'The Regiment!'

'It's not customary to drink to the Regiment after dinner,' Major Sykes corrected me quietly. 'Except on formal evenings in the Mess.'

So I drank, but not to the Regiment, and the Colonel got up and went to a small grand piano in the corner of the Mess. He sat on the piano stool, gently massaging his fingers and, as this was more as I expected an evening among soldiers would be, I started to sing 'Roll out the Barrel' just as we had sung it during the late war:

> 'Roll out the barrel,
> We'll have a barrel of fun
> Drink to the barrel
> We've got the blues on the run...'

And then I fell silent, feeling exceedingly foolish as Colonel Undershaft began to play what even I could recognize as Beethoven's Moonlight Sonata. Over a soft passage he spoke to no one in particular: 'Perhaps we are all practising idiotically for a war which would begin by obliterating us all. But we're still responsible, aren't we? Responsible for our soldiers. Boys like Danny Boy. We pick them out of a back-street in Glasgow and give them clean boots and a haircut. We feed them and water them and teach them to kill people in all sorts of ingenious ways, and then we can't even offer them a proper soldier's war to do it in. Can we expect them to turn into nice, quiet members of the Salvation Army? We're responsible for Danny Boy'—he stopped playing and looked at me—'which is why we've got to take all possible steps to see that he's acquitted.'

'I'm sorry,' I said in the ensuing silence.

'Why?' the Colonel asked.

'Sorry about that "Roll out the Barrel" business. It seems that I got things rather wrong.'

Later Sandy took me across the square to a comfortable guestroom with a bathroom attached. On the way I asked him to show me the married quarters. I saw the late sergeant's flat up a short, iron staircase at the foot of which two or three large dustbins stood against a wall; and, on ground level, I saw Trooper Danny's small accommodation. There were lights on up and below the outside staircase. Two wives, parted from their husbands, were, it seemed, unable to sleep. When we got to my room, Sandy said we would see Danny in the morning and asked if I had all the 'paperwork' I needed.

'Oh yes. An interesting little brief, especially the post-mortem photographs. Quite a lot to be learned from them.'

'What about?' Captain Sandy Ransom didn't sound particularly interested.

'About the time of death. It's the hypostasis, you see, the post-mortem staining of the body that shows the time when the blood settles down to the lowest level.'

'Time of death? I shouldn't have thought it was the time that mattered. It's *who* dunnit.'

'Or it's *when* dunnit?' I suggested. 'Perhaps that's what makes this case interesting.'

The next morning I found myself alone at breakfast-time in the Mess with Major Sykes, who was now in uniform and methodically consuming eggs, bacon and sausages. 'Sandy told us you were brilliant at murders,' he said, an accusation to which I had to plead guilty.

'Of course Sandy's a great one for jokes, usually of the practical variety.'

'I can imagine that.'

'Oh yes.' The Major gave me an instance: 'We had some sort of man from the Ministry out here—Under-Secretary at Defence, something like that. And Sandy turned up in the Mess pretending to be a visiting German officer. He'd got hold of the uniform somewhere. God knows where. Of course Sandy speaks German. About the only one of us who does. Anyway, he started doing Nazi salutes and singing the "Horst Wessel". Nearly scared the fellow from the Ministry out of his few remaining wits.'

'Does your colonel allow that sort of thing?' I wondered.

'Oh, Hugh was away that night, somewhere at Brigade H.Q. But no one can really be angry with Sandy. He's a sort of licensed jester. Puts on the panto, you know. *Aladdin* last year. I was the Dame.' He turned and nodded to one of the many framed regimental photographs on the wall behind him. It showed Major Sykes with other members of the pantomime cast.

'You have hidden talents, Major,' I had to admit my surprise.

'Oh, it's Sandy brought it out in me. He's such a wonderful "producer"—is that the word for it? He can get the best out of everyone. Tell me. How do you find the U.K.?'

'Go out of that door, turn West and keep straight on.' I shouldn't have done it and the Major didn't smile.

'You're a joker, aren't you?' he said. 'Like Sandy. I only asked because I'm retiring next year. Got to. Back to live with my sister in Surrey. I never married—not to anyone except the Regiment.'

'Now you've got to divorce?'

'It'll be a bit of a wrench, although I wasn't born into it. I'm not like Sandy; his father was a colonel, of course, and his grandfather a lieutenant-general. Sandy was born into the Cavalry.'

'With a silver bit in his mouth?'

'Oh, he's got plenty of money. But generous with it. He's paying for you, you know...'

'For *me?* No. I didn't know that.' It came as a surprise, and I didn't know whether I wanted to feel so much indebted to the young Defending Officer.

'When anyone's in trouble, like this young Trooper Boyne'—the Major explained the situation—'Sandy'll always come to their rescue. He'd do anything for the Regiment.'

'Even making you a Dame?' At which point Major Sykes folded his arms and did a surprising Dame's North country accent.

'Where's that naughty boy Aladdin now?' he crowed, and then added, in his own voice, 'Yes. He'd even do that.'

After breakfast Sandy Ransom, an officer so popular, I later discovered, that it seemed inevitable that Trooper Danny Boyne should choose him for his defence, and I sat in a small office set aside in the guard room and interviewed our client. He seemed shy, indeed nervous, of me, and directed many of his answers to Captain Sandy Ransom, who perched on a small upright chair beneath which slept his favourite lurcher.

'You said Sergeant Jumbo Wilson picked on you,' I started at the beginning. 'Why do you think that was?'

'I don't know.'

'No idea?'

'I don't know, I told you.' And then he turned to Sandy as if to explain, 'I told him.'

'Mr Rumpole's here to help you. Trust him.' It was, I supposed, an order from a superior officer, but it didn't seem to have a great deal of effect. I picked up Danny's statement and went on to one of the most damaging parts of the evidence.

'Did you ever say you'd carve him up?'

'That was a long time ago.'

'About three weeks, apparently, before he died.'

'Jumbo Wilson came into the disco, throwing his weight about like he always did'—the Trooper started to talk more easily—'shouting, so people'd notice him. I may have said that to some boys by the bar.'

'Some boys who're coming to give evidence!' I reminded him.

'Witnesses from another regiment,' Sandy said as though that disposed of the matter. 'Of course,' I remembered, 'seraphs wouldn't give evidence against each other —but you admit you said it?' I asked Danny.

'Like you'd say about anyone that picked on you: "I'll carve him up." It's like a common saying.'

'Danny comes from Glasgow.' Sandy supplied what must have seemed to him an obvious explanation. 'Is that going to be our defence?' Not if I have anything to do with it, I thought. I came on to the fatal occasion. 'On that evening, Saturday November 22nd . . .'

'We were practising for the panto Captain Ransom puts on at Christmas.' Danny now seemed more confident.

'I can confirm that.' Sandy confirmed it.

'Until when?'

'It was about nine o'clock.'

'Or 21.00 exactly.' I wasn't sure whether I was getting the answers from the client or the Defending Officer.

'I went back to the married quarters block. I changed and went out again. I was meeting my mates in the square. Just in front of my quarters.'

'Where?'

'Just on the square. In front of the quarters.'

'And there you met . . . ?'

'Finchie and Goldie.'

'Troopers Finch and Goldsmith,' Sandy gave me the names and added, for good measure, 'I can confirm that too. I happened to see them. I stayed on a little while after the rehearsal and then I saw the three men when I came out.'

'Where did you three go to?'

'The disco.'

'The Rosenkavalier?'

'Got there about 21.30, didn't you?' Sandy asked, and Danny Boy said, 'About that. Yes, sir.'

'Did you see Sergeant Wilson?' I asked.

'He was there, yes. In a corner.'

'Your statement says the place was dark and very crowded. Are you sure you recognized the Sergeant?'

'I could tell that bastard anywhere.' At least he was sure about that, but I thought he could do with a little training as a witness. 'When you give your evidence, Trooper Boyne,' I told him, 'please try not to call the dear departed a bastard. It won't exactly endear you to the tribunal. How was the Sergeant dressed?'

'Casual—a sports jacket, I think. A shirt without a tie.'

'Not in a frock?'

'Not when I saw him.' He seemed a little puzzled, but when I asked, 'And then you saw this other man?', he answered with quiet conviction, 'I saw this German.'

'How did you know he was German?'

'He was speaking Kraut to the girl by the door. Then he spotted Wilson and went over to his table.'

'A man in a black leather jacket. With spiky hair...' I read from the statement our client had made to the Investigating Officer.

'This punk.' Danny spoke with a good deal of dislike. Basically, I thought, he was a very conventional young man.

'Did the Sergeant speak to him at all?'

'Just "Helmut". We heard him call out, "Helmut."'

'What else?'

'We didn't hear what they said. They sat together in the corner; they were still there when we left.'

'Which was at, approximately?'

'01.00 hours, wasn't it, Danny?' Again Captain Sandy Ransom supplied the time and our client nodded his head.

'And you never saw Sergeant Jumbo Wilson alive again?'

'Never!'

'And you got back into the barracks over the back wall?'

'We don't bother about booking in and out at the guard room.'

'Especially as you were confined to barracks.' Sandy smiled indulgently as a schoolmaster might at the prank of a favourite pupil.

'That was after a wee fight I had. A couple of weeks ago. Down at the disco . . .' Danny started to explain, but again the Defending Officer took up the story. 'That was the fight when he got the blood on his cuff. It's in the evidence.'

'Tell me'—I spoke to our client who wouldn't have a favourite captain to help him give evidence in Court—'just tell me in your own words.'

'It was a German boy what was taking the mickey out of my wife. Out of Hanni. I took him outside and gave him a couple of taps. He must have bled a bit.'

'A German boy with a Class AB Blood Group just like the Sergeant's?' I asked, feeling my side was getting over-confident. 'A blood group only enjoyed by 3 to 4 per cent of the population?' I stood up, put away my pen and started to tie up my brief. 'So it comes to this. You saw the Sergeant alive at one in the morning. And he was found at 4 a.m. after the Military Police got an anonymous phone call.'

'From a German,' Sandy reminded me.

'In German, anyway. So. Giving the Sergeant time to leave the bar, slip into his frock—wherever he did that— quarrel with whoever he quarrelled with . . .' His friend, Helmut. Isn't that the most likely explanation?' Sandy interrupted, but I went on. 'When he was found he couldn't have been dead much more than two and a half hours.'

'The fellows prosecuting accept that,' Sandy was reassuring me.

'But do I accept it?' I asked, and Danny, who had been looking at me doubtfully, spoke, for the first time I thought, his mind. 'Don't you believe me, Mr Rumpole?'

'I'm not here to believe anything, I'm here to defend you,' I told my client. 'But some time or another it might be a bit of a help, old darling, if you started to tell me the truth.'

After we had left our client, I asked Sandy to drive me to the scene of the crime. The Rosenkavalier disco-bar looked small and somewhat dingy by daylight with its neon sign —an outline of a silver rose—switched off. The place was locked up and we inspected the side alley which was, in fact, a narrow lane which joined the streets in front of and behind the disco, so a body might have been driven up from behind the building and delivered at the side entrance. On the other side of the lane was the high wall and regular windows of a tallish block of flats. Sandy's lurcher was sniffing at the side entrance, perhaps scenting old blood. I asked the Captain, 'None of the neighbours saw or heard anything?'

'They wouldn't, would they?'

'Why do you say that?'

'They're all Germans.'

'The telephone call was made in German.'

'By his boyfriend perhaps.' The Defending Officer clearly had his own explanation of the crime.

'Boyfriend?'

'Helmut. He might not have been sure if he'd killed Jumbo Wilson. Perhaps he had a fit of remorse.'

'Why do you think "Jumbo" had a boyfriend? He was married.'

'What's that got to do with it?' Sandy smiled and then said seriously, 'You were right, of course, Danny wasn't telling you the whole truth. You know why Jumbo picked on him?'

'Tell me.'

'Because the Sar'nt made a heavy pass and Danny Boy told him to satisfy his lust on the regimental goat, or words to that effect.'

I tried to think of the sequence of events. The Sergeant had left the disco and gone somewhere, perhaps into the block of flats, changed into a bizarre costume, been knifed and dumped in the lane. 'So Helmut stabbed Jumbo in a lovers' quarrel after a bit of convivial dressing up?' I considered the Captain's theory.

'Isn't that the obvious solution?' Sandy obviously regarded the problem as solved.

'I suppose it'd get you out of trouble,' I said, and when he laughed and asked, 'Me?', I explained, 'I mean, the Regiment, of course.'

I was tired that night and I left the Mess early. I got a torch from Borrow, the Mess Attendant, to light my way across the darkened square. As I left, Sandy had sat down to the piano, and I heard him singing: 'Kiss me goodnight, Sergeant Wilson, Tuck me in my little wooden bed . . .'

I came to the corner of the married quarters wing. I could hear the thin wail of the Boynes' baby, awake and crying, and I saw a curtain pulled back for a moment and a grey-haired, handsome woman, whom I took to be Mrs Wilson, looked out frowning with anger towards the source of the sound. Then she twitched the curtain across the window again, and I sank to my knees behind the dustbins at

the foot of the iron staircase, and made a close examination, with the help of Borrow's torch, of the ground and the
bottom stair.

I was in that position when Lieutenant Tony Ross, the
Duty Officer in uniform that night, discovered me and
looked down, as I thought, rather strangely. 'Hail to thee,
bright seraph,' I greeted him. 'Thought I'd dropped a few
marks down here. Must've had a hole in my pocket.'

'Can I help at all, sir?' the young officer asked.

'Not at all. No.' I struggled to my feet. 'Sleep well,
Lieutenant. It's only money, isn't it?'

The court martial, which I don't think anyone suspected
was my first, took place in an ornate nineteenth-century
German civic building, and in a room with a great deal of
carved stonework and a painted ceiling. Everyone was
clearly identified, like the members of a television chat-
show panel, by a little board with their title painted on it
set on the table in front of them. The tribunal appointed to
try Danny Boyne consisted of a president (a Brigadier
Humphries of the Transport Corps, Sandy told me), a lieutenant-colonel, a major and two captains, one of whom
was a uniformed, lady W.R.A.C. officer. And seated beside the President, I was surprised to see my old friend and
one-time Chamber mate, George Frobisher, who had de-
serted the dusty arena down the Bailey (well, George was
never much of a cross-examiner) for the security of the
Circuit Bench, and then, apparently in search of adventure,
become a judge advocate, stationed in Germany advising
court martials on the legal aspects of soldiers' trials.
George sat beside the President now, wearing his wig and
gown, and explained every point in the proceedings with
tireless courtesy to the accused trooper, in a way which

seemed to show the Military as more civilized than some of the learned judges down the Bailey, notably his Honour Roger Bullingham known to me as the Mad Bull.

So, 04916323, Trooper Boyne of the 37th and 39th, the Duke of Clarence's Own Lancers, was charged with 'a civilian offence contrary to Section 70 of the Army Act of 1955, that is to say, murder, in that on the 22nd and 23rd days of November last he murdered 75334188, Sergeant J. Wilson of the Duke of Clarence's Own'. A plea of not guilty was entered and after George had painstakingly explained the roles of everyone in Court, and advised Danny to relax and sit comfortably and make any comment that occurred to him to Mr Rumpole, his barrister, Lieutenant-Colonel Watford, was invited to rise from the prosecution table and outline the case against the Trooper.

Sandy Ransom (at last parted from his lurcher, who was being cared for in the Special Investigations Branch Office) and I sat at the defence table next to our client, who had an N.C.O. beside, and one behind him, holding his hat and belt, which he wouldn't wear, so Sandy explained, until he gave evidence. There was no dock, which again seemed a better arrangement than at the Bailey, where an accused person is penned into a sort of eminence which hints at their guilt. Taking George's advice, I sat comfortably and let the Prosecuting Officer begin.

And here was another plus. Lieutenant-Colonel Michael Watford, O.B.E., the Army Legal Services, was tall, youngish (almost everyone seems youngish to me), bespectacled and sensible. He had trained as a solicitor, and had, as it so happened, been well known to me as young Mike Watford, articled clerk with Butchers & Stringfellow, a firm who had often briefed me at the Bailey and who sent young Mike out to help with taking notes and witness statements, a task he performed a great deal better than the senior partners. So, from the whirligig of time, Mike Watford was known to me as a good egg; in fact, I would go so far as to say that he was a double yoker.

As Lieutenant-Colonel Mike outlined his case, my eyes strayed to our judges or, would they more correctly be called, the Jury of Army Officers, because they would decide all the facts and leave the law to George. I had never had to face a jury in uniform before. I tried flashing a charming smile at the W.R.A.C. officer but it had no effect on her whatever. She was listening to Mike's opening with a frown of fierce concentration.

Mike's first witness was a young lady with a good deal of rather dried-up blonde hair, tricked out in tight, artificial leopard-skin trousers and a low-cut black silk vest. Chains and bracelets clinked as she moved, and she looked as though she had better things to do than take part in the army exercises of a foreign power. Her English was, however, so much better than my non-existent German that it was fully equal to all the demands made on it that day.

Mike Watford got her to admit that her name was Greta Schmerz, and she worked at hanging up the coats in the Rosenkavalier; when business was brisk, apparently, she also helped out at the bar. She identified the photograph of Sergeant Wilson as someone she had seen on occasions at the disco-bar. Mike then went so far as to tell her that we knew that, on the night in question, the Sergeant was stabbed outside the disco-bar.

'We know nothing of the sort,' I rose to protest, and drove on through a mild 'Don't we, Mr Rumpole?' from George. 'We know he was found dead outside the disco. We haven't the foggiest idea where he was stabbed.'

'Very well'—Mike Watford conceded the point—'he was found dead. Had you seen him in the disco that night?'

'I can't remember,' Greta told us after a pause.

'And *that* young man, Trooper Boyne, sitting there, was *he* in the disco that night?' the Prosecutor asked.

'He was there, I remember him.' Miss Schmerz was sure. Having achieved this, Watford sat down and Rumpole arose.

'Fraulein Schmerz. So far as Sergeant Wilson, the man in the photograph, was concerned, he may have been there that night, or he may not. You simply don't know?'

'He was there. Danny and the other two saw him.' I got a loudly whispered reminder from the Defending Officer.

'Please, Captain. I do know your case!' I quieted Sandy and addressed the witness. 'Do you remember someone coming to the disco with spiky hair and black leather jacket?'

'I do remember.'

'Helmut!' Sandy whispered again triumphantly, and I muttered, 'I know it's much more exciting than manoeuvres, but do try and stay relatively calm.' I asked Miss Schmerz, 'What time did you see him?'

'How should I know that?'

'How indeed? Was it late?'

'I think . . . perhaps midnight . . .'

'Well, that's very helpful. Did he speak to you?'

'The punk man? He spoke to me.'

'In German?'

'Yes. He asked if I had seen the English sergeant.'

'Did he say the name Wilson?'

'He said that.'

'Tell me, Fraulein Schmerz.' I was curious to know. 'All the soldiers came to the disco in civilian clothes, didn't

they? Jeans and anoraks and plimsolls—that sort of costume?'

'They weren't in soldier's dress,' she agreed.

'So you couldn't tell if that man in the photograph was a
sergeant or not?'

'No.'

'Did you know his name was Wilson?'

'I didn't know his name.'

'So there seems very little point in the punk asking you
the question? Yes, thank you, Fraulein Schmerz.'

I sat down, and Sandy looked at me with obvious dis-
pleasure. I was, it must have seemed to him, a very ordinary barrister indeed. 'What are you trying to do?' he
asked me, and all I could whisper back was, 'Strangely
enough, my dear old Defending Officer, I think I'm trying
to find out the truth.'

The Court was still and respectful when the Sergeant's
widow was called to give her evidence. George asked her
if she'd care to sit, and when she preferred to stand, tall,
grey-haired and dignified, by the witness chair, he assured
her that she wouldn't be kept there long. In fact, Mike
Watford only asked her a few questions. She identified the
photograph of her dead husband, whom she had last seen
alive when he left their flat in the married quarters not very
long after nine o'clock on the night of 22 November. When
I rose to cross-examine I told the witness that we all sym-
pathized with her in the tragic situation in which she found
herself, and went on to ask if Trooper Boyne and his German wife, Hanni, didn't live very near her little flat?

'Almost next door.' The voice was disapproving and the
face stony.

'Did you see anything of them?'

'She was always at the dustbins. Putting things in them. Things the baby dirtied, most like.'

'Most likely.' I turned to another topic. 'You were at home all the evening and the night when your husband died?'

'Yes, I was. I never went out.'

'And Trooper Boyne was never in your flat at any time?'

'No.' The answer was decided.

'Did you ever ask either Mr or Mrs Boyne to your home?'

'Of course not.' The suggestion clearly struck her as ridiculous.

'Did you not invite them because your husband was a sergeant and my client was a humble trooper?'

'Not *just* because of that. She was one of them, wasn't she?'

'One of what?'

'One of them Germans.'

'You don't like Germans, Mrs Wilson?' The question seemed unnecessary; I asked it all the same.

'*They* did it.'

'They did what?'

'That's why he was out there in the street, out there dressed like that! They took him . . . He . . . He was gone . . . Gone . . .'

'Don't distress yourself, Madam.' George was using his best bedside manner. 'Which Germans do you mean killed your husband?'

'I don't know. How could I know?' She was talking very quietly and calmly, like someone, I thought, on the verge of tears.

'You say some Germans killed him?'

'With respect'—I had to correct him—'she didn't say

that. She said Germans "took" him. Perhaps the shorthand writer...' The lady with the shorthand book stood and found the phrase with unusual rapidity. 'She said "they took him...He was gone..." '

'I assume by "took" she meant kill.' George seemed to have little patience with my interruption.

'In my submission it would be extremely dangerous to assume anything of the sort,' I had to tell him. 'She said "took". The person who killed him may be someone entirely different.'

'What exactly are you suggesting, Mr Rumpole?' George frowned at me. It wasn't a fair question to an old Chambers mate who was, as yet, not entirely clear what he was suggesting. 'I hope that may become quite clear in my cross-examination of other witnesses,' I said to keep him quiet. 'I really don't want to prolong this witness's ordeal by keeping her in the witness-box a moment longer.' So I sat down and Sandy gave me another of his cross whispers, 'Why don't you ask her the vital question?'

'Which is?'

'Wasn't Jumbo Wilson a pooftah?'

'For a soldier, old darling,' I whispered back, 'you really know so little about murder. You don't endear yourself to the Court by asking the weeping widow if her husband wasn't a pooftah. It sort of adds insult to injury. No, I didn't ask the vital question. But I got the vital answer.'

'What was that?' Captain Sandy looked doubtful.

'They "took" him. That's what she said. Now wasn't that rather a curious way of putting it?' And as we sat in silence waiting for the next witness, some lines of old Robert Browning wandered idly into my mind: 'Some with lives that came to nothing, some with deeds as well undone,/ Death stepped tacitly and *took* them where they never see the sun . . .' So did Mrs Wilson mean that death had taken Jumbo, or did she mean something else entirely?

Now the door opened and an important-looking gentleman in the uniform of the Royal Army Medical Corps came to the witness table and was sworn by a member of the Court. I knew he would be the subject of my most important cross-examination, and I gazed at him with the close attention a matador gives to a bull as it enters the ring and does its preliminary business with the picadors. Lieutenant-Colonel Basil Borders, Doctor of Medicine and Fellow of The Royal College of Pathologists, was a tall, pale man with a thickening waist, ginger hair going thin, and rimless spectacles. He appeared, from the way he took the oath and answered Mike Watford's early questions, to have a considerable opinion of his own importance, and when he was asked to give his post-mortem findings he answered clearly enough.

'The deceased was a well-nourished man, forty-five years old, with no signs of disease,' Lieutenant-Colonel Borders told us. 'There were indications of a fairly recent high consumption of alcohol and a heavy meal. Death had been caused by a stab wound, with a flat, sharp object such as a knife which entered the abdomen and penetrated the abdominal aorta.'

I will not weary the reader with an account of the Army Pathologist's evidence-in-chief. It followed the lines of his statement and was thorough, painstaking and predictable. I opened my cross-examination with a dramatic performance which Captain Sandy had suggested and now staged with relish. He stood up with his back to me as I put an arm about his neck and appeared to stab him from behind with my pencil.

'One arm across the windpipe to stop the victim crying

out and an upward stab from the back, penetrating the heart. Isn't that the accepted military manner of using a knife, Doctor?' I asked as I acted the commando role.

'That is the method taught in commando training.' Borders was clearly distressed by our courtroom histrionics.

'But the Sergeant had a knife jabbed into the stomach?'

'Yes, indeed.'

'So inexpertly that it might not even have been fatal?'

'It might not have been.'

'If it hadn't happened to penetrate the aorta?'

'Indeed.'

'It looks far more like a civilian than a military job, doesn't it, Doctor?'

'Perhaps,' was as far as the witness would go, but Sandy whispered, 'Oh, I like it,' as he resumed his seat, his great moment over. I just hoped he would enjoy the rest of my cross-examination as much.

'And the knife—there's nothing to indicate that it was a bayonet?' I asked the Pathologist.

'As I have said, I believe the blade was flat.'

'Not a bayonet or any sort of army knife?'

'There is no particular indication of that,' Borders agreed.

'It could've been the sort of sharp, pointed carving-knife available in any kitchen?'

'Yes, indeed.' He was finding the cross-examination easier than he had expected and was relaxed and smiling round the court. No one, I noticed, smiled back.

'Available to any civilian?'

'Available to Helmut!' the irrepressible Captain Sandy whispered as the witness answered, 'Yes.'

So far so good but I knew I was coming to an area of

likely disagreement. I decided to lull the witness into a feeling of false security, hoping he would be taken by surprise when the attack was launched. I leant forward, spoke in a silken voice and I poured out a double dose of flattery: 'Lieutenant-Colonel Borders, you are a very distinguished and experienced pathologist and no doubt you carried out a most thorough post-mortem examination.'

'Thank you.' The witness preened himself visibly. 'Indeed I did.'

'And we are all *most* grateful for the enormous trouble you have clearly taken in this matter.' George joined in the smiles now and the witness was even more grateful. 'Thank you very much.'

'Rarely have I heard such absolutely expert evidence!' Well, *I* wasn't on oath.

'You're very kind.'

'Just one small detail. What were your conclusions about the frock?'

'The frock?' He looked puzzled and I knew I was on to something.

'There is a cut in the scarlet frock the Sergeant was wearing and a good deal of staining. Of course you fitted the hole in the dress to the hole in the body?' I assumed politely.

'I don't think I did.' The Lieutenant-Colonel looked at the Court as though it were a point of no importance, and I looked at him with rising and incredulous outrage. Finally, I managed a gasp of amazement on the word *'Indeed?'*

'The dress was a matter for the Scientific Officer. I don't believe I examined it at all.'

'Lieutenant-Colonel Borders!' I called the man to order. 'Are you representing yourself as an expert witness?'

'I am.' There was a flush now, rising to the roots of the ginger hair.

'A person capable of carrying out a post-mortem examination in a reasonably intelligent way?'

'Of course!'

'And you can't even tell this Court'—I spoke with rising fury—'if the Sergeant was wearing the frock when he was stabbed, or if it was cut and put on him *after his death?*'

'No, I can't tell you that, I'm afraid.' Again he did his best to make it sound as irrelevant as the weather in Manchester.

'You're afraid?' I gave my best performance of contemptuous anger. 'Then I'm afraid you're unlikely to have sufficient expertise to be of much assistance to the Court on another vital matter.'

'Mr Rumpole . . .' George was trying to call a halt to this mayhem, but I had done with the cape and was moving in with the sword and not to be interrupted. 'I refer to the time of death. Have you any useful contribution to make on that matter?'

'Mr Rumpole.' George could contain himself no longer. 'I know that you are in the habit of conducting murder cases at the Old Bailey with all the lack of inhibition of, shall we say, a commando raid.'

'Oh, sir.' I smiled at the old darling. 'You're too kind.'

'I think I should make it clear that the Army expects far more peaceful proceedings.' George spoke as severely as he knew how. 'The Military Court is accustomed to seeing all witnesses treated with quiet courtesy. I hope you'll find yourself able to fall into our way of doing things.'

'I'm extremely grateful, sir.' I thought it best to apologize. 'The Court will excuse me if I showed myself, for a moment, to be as clumsy and inexpert in my profession as this officer clearly is in his...'

'Mr Rumpole!' George was about to launch another missile in my direction, but I turned to the witness. 'Lieutenant-Colonel. Tell me, is that higher than a colonel?'

'No, lower.' Borders was not pleased.

'Oh, I'm sorry. I'm sure you'll soon earn promotion. You came from England to do this post-mortem?'

'Yes. I was flown out from the U.K.'

'And were you told the brief facts of the case?'

'I was told that the suspect had been in a disco where the Sergeant had been seen by witnesses around 01.00 hours.'

'And a telephone call about the stabbing had been received by the Police at 03.45 hours. So when the Army Doctor arrived at 04.15 hours the Sergeant could only have been dead, say, about three hours?'

'That is so.'

'And yet there was a definite progress of rigor mortis?'

'Yes. That was found.' Borders was wary of another attack, and this was the vital part of my case. I pressed on quickly: 'Which you would not normally expect in the first three hours after death?'

'Rigor has been known to occur within thirty minutes,' he told *me,* who had won the Penge Bungalow case on rigor, among other factors.

'In *very* exceptional cases,' I told him.

'Well, yes...'

'And the temperature of the body had dropped by some six degrees.'

'Yes.'

'I have here Professor Ackerman's work *The Times of Death* in which he deals with falling temperatures.' In fact this volume, together with my old *Oxford Book of English*

Verse, had been my constant bedtime reading in Germany. 'Let me put this to you. Normally wouldn't that indicate death at least six hours before?'

'It was a cold night in November, if you remember.'

'That is your answer?' I hope I sounded as though I couldn't believe it.

'Yes.' Borders looked at the faces of the Court members for comfort and received none. *'Hypostasis,'* I gave him the word as though I thought he might not have heard it before. 'The staining caused by blood settling down to the lower parts of the body after death. Were there not large areas of staining when the body was found? Just look at the photographs.' Borders opened the volume of post-mortem photographs on the witness table in front of him and I thought that he did so somewhat reluctantly. 'Isn't that degree of staining consistent with death, let's say, some six hours earlier?'

'It might be consistent with that, yes,' he admitted reluctantly. 'Hypostasis is subject to many variations.'

'In fact everything in those photographs is consistent with death having occurred around nine o'clock on the previous evening!'

'Mr Rumpole . . .' George was now looking genuinely puzzled.

'Yes, sir?'

'Aren't you forgetting your own client's statement? And the statements of Troopers Finch and . . .'

'Goldsmith, sir,' I helped him.

'Goldsmith. Exactly so. They saw the Sergeant in the disco at 1 a.m. He could hardly have died at nine the previous evening.'

'Oh, I don't know. Isn't there some sort of biblical parallel?' This was all the help I'd give old George. I said to the witness, 'One other little matter on the photographs. Are there not a number of pale patches on the stains?'

'Yes, there are.' He was looking at the pictures as though he hated them.

'Representing places where the body rested. Doesn't that indicate one thing clearly to you?'

'What do you mean exactly?'

'What do I mean? Exactly? I mean that the body had been moved after death. That's what I mean.'

There was a long pause, and then another reluctant admission from the witness who said, 'I think that may very well be so.'

It was over. A bit of a triumph, as I hope you will agree. I awarded myself two ears and a tail as I said, 'Thank you very much, Lieutenant Borders,' extremely politely and sat down.

Modestly satisfied as I had been with my cross-examination of the Army Pathologist, it had in no way delighted Captain Sandy Ransom, who sank lower in his seat during the course of it. As we came out of Court at the end of the day he was grumbling, 'Died by nine o'clock. He couldn't have! By nine o'clock he hadn't even met Helmut.'

'Helmut, of course.' I did my best to sound apologetic. 'Why do I always seem to forget about Helmut?'

'We thought we were getting an ordinary barrister. Do ordinary barristers try so damned hard to get their clients convicted?' Sandy was very angry. '*Someone's* got to do something for that boy!' And he moved off to liberate his lurcher.

Then I heard the soft voice of a young woman who had clearly learnt to speak English with a Glasgow Irish accent.

'Mr Rumpole! About the blood on Danny's cuff...' I

turned to her and it was impossible, in spite of Mrs Wilson's evidence, to think of her as English or German—she was just an extremely beautiful girl in very great distress. 'Yes, I am Hanni Boyne. It was the old shirt,' she told me. 'He wore it when he had the fight. I hadn't washed it, you see. Then he wore it again that night. He didn't remember. I will say all that to them.'

I bet you will, I thought. What lies love makes people tell, for I couldn't imagine Hanni failing to wash Danny Boy's shirts. 'I really shouldn't be talking to you about your evidence,' I told her. Out of the corner of my eye I could see Lieutenant-Colonel Mike Watford coming out of Court.

'You will do your best for Danny, sir. We have been so happy, so awfully happy. The three of us.' I knew she was telling the truth then, but all I could do was mutter something about the case going reasonably well—nothing of any real use to her when she was sick for certainties—and take Mike Watford's arm and steer him to a quiet end of a marble-paved corridor and under the ponderous stone arches.

'Soft you, a word or two before you go, Mike,' I started, doing my best to cash in on the past. 'We used to get on moderately well, didn't we, when you were an articled clerk with Butchers & Stringfellow.'

'I always enjoyed our cases,' Mike admitted.

'Went after the evidence, didn't we, and got at the truth on more than one occasion?'

'You always had a nose for the evidence, Mr Rumpole.'

'So did you, as a young lad, Mike.'

'All this flattery means you're after something.' Lieutenant-Colonel Watford was not born yesterday.

'Oh, young Mike, as astute as ever. Be honest, you're

not happy about the evidence on the time of death are you?'

There was a silence then. Mike Watford stopped walking and looked at me. I knew it would not be his style to tell me anything less than the truth. 'To be honest, not particularly.' And then he asked me. 'When do you think it was?'

'The time? Around 21.00 hours, as you would say,' I told him. 'The place, the bottom of the iron staircase outside the Sergeant's married quarters. Looked for any blood traces round there, have you?'

'No. As a matter of fact.' He looked thoughtful. 'No.'

'Oh, young Mike Watford! What do you want to do? Win your case or discover the truth?'

'I think the Army would want us to discover the truth.' He had no doubt about it.

'Then, old darling, may I make a suggestion?' And I walked on with him, giving him a list of things to do as I had when we had worked together so happily down the Old Bailey.

When I got back to the barracks I sought an appointment with the Colonel. After I had seen him, I went back to my quarters and soaked for a long time in the excellently hot water provided by the British Army. I wondered how many times I had washed away the exhaustion of a day in Court, and the invisible grime which comes from a long association with criminal behaviour, in an early evening bath-tub. Then I put on a clean shirt and walked across the darkened barracks square to the Mess.

My journey was interrupted by the roar and rattle of a jeep which drew up beside me. Captain Sandy Ransom and his lurcher jumped out, and I saw, with some sinking of the heart, that he was holding a rather muddy black leather jacket. 'Triumph!' he shouted at me. 'I've found it. I've found the evidence.'

It seemed that he had gone for a walk by the old Bad-weisheim canal after what he regarded as an extremely un-satisfactory day in court. The lurcher had started to sniff around in a pile of loose earth, and there, by chance, some-one had tried to bury the clear indication of their guilt. 'It's Helmut's jacket.' Sandy had no doubt about it.

'Of course it is,' I agreed, and went on to a more impor-tant matter. 'I've spoken to your colonel and he's dining in the Mess tonight. I hope you can join us.'

'Aren't you going to ring Watford?' For a moment Sandy looked like a schoolboy deprived of a treat. 'Aren't you going to tell the Prosecution about the new evidence?'

'I really think that can wait until after dinner.'

We were once again a small gathering in the Mess: Colo-nel Undershaft, Major Sykes, Captain Ransom, Lieutenant Hammick and Ross, who was that night's Duty Officer. When the port was on the table I sat back and addressed them, having refused to answer any questions during the service of the usual excellent dinner. I felt that I was speaking to them as though I were in Court, and they formed the tribunal who would finally have to decide the strange case of the murder of Sergeant Jumbo Wilson. First I filled my glass and sent the decanter on round the table.

'I know you don't usually toast the Regiment after din-ner,' I started, 'except on formal evenings in the Mess. But it's such a power over you all, isn't it, the Regiment? Blenheim, Malplaquet, Waterloo, Balaclava, El Alamein,' I intoned, looked round at them and raised my glass:

> 'This seraph-band . . .
> It was a heavenly sight!

They stood as signals to the land,
Each one a lovely light.

And the Regiment always rallies round a seraph in trouble.
You told me that, didn't you, Sandy?'

'Of course we do.' Sandy was opposite me, nodding
through the candlesticks. 'That's why we got you out here.
Not that you've done much for the boy so far.'

'So when Sergeant Wilson was stabbed to death,' I went
on with my final speech, 'you couldn't have it said that it
was done by a seraph, could you? Not by one of the heav-
enly band. Far better that the crime should have been com-
mitted by an unknown German called Helmut with a black
leather jacket and a punk hairdo. Who better to take the
blame, after all, than one of the old enemy? An enemy
from the war you're all too young to remember.'

'Are you suggesting that the officers of this regiment...?' The Colonel had never looked more deeply disturbed.

'Not the officers, Colonel,' I hastened to answer him.
'One officer, the joker in the pack. Of course, pinning the
crime on the mysterious Helmut took a lot of organization
and a good many risks. But perhaps that was part of the
attraction. It took the place of war.'

The Mess was very quiet; Borrow had left us. Old
generals and defunct colonels on their rearing chargers
looked down on us. Behind the flickering candles, Sandy
was smiling. Hugh Undershaft asked me exactly what I
knew.

'I'm not sure what I *know*, Colonel. Not for certain. But
I'll tell you what I think. I think Danny Boy and his mates
met by the dustbins at the foot of the Sergeant's staircase
and found him there. Dead. I think they told an officer. An

officer who was there. With a jeep—his usual method of
transport. Danny helped this officer move the body, hence
the blood on his cuff. It was the Sergeant's blood not the
blood of another mysterious German. Then the lads, the
young seraphs, went into *Der Rosenkavalier* so they could
lie and say they'd seen the Sergeant there after midnight.
Meanwhile, the Captain of the Seraphs was unloading a
body in a dark alley...'

'Dressed in a frock?' the Colonel asked.

'That was your joker's contribution. Did he have a dress
among the props for the pantomime, one large enough for
the Dame? I think he dressed up a dead body.'

'Why on earth should anyone do that?' Sandy sounded
incredulous.

'Why? To make some sort of homosexual crime of pas-
sion more credible, or as a sign of disapproval? The Sergeant brought no credit on the Regiment by having himself
murdered, did he?'

There was a long silence then; the officers were looking
at me, and I felt an intruder, never particularly welcome, in
their private world. Then Sandy said, 'Aren't you forgetting Helmut?'

'Oh, I never believed in Helmut, the mysterious German
who came so conveniently and asked for the Sergeant by
name. All the girl remembered was the spiky hair. What do
you use in the pantomime, Sandy? Hair lacquer? Hair gel?
Was that your own black leather jacket you found so conveniently?' The port had returned to me and I refilled my
glass. I felt tired after a long case, and I wanted to leave
them, to go home and forget their problem. 'I suppose, in a
way, you were a first-rate Defending Officer. You wanted
to get Danny Boy out of trouble and you thought he was
guilty. I always believed he was innocent; he was a boy

from Glasgow with the good sense to marry a German girl because they loved each other.'

There was another long, thoughtful silence, and then the Colonel spoke to me, 'So, may we ask, who, in your opinion, killed Sar'nt Wilson?'

'Oh, don't worry,' I could reassure him, 'the joker never went so far as that. He could move his body, dress him in a frock, but not murder him.'

'Then *who* . . .'

'I always thought that it must've been bad enough to have been fancied by Sergeant Wilson. It must have been hell on earth to be married to him.' As I said it, in the warm Mess, I shivered slightly. I was doing a job which wasn't mine, making accusations and bringing home guilt.

While I was talking to the officers of the Duke of Clarence's Own Lancers, a Captain Betteridge of the Special Investigations Branch called at the flat up the iron staircase in the married quarters. He found it spotlessly clean and shining. He saw the polished furniture and the framed photographs of Sergeant and Mrs Wilson on their wedding day, and of Mrs Wilson's father, a sergeant-major who had been killed at Arnhem. He opened a drawer in the sideboard and saw the gleaming, black-handled carving-knife, and he told Mrs Wilson that he wanted to question her further about the events around nine o'clock on the evening her husband died. It was not long before she told him everything, as she had been secretly longing to do since the day she killed Sergeant Wilson.

> Farewell the plumed troop and the big wars,
> That make ambition virtue! O, farewell!
> Farewell the neighing steed and the shrill trump,

> The spirit-stirring drum, the ear-piercing fife,
> The royal banner, and all the quality,
> Pride, pomp and circumstance of glorious war!

Farewell, anyway, to the barracks of the 37th and 39th Lancers at Badweisheim. Lieutenant Tony Ross drove me to the airport and Captain Ransom, for some reason, didn't turn out to say goodbye. Danny Boy thanked me a little brusquely, as though I had, after all, let down the Regiment. Only his wife, Hanni, was genuinely and, I expect, everlastingly, grateful. I went back to Civvy Street and, in due course, I was ensconced with Hilda in the bar of the Old Gloucester.

'Where's ex-Major Johnnie?' I asked her.

'He got a job as secretary of a golf club in Devon. We had a farewell lunch. He bought me champagne.'

'Decent of him.'

'We had a really good chat. When you're with us, he told me, you do all the chatting.'

'Oh, do I?'

'He got me wondering.'

'Oh, really. What about?'

'I suppose what my life would have been like if I hadn't got you to marry me, Rumpole.'

'Did you do that?'

'Of course. You don't decide things like that on your own.'

She was right. I can make all sorts of decisions for my clients, but practically none for Rumpole.

'I might have kept up my singing,' Hilda told me, 'if I hadn't married you, Rumpole. I can't help thinking about that.'

'No future in that, Hilda. No future at all in thinking about the past, or what we might have done. Let me give you a toast.' I raised my glass of indifferent claret. 'To the Regiment! Coupled,' I murmured under my breath, 'with the name of She Who Must Be Obeyed.'

Rumpole and the Winter Break

'What you need, Rumpole, is a break.'

My wife Hilda, known to me only as She Who Must Be Obeyed, was, of course, perfectly correct. I did need a break, a bit of luck, like not all my cases being listed before Judge Roger Bullingham, the Mad Bull of the Old Bailey, and not being led by an ineffective Q.C. named Moreton Colefax, not being prosecuted by Soapy Sam Ballard, the Savonarola of our Chambers, and not having as a client in my current little murder a shortsighted Kilburn greengrocer who admitted placing his hands about his wife's throat to reason with her. When this happened she dropped dead and he concealed her body, for some time, in a large freezer in the stock-room, that is, until he lost his nerve and called in the Old Bill.

'Of course, I need a break, Hilda. Anyone would think the Bull's the only judge left down the Bailey.'

'Not that sort of break. I mean a winter break. Now, for

£236 each, we could have seven nights on Spain's Sunshine Coast, with sea-view, poolside barbecue, sports facilities and excursions, including cocktails aboard the hotel's
old-time Pirate Galleon! Dodo's been to Marbella, Rumpole, and we never have a winter holiday.'

'Oh, yes,' I said. 'I can see your old school-friend,
Dodo Mackintosh, with a cutlass between her teeth shin-
ning up the ratlines to board the Pirate Galleon for a com-
plimentary cocktail.'

'I'll book up,' Hilda said.

'Not yet,' I told her, and thought to avoid further argument with a perfectly safe bet. 'We'll go,' I promised, 'if I
win *R*. v. *Gimlett*. We'll go as a celebration.' Hilda appeared, for the moment, to be satisfied and I knew that
never, in the whole Rumpole career, had there been such a
certain loser as the case of the gentle greengrocer from
Kilburn.

'It's true, is it not?' I asked Professor Ackerman, pathologist *par excellence* and uncrowned King of the Morgues,
across a crowded Courtroom a few days later, 'that a very
slight pressure on the vagal nerve at the throat may stop the
heart and death may follow speedily?'

'That would be so,' the Professor agreed. He and I had
discussed many a deceased person together and so, over
the years, although always opponents, we had achieved a
great deal of rapport. 'But of course, my Lord, as Mr
Rumpole knows, the pressure would have to be just on the
right spot.'

'Of course Mr Rumpole knows that!' The Bull lowered
his head in my direction and pawed the ground a little. 'Are
you suggesting that your client sought out the right spot
and pressed on it?'

'Certainly not, my Lord. He pressed on it by the sort of accident your Lordship or any of us might have—pressing on a gold collar-stud, say, putting on a winged collar before the start of a day in Court.'

'That sort of pressure?' I could see the Bull pale beneath his high blood pressure, and a nervous but stubby finger went to the space between the purplish folds of his neck and his off-white starched stand-up size nineteen. 'Do you mean by a collar-stud?' he asked the Professor.

'I think Mr Rumpole is exaggerating a little.' Ackerman gave me the tolerant smile he might reserve for a favourite pupil who had gone, for once, a little too far. 'But the pressure could be comparatively slight.'

'Mr Rumpole is exaggerating!' His Honour Judge Bullingham, senior Old Bailey judge, and as such, entitled to try murders, seemed to be remembering my previous convictions. 'That doesn't surprise me in the least.' And he gave the Jury one of his well-known meaningful smiles; no doubt it frightened the wits out of them.

'The sort of pressure which might arise if a man put his hand round his wife's neck for the purpose of restraining her?' I asked the witness.

'Restraining her, Mr Rumpole?' the Bull growled.

'Oh yes, my Lord. Restraining her from attacking him in one of her frequent outbursts of fury. Restraining her from following him into the shop and abusing him in front of the clientele as he weighed out a couple of pounds of Golden Delicious.'

I got a small titter from the Jury, a cry of 'Silence!' from the Usher, a glare from the Bull, and an absolutely charming answer from the fair-minded forensic expert.

'If he restrained her with some force, the vagal nerve

might be inhibited, particularly if she were pressing against
his hand. I suppose that is possible. Yes.'

'Thank you, Professor!' And I sat down silently wishing
the pale Ackerman a long life and happy dissecting.

But why was I, Horace Rumpole, a junior barrister in
status if not in years (I go back to the dawn of time when
Lord Denning was a stripling judge in the Divorce Division), why was I, who had a none-too-learned leader in the
shape of Moreton Colefax, Q.C., cross-examining the Pathologist called by the Crown?

The short answer was that Colefax, after a long delay,
had been called to higher things, that is, the Bench, and, as
our timid client appeared to feel safe in the Rumpole
hands, I was left in the firing-line, a target for the Bull's
blunderbuss and the sniping of my opponent and fellow
member of Chambers, Sam Ballard, Q.C.

'You say your married life was unhappy, Mr Gimlett?'
Ballard started his cross-examination when the prisoner at
the Bar had given evidence.

'She had a terrible temper when roused.' Gimlett looked
at the Jury in a woebegone sort of way. 'Her chief delight
seemed to be to show me up in front of my customers. Talk
about screaming; they say you could hear it all the way
down to Sainsbury's.'

'You have some experience of married life though,
haven't you? You have been married before?'

'My Lord. What on earth can be the relevance . . . ?' I
reared to my hind legs to protest and the Bull bared his
teeth in some sort of grin. 'I don't know, Mr Rumpole.
Unless Mr Ballard is trying to suggest that your client is
something of a Casanova.'

Ballard passed swiftly on to other matters and abandoned that line of cross-examination, but I sat in a sort of

glow because the Bull had delivered himself into my hands. Nothing in the world could have looked less like Casanova than the meek and middle-aged Harold Gimlett, with his pinkish bald head and National Health specs, who looked out of place without a brown overall, a slightly runny nose and cold hands among the Jersey potatoes. I would make him, before I finished with the Jury, the very image and archetype of the hen-pecked husband.

'Members of the Jury,' I told them in my final speech. 'My client has been presented to you as a Casanova, a Valentino, even (I had got the name from Mizz Liz Probert, the youngest member of our Chambers), a Jagger. Look at him! Can you imagine teenagers swooning over him at the airport? (Laughter, at which the Bull growled menacingly.) Is he a Lothario or a Bluebeard? Does he fill you with terror, Members of the Jury, or is he simply a put-on, timid and long-suffering human being who only wanted peace in his home and prosperity for his little grocery business? Of course, after this terrible accident, when he managed to make contact with his wife's neck in a way that he never dreamt could be so dangerous, he lost his head. For a futile moment he tried to conceal the body in that freezing cabinet you have all seen in the photograph, but soon he was his honest, straightforward self again and walked, of his own free will, into Kilburn Police Station, anxious only to face you fairminded, sensible ladies and gentlemen of the Jury, and receive justice at your hands...'

'You look tired, Mr Rumpole. You need a holiday.'

We sat together, Harold Gimlett and my learned self in the cells under the Old Bailey, waiting for the Jury to come back with a verdict. Such times are always embarrassing.

You don't quite know what to say to a client. You could say, 'Win a few, lose a few,' or, 'See you again, in about fifteen years,' but such remarks would be scarcely welcome. On this occasion it was the greengrocer who kept up the small talk.

'I've always enjoyed a holiday, speaking personally,' he said. 'Things happen sometimes, on a holiday.'

'What sort of things?'

'Well, for instance. It was on holiday that I met the ladies who became my wives.'

I left him then and paced up and down outside the Court, smoking a small cigar and nervously dropping ash down the front of the waistcoat. I don't know why, after so many years of waiting for juries to return, it never gets any better. The sad face of Sam Ballard, my devout prosecutor, hove into view.

'Ballard,' I said, 'why did you embark on that line about the previous wife? I mean, she died quite naturally, didn't she?'

'Natural causes, yes,' he agreed in a sepulchral tone. 'With quite a hefty life insurance made out in your client's favour. As was the case with the last Mrs Gimlett.'

'The trouble with you members of the Lawyers As Christians Society,' I told him, 'is that you have the most morbidly suspicious minds.' What he said had unsettled me a little, I confess. I felt a momentary sense of insecurity, but within ten minutes the Jury, to the Bull's evident chagrin, returned to find Harold Gimlett 'not guilty'. It was only then, and with a sickening heart, that I remembered the promise I had made to She Who Must Be Obeyed.

Three weeks later we had checked in at Gatwick airport, *en route* to the Costa del Sol.

• • •

'What you will find in the Hotel Escamillo, Mr and Mrs Rumpole, is never a dull moment. We lay on the usual wet-suit water-skiing on clear days—all that sort of activity. Hardly your line, Mr Rumpole, is it? Well, you'll be well pleased with the miniature golf, the Bingo and the bowling-green. We offer a full day, taking in Gibraltar and a packed lunch. The caves, now that makes a very nice excursion. And the hotel offers the Carmen Coffee Shop, the Mercedes Gourmet French Restaurant, the Michaela for snacks and grills, and the usual solarium and gym equipment if you want to keep in trim, Mr Rumpole.'

'Thank you. I have no desire whatever to keep in trim.'

'And for Mrs Rumpole, the Beauty Parlour—not that you need that, Mrs Rumpole. I must say we all, in hospitality, take particular care of our more mature ladies. Tonight, just as a for instance, there's a Senior Citizens' Happy Hour in the Don José American bar. Any problems at all, and you come straight to me. My name's Derek and I'm happy to host your stay.'

I could tell his name was Derek because he had it written in gold letters on a plastic label attached to his green blazer. He had soft brown eyes and a sort of Spanish-style gaucho moustache, although his accent was pure Ealing Broadway.

'Now, have you any questions at all, Mrs Rumpole, Mr Rumpole?'

'Yes,' I said. 'Where can I get *The Times*?'

'The Frasquita Drugstore on the mezzanine floor,' Derek told me, 'is continually at your service.'

But when I got there, they had nothing left but the *Mirror* and the *Sun*. I found the crosswords in those periodicals extremely puzzling.

'I don't know about you, Rumpole,' said She Who Must Be Obeyed, 'but I intend to take full advantage of all the facilities provided.'

'Pity I've got a touch of leg coming on.' I limped elaborately a few steps behind Hilda on the way to the lift. 'But of course, I want you to enjoy the full day in Gibraltar.'

So our days fell into a sort of pattern. The sun rose palely behind the tower blocks of the hotels, which in their turn cast a dark shadow upon the strip of beach. Each morning we took the Continental in the bedroom, as the Escamillo version of the full British breakfast arrived very cold and greasy, as though it had been flown out, tourist class, from England. I usually woke tired; the bedroom walls seemed made of thinnish hardboard, and the young family in the next room apparently enjoyed round games and pop music far into the night. Hilda was always in a hurry to get ready, to find her purse, her straw peasant-style shopping-basket, her hardly needed sun-hat and shaded specs, because the day's tour, or expedition, was always assembling round dawn in the foyer, to be taken by Derek on a bus journey to some distant point of interest.

I would skulk in bed until she had set out, and then get up slowly and wait for the hot water which apparently also arrived from a long way off. Once togged up in a pair of old flannels and a tweed jacket, I would leave the delights of the Escamillo Hotel. I would walk, my leg having rapidly recovered, into a sort of village where there were still dark and narrow streets, a dripping fountain and a square. On the square was a dark shop—a jumble of tinned food, sun-hats, paperback books, lilos and shrimping-nets—kept by an old woman in a black dress, with a gold tooth and a stubby moustache, who managed to save me copies of *The Times*. I would then go and sit in the comforting, incense-filled gloom of the church and do the crossword. Once it was finished, I transferred my patronage to a small, tiled bar which smelled of carbolic soap and wet dogs, where I ate shrimps, drank a red wine which bore about the same relationship to Pommeroy's plonk as Château Thames Embankment does to Latour 1961, and read my way backwards from the obituaries to the front-page news.

I was always back at the hotel in time to meet Hilda, who arrived home footsore and very weary with her basket full of fans, mantillas, bullfighting posters, sword-shaped paper-knives and other trophies of the chase. We had dinner together and after a terrible encounter with an antique hen lurking under a sweetish sauce, which called itself 'Caneton à l'Orange', in the Mercedes Gourmet Restaurant, we patronized the Michaela for snacks and grills. Every evening Hilda would recount the adventures of the day, repeat several of Derek's jokes, and tell me of the friendliness shown to her by everyone, but particularly by a Mr Waterlow, a visitor from England.

'Mr Waterlow's quite obviously a seasoned traveller. He came into the shop with me and managed to beat them down quite marvellously over the mantilla I bought as a present for Dodo Mackintosh.'

'I always thought old Dodo would look a lot better, heavily veiled.'

'What did you say?'

'You were going to tell me where you sailed . . .'

'Sailed? We didn't sail anywhere, Rumpole. We went on a bus. Mr Waterlow sat at my table at lunch in the Parador. Such a charming man and so distinguished-looking. He

wears one of those white linen shirts with short sleeves.
What do you call them? Bush-whacking shirts?' I said I
didn't call them anything.

'I think it's "bush-whacking". Anyway, you ought to get
a shirt like that, Rumpole.'

'Did you happen to tell this Waterlow person that you
were here with your husband?'

'Oh, Rumpole! We didn't talk about my life; I don't
suppose he even knows my name. He told me a little about
himself though; he says he's all alone in the world now. He
does seem rather sad about it.'

So life continued and each evening Hilda regaled me with her
travels round the Iberian peninsula and told me of the charm
and general helpfulness of the man Waterlow. Strangely we
never saw this paragon about the hotel. He knew, Hilda told
me, a lot of little restaurants along the coast. 'Places where
the continentals go, Rumpole. But then, of course, Mr Waterlow speaks absolutely perfect Spanish.'

On the last but one night of our stay dinner was laid out
in the nippy darkness beside the pool. The ladies pulled on
cardigans over thin dresses, the men brought out sweaters,
and a group of shifty-looking customers in big hats and
frilly shirts sang 'Deep in the Heart of Texas' and such-like
old Spanish folk-songs. Derek was tablehopping, telling
his jokes and flirting in a nauseating manner with the female senior citizens, when Hilda looked up from a battle
with a slice of singed bull which had no doubt weathered a
good many corridas, and almost shrieked, 'Why, Rumpole.
There he is!'

'There who is?'

'Why, Mr Waterlow, of course.'

I saw him then, sitting among the group who were so often poolside with their ladies. He saw Hilda and my back only. He raised his Sangría when she looked at him, but when he saw me he seemed to freeze, his glass an inch from his lower lip.

'Hilda,' I said, with all the determination I could muster, 'you must never speak to that man again!'

I looked back and he had gone, out of the poolside lights perhaps, and was still lingering in the shadows.

'But why, Rumpole? Why ever do you say that?'

I couldn't tell her about the man with whom she had struck up a friendship. Even if he had changed his name, substituted contact lenses for National Health specs and a safari suit and a gold medallion for a greengrocer's overall, I knew exactly who he was. I may have cherished uncharitable thoughts about She Who Must Be Obeyed at times, when a cold wind was blowing around Casa Rumpole, but I never wanted to see her end up in a freezer cabinet.

'Why mustn't I speak to him again?'

'Because I say so.'

'Rumpole, you silly old thing.' Hilda's face was wreathed in smiles. She looked some years younger, and intensely flattered. 'I do believe you're jealous.'

'Jealous?'

'Of Mr Waterlow. It's so silly, Rumpole. But it's nice to know that you really care as much as that. I do think that's awfully nice to know.' She's eyes were smiling. She put out her hand and took mine in a fairly moist embrace.

'You know, there's no one else really, don't you? Mr Waterlow was very charming, but what I really liked about him was he made you jealous! Would you like to dance with me, Rumpole?'

'No, Hilda.' I disengaged my hand as gently as possible. 'I don't really think I would.'

The next day was our last and Hilda forswore all trips. She came with me when I bought *The Times* and sat beside me in the church making some unhelpful suggestions for One Across. I didn't take her to the tiled bar, but we chose a restaurant by the sea where we ate calamares, food that tasted much like India rubber teething-rings. Hilda was smiling and cheerful all day. Harold Gimlett, the Kilburn greengrocer, seemed to have greatly improved my married life by giving Rumpole an undeserved reputation as a jealous husband.

Rumpole's Last Case

P icture, if you will, a typical domestic evening, *à côté de chez* Rumpole, in the 'mansion' flat off the Gloucester Road. I am relaxed in a cardigan and slippers, a glass of Jack Pommeroy's Very Ordinary perched on the arm of my chair, a small cigar between my fingers, reading a brief which, not unusually, was entitled, *R*. v. *Timson*. She Who Must Be Obeyed was staring moodily at the small hearthrug, somewhat worn over the ages I must admit, that lay in front of our roaring gas-fire.

'The Timsons carrying a shooter!' I was shocked at what I had just read. 'Whatever's the world coming to?'

'We need a new one urgently,' Hilda was saying, 'and we need it *now*.' She was still gazing at our hearthrug, scarred by the butt ends of the small cigars I was aiming at the bowl of water that stood in front of the fire.

'It's like music in lifts and wine in boxes.' I was lamenting the decline of standards generally. 'We'll be having Star Wars machines in Pommeroy's Wine Bar next. Decent, respectable criminals like the Timsons never went tooled up.'

'Rumpole, you've done it again!' Hilda recovered the end of my cigar from the rug and ground it ostentatiously out in an ashtray as I told her a bit of ash never did a carpet any harm, in fact it improved the texture.

'There's a perfectly decent little hearthrug going in Debenhams for £100,' Hilda happened to mention.

'Going to someone who isn't balancing precariously on the rim of their overdraft.'

'Rumpole, what on earth's the use of all these bank robberies and the rising crime-rate they're always talking about if we can't even get a decent little hearthrug out of it?' Hilda was clearly starting one of her campaigns, and I got up to recharge my glass from the bottle on the sideboard. 'Remembering what they're paying for legal aid cases nowadays,' I told her firmly. 'It hardly covers the fare to Temple station. And there's Henry's ten per cent and the cost of a new brief-case . . .'

'You're never buying a new brief-case!' She was astonished.

'No. No, of course not. I can't afford it.' I took a quick sustaining gulp and carried the glass back to my armchair. '. . . And there's a small claret at Pommeroy's to recover from the terrors of the day.'

'That's your trouble, isn't it, Rumpole.' She looked at me severely. 'If it weren't for the "small claret" at Pommeroy's we'd have no trouble buying a nice new hearthrug, and if it weren't for those awful cheroots of yours we shouldn't need one anyway. I warn you I shall call in at Debenhams tomorrow; it's up to you to deal with the bank.'

'How do you suggest I deal with the bank?' I asked her. 'Tunnel in through the drains and rob the safe? Not carrying a shooter, though. A Timson carrying a shooter! It's the end of civilization as we know it.'

Counsel is briefed for Mr Dennis Timson. He will 'know the Timson family of old'. It appears that Dennis and his cousin Cyril entered the premises of the 'Penny-Wise Bank' in Tooting by masquerading as workers from British Telecom inspecting underground cables that were laid in Abraham Avenue. Whilst working underground the two defendants contrived to burrow into the 'strong-room' of the 'Penny-Wise' and open the safe, abstracting therefrom a certain quantity of cash and valuables. As they were doing so, they were surprised by a Mr Huggins, a middle-aged bankguard. It is clear from the evidence that Huggins was shot and wounded by a revolver, which was then left at the scene of the crime. The alarm had been given and the two Timson cousins were arrested by police officers who arrived at the scene of the crime.

Mr Dennis Timson admits the break-in and the theft. He says, however, that he had no idea that his cousin Cyril was carrying a 'shooter', and is profoundly shocked at such behaviour in a member of the family. He is most anxious to avoid the 'fourteen', which he believes would be the sentence if the Jury took the view he was party to the wounding of Mr Huggins. Cyril Timson, who, instructing solicitors understand, is represented by Mrs Phillida Erskine-Brown, Q.C., as 'silk' with Mr Claude Erskine-Brown as her 'learned Junior', will, it seems likely, say that it is all 'down to' our client, Dennis. He has told the police (D.I. Broome) that he had no idea Dennis came to the scene 'tooled up', and that he was horrified when Dennis shot the bankguard. It seems clear to those instructing that Cyril is also anxious to avoid the 'fourteen' at all costs.

Counsel will see that he is faced with a 'cut-throat' defence with the defendants Timson blaming each other.

Counsel will know from his long experience that in such circumstances the Prosecution is usually successful, and both 'throat-cutters' tend to 'go down'. Counsel may think it well to have a word or two with Mr Cyril Timson's 'silk', Mrs Phillida Erskine-Brown, who happens to be in Counsel's Chambers, to see if Cyril will 'see sense' and stop 'putting it all down' to Mr Dennis Timson.

Counsel is instructed to appear for Mr Dennis Timson at the Old Bailey, and secure his acquittal on the charges relating to the firearm. Those instructing respectfully wish Learned Counsel 'the best of British luck'.

Dear old Bernard, the Timsons' regular solicitor, was a great one for the inverted comma. He had put the matter clearly enough in his instructions with my brief in *R. v. Timson,* and the case as he described it had several points of interest as well as a major worry. Both Cyril and Dennis were well into middle-age and, at least so far as Cyril was concerned, somewhat overweight. The whole enterprise, setting up a tent over a manhole in the road and carrying out a great deal of preliminary work in the guise of men from British Telecom, seemed ambitious for men whom I should never have thought of as bank robbers. It was rather as though the ends of a pantomime horse had decided to get together and play Hamlet. Den and Cyril Timson, I thought, should have stuck to thieving frozen fish from the Cash & Carry. The Penny-Wise affair seemed distinctly out of their league.

The fly in the ointment of our case had been accurately spotted by the astute and experienced Bernard. In a cut-throat defence, two prisoners at the Bar blame each other. The Prosecutor invariably weighs in with titbits of information designed to help the mutual mayhem of the two defendants and the Jury pot them both. The prospects were not made brighter by the fact that his Honour Judge Bullingham was selected to preside over this carnage. On top of all this anxiety, I was expecting my overdraft, already bursting at the seams constructed for it by Mr Truscott of the Caring Bank, to be swollen by Hilda's extravagant purchase of a new strip of floor-covering.

And then an event occurred which set me on the road to fortune and so enabled me to call this particular account 'Rumpole's Last Case'.

My luck began when I called in at the clerk's room on the first morning of *R*. v. *Timson* and found, as usual, Uncle Tom getting a chip shot into the waste-paper basket, Dianne brewing up coffee, and Henry greeting me with congratulations such as I had never received from him after my most dramatic wins in Court (barristers, according to Henry, don't win or lose cases, they just 'do' them and he collects his ten per cent). 'Well done, indeed, Mr Rumpole,' he said. 'You remember investing in the barristers clerks' sweepstake on the Derby?' In fact I remembered his twisting my arm to part with two quid, much better spent over the bar at Pommeroy's. 'You drew that Dire Jeans,' Henry told me.

'I drew what?'

'Diogenes, Rumpole.' Uncle Tom translated from the original Greek. 'Do you know nothing about the turf? It came in at a canter. I said to myself, 'That's old Rumpole for you. He has all the luck!" '

'Oh. Got a winner, did I?' I tried to remain cool when Henry handed me a bundle and told me that it was a hundred of the best and asked if I wanted to count them. I told him I trusted him implicitly and counted off twenty crisp fivers. It was an excellent start to the day.

'You know what they say!' Uncle Tom looked on with interest and envy. 'Lucky on the gee-gees, unlucky in love. You've never been tremendously lucky in love, have you, Rumpole?'

'Oh, I don't know, Uncle Tom. I've had my moments. One hundred smackers!' I put the loot away in my hip-pocket. 'It's not every day that a barrister gets folding money out of his clerk.' Uncle Tom looked at me a little sceptically. Perhaps he wondered what sort of moments I had had; after all he had enjoyed the privilege of meeting Mrs Hilda Rumpole at our Chambers parties.

As I sat in the café I said to myself,
They may talk as they please about what they call
    'pelf',
They may sneer as they like about eating and drink-
    ing,
But I cannot help it, I cannot help thinking...
How pleasant it is to have money, heigh ho!
How pleasant it is to have money...
So pleasant it is to have money...

The lines went through my head as I took my usual walk down Fleet Street to Ludgate Circus and then up to the Old Bailey. As I walked I could feel the comforting and un-usual bulge of notes in my hip-pocket. As I marched up the back lanes to the Palais de Justice, I passed a newspaper kiosk which, I had previously noticed, seemed to mainly cater to the racing fraternity. There were a number of papers and posters showing jockeys whose memoirs were printed and horses whose exploits were described, and I noticed that morning the advertisement for a publication entitled *The Punter's Guide to the Turf* which carried a

story headed FOUR-HORSE WINNER FATHER OF THREE TELLS
HOW HE HIT QUARTER OF A MILLION JACKPOT.

Naturally, as a successful racing man (a status I had
achieved in the last ten minutes), I took a greater interest in
the familiar kiosk. I had, clearly, something of a talent for
the turf. The Derby one day, perhaps the Grand National
the next—was it the Grand National or the Oaks? With a
few winners, I thought, a fellow could live pretty high on
the hog—I took a final turning and the Old Bailey hove
into view—a fellow might even be able to consider giving
up the delights of slogging down the Bailey for the dubious
pleasure of doing a cut-throat defence before his unpredict-
able Honour Judge Roger Bullingham.

And then, walking on towards the old verdict factory, I
heard the familiar voices of Phillida Erskine-Brown, Q.C.,
and her spouse; fragments of conversation floated back to
me on the wind.

'Rumpole's got Probert taking a note for him,' our Portia
said. 'Do try not to dream about taking her to the Opera
again.'

'I only took her once. And then she didn't enjoy it.' This
was Claude's somewhat half-hearted defence.

'I bet she didn't. You would have been better off inviting
her to a Folk Festival at the Croydon Community Centre.
Much more her style.'

'Philly! Look, aren't you ever going to forget it?'

'Frankly, Claude, I don't think I ever am.'

They crossed the road in front of me and their voices
were lost, but I had heard enough to know that all was not
sweetness and light in the Erskine-Brown household. I
hoped that our Portia's natural irritation with her errant
husband would not lead her to sharpen her scalpel for the
cut-throat defence.

Half an hour later I knew the answer to that question. I was robed up with Liz Probert and Mr Bernard in tow on my way to a pre-trial conference with my client Dennis Timson, when we met Phillida Erskine-Brown and her husband on a similar mission to Den's cousin, Cyril.

'Ill met by moonlight, proud Titania.' I thought this was a suitable greeting to the lady silk in the lift.

'Rumpole! What's all this about proud Titania?'

'You're not going to listen to me?'

'I'll certainly listen, Rumpole. What've you got to say?'

'You know it's always fatal when two accused persons start blaming each other! A cut-throat defence with the Prosecutor chortling in his joy and handing out the razors. That's got to be avoided at all costs.'

'Why don't you admit it then?'

'Admit *what?*'

'Admit you had the shooter? Accept the facts.'

'Plead guilty?' I must admit I was hurt by the suggestion. 'And break the habit of a lifetime?' We were out of the lift now and waiting, at the gateway of the cells in the basement, for a fat and panting screw, who had just put down a jumbo-sized sandwich, to unlock the oubliettes. 'Who's prosecuting?' I asked Phillida.

'Young fellow who was in our Chambers for about five minutes,' she told me. 'Charles Hearthstoke.'

'My life seems to be dominated by hearthrugs,' I told her.

'He's rather sweet.'

'If you can possibly think Hearthrug's sweet'—I must say I was astonished—'no wonder you suspect Dennis Timson of carrying a shooter.'

'Dennis Timson was tooled up.' She was positive of the fact.

'Cyril was!' I knew my Dennis.

'Moreover, he shot the bankguard extremely ineffi-
ciently—in the foot.'

'Come on, proud Titania. Plead guilty...' I tried a win-
some smile to a minus effect.

'Not for thy fairy kingdom, Rumpole!'

'What *do* you mean?'

'Isn't that what Titania tells him. At the end of the
scene? I suppose it means "no deal".' We parted then, to
interview our separate clients, and I was left wondering if,
when she was a white-wig, I had not taught young Phillida
Trant, as she then was, far too much.

We, that is to say, Liz, Mr Bernard and I, found Dennis
in one of the small interview rooms, smoking a little snout
and reading *The Punter's Guide to the Turf*. I thought I
should do best by an appeal to our old friendship and business association. 'You and I, Dennis,' I reminded him,
'have known each other for a large number of years and
I've never heard of you carrying a shooter before.'

'You're a sporting man, Mr Rumpole,' the client said
unexpectedly. I had to admit that I had enjoyed some recent
success on the turf.

'Bloke in here cleared quarter of a million on the
horses.' And Dennis was good enough to show me his
Punter's Guide. 'Well,' I told him, 'I've had handsome
wins in my time, but nothing to equal...'

'He's seen boarding an aeroplane for the Seychelles.'
Dennis showed me the picture in his *Punter's*.

'The Seychelles, eh?' I was thoughtful. 'Far from Judge
Bullingham and the Old Bailey.'

'I could make more than that on a four-horse accumulator. If I had a ton,' our client claimed.

'A ton of what?'

'A hundred pound stake.'

'A hundred pounds?' That very sum was swelling in my back pocket.

'I reckon I could top three hundred grand in the next few days.'

I pulled myself together and reluctantly came back to the matter in hand. 'You know what's going to happen when you and Cyril blame each other for carrying the shooter? The Mad Bull's going to tell the Jury you agreed to go on an armed robbery together. He'll say that it doesn't really matter who was in charge of the equipment. You're *both* guilty! Did you say ... three hundred thousand pounds?'

'From a four-horse accumulator.' Dennis made the point again.

'Four-horse what?'

'Accumulator.' He consulted his paper again. 'I could get 9 to 1 about Pretty Balloon at Goodwood this afternoon.'

'Do you want me to take this down?' Mizz Probert was puzzled at the course the conference was taking. I told her to relax but I pulled out a pencil and made a few notes on the back of my brief. I am ashamed to have to tell you they were not about the case.

'So there'd be a grand to go on Mother's Ruin at Redcar. 5 to 1, I reckon. That'd give us six thou.' Dennis went on as though it were peanuts. 'And that'd be on Ever So Grateful ... which should get you fours at Yarmouth. So that's thirty grand!'

'Ever So Grateful, sounds a polite little animal.' I was taking a careful note.

'Now we need 10 to 1 for a bit of a gamble.' Dennis was studying the forecasts.

'What's it been up to now?'

'A doddle,' he told me calmly.

'Easy as tunnelling into a bank vault?' I couldn't help it.

'Do me a favour, Mr Rumpole, don't bring that up again.' His pained expression didn't last long. 'Kissogram at Newbury on Wednesday,' he read out in triumph. 'Ante-post price should bring you, let's say three hundred and thirty grand! Give or take a fiver.'

'In round figures?'

'Oh, yes. In round figures.'

I put away my pen and looked at Dennis. 'Just tell me one thing.'

'About the shooter?' His cheerfulness was gone.

'We'll come back to the shooter in a minute; I was thinking that you've been in custody since that eventful night.'

'Six months, Mr Rumpole,' Bernard told me and Liz Probert added, 'We should get that off the sentence.'

'I suppose, being in Brixton and now here, it's difficult to place a small bet or two? Not to mention a four-horse accumulator?'

'Bless your heart, Mr Rumpole. There's always screws that'll do it for you, even down the Old Bailey cells.'

'Screws that'll put on bets?' I was surprised to hear it.

'You know Gerald, the fat one at the gate, the one that's always got his face in a bacon sarny?'

'Gerald.' I was grateful for the information. And then I stood up; we seemed to have covered all the vital points. 'Well, I think that's about all on the legal aspect of the case. Just remember one thing, Dennis. The Timsons don't carry weapons and they don't grass on each other.'

'That's true, Mr Rumpole. That has always been our point of honour.'

'So don't you go jumping into that witness-box and blame it all on your cousin Cyril. Let the Prosecution try and prove which of you had the gun; don't you two start cutting each other's throats.'

'Cyril goes in the first, don't he?' Dennis had a certain amount of legal knowledge gained in the hard school of experience.

'If he goes in at all, yes. You're second on the indictment.'

'I'll have to see what he says, won't I?'

'But you wouldn't grass on him?'

'Not unless I have to.' Dennis didn't sound so sure.

'"What is honour? A word. What is that word, honour? Air!"' Happily the allusion was lost on my client, so I went off to try a few passes at the Mad Bull after a word in confidence with the stout warder at the gate.

'Gerald.' I accosted him after I had told Liz and Mr Bernard to go on up and keep my place warm in Court. "Yes, Mr Rumpole. Got a busy day in Court ahead, have you?' The man's voice came muffled by a large wadge of sandwich.

'I am a little hard-pressed; in fact I'm too busy to get to my usual bookmakers.' 'Want me to put something on for you?' Gerald seemed to follow my drift at once.

'A hundred pounds. Four-horse accumulator. Start this afternoon at Goodwood'—I consulted the notes on my brief—'with Pretty Balloon. I reckon you can get 9 to 1 about it.'

'Will do, Mr Rumpole. I'll be slipping out soon, for a bit of dinner.'

'And I'm sure you'll need it . . .' I looked at the man with something akin to awe and gave him the name of my four hopeful horses. Then I put my hand in my back pocket, lugged out the hundred pounds and handed it all to Gerald. As some old gambler put it:

He either fears his fate too much,
Or his deserts are small,
That puts it not unto the touch,
To win or lose it all.

It was after I had placed the great wager with Gerald that I went upstairs. Outside Judge Bullingham's Court, I found three large figures awaiting me. I recognized Fred Timson, a grey-haired man, his face bronzed by the suns of Marbella, wearing a discreet sports jacket, cavalry-twill trousers and an M.C.C. tie. He was the acknowledged head of the family, always called on for advice in times of trouble, and with him I had also a longstanding business relationship. Fred was flanked by two substantial ladies who had clearly both been for a recent tint and set at the hairdressers; they were brightly dressed as though for a wedding or some celebration other than their husbands' day in Court. They, as I was reminded, were Den's Doris and Cyril's Maureen. Fred hastily told me of the family troubles. 'We're being made a laughing stock, Mr Rumpole. There's Molloys making a joke of this all over South London.' Of course, I knew the numerous clan Molloy, rival and perhaps more deft and successful villains, who were to the Timsons what the Montagues were to the Capulets, York to Lancaster or the Guelfs to the Ghibellines of old.

'I've been called out to in the street by Molloy women,' Den's Doris complained. 'Maureen's been called out to in Tesco's on several occasions.'

'They're laughing at our husbands'—this, from Cyril's Maureen—'grassing on each other.'

'Is *that* what they're laughing at?' I wondered.

'Oh, the Molloys is doing very nicely, that's what we

hear. They pulled off something spectacular.' Fred had the
latest information.

'They got away with something terrific, they reckon,'
Maureen and Doris added. 'And they calls out that all the
Timsons can do is get nicked and then grass on each other.'

'These Molloys aren't ever going to let us hear the last
of it.' Fred was gloomy. 'Young Peanuts Molloy, he called
out that all the Timsons is good for is to use as ferrets.'

'Ferrets?' I looked at him with some interest. 'Why on
earth did he say *that*, I wonder?'

'You know the way they talk.' Fred was full of contempt
for Molloy boasting. 'We wants you to go in there, Mr
Rumpole. And save our reputation.'

'I'll do my best,' I had to promise. After all, the Timson
family had done more for the legal profession than a
hundred Lord Chancellors.

A standard opening gambit, when faced with the difficulties of a cut-throat defence, is to apply to the Court,
before the Jury is let in and sworn, for separate trials for
the defendants. If they are tried on different occasions they
cannot then give evidence which will be harmful to each
other. Such applications are usually doomed, as the Judge
is as keen as the Prosecution to see a couple of customers
convicting each other without the need for outside assistance.

'A separate trial,' the Bull growled when I stood on my
feet to make the application, 'for Dennis Timson? Any
reason for that, Mr Rumpole, apart from your natural desire to spin out these proceedings as long as possible? I
assume your client's on legal aid?'

I am sorry to say that not only the handsome young
Hearthstoke but Phillida laughed at Bullingham's 'joke',
and I thought that if I were to win the four-horse accumu-

lator, I could tell his Lordship to shut up and not be so
mercenary.

'The reason, my Lord,' I told him, 'is my natural desire
to see that justice is done to my client.'

'Provided it's paid for by the unfortunate rate-payers of
the City of London.' The Bull glared at me balefully. 'Go
on, Mr Rumpole.'

'I understand that my co-defendant, Mr Cyril Timson,
may give evidence accusing my client of having the
gun.'

'And you, no doubt, intend to return the compliment?'

'I'm not prepared to say at this stage what my defence
will be,' I said with what remained of my dignity.

'But it may be a cut-throat?' the Bull suggested artlessly.

'That is possible, my Lord.'

'These two...'—he looked at the dock with undisguised contempt—'*gentry!* Are going to do their best to cut
each other's throats?'

Gazing at his Lordship, I knew how the Emperor Nero
looked when he settled down in the circus to watch a glad-
iator locked in hopeless combat with a sabre-toothed tiger.
I glanced away and happened to catch sight of a pale,
weaselly-faced young man with lank hair and a leather
jacket leaning over the rail of the Public Gallery, listening
to the proceedings with interest and amusement. I immediately recognized the face, well known in criminal circles,
of Peanuts Molloy, who also appeared to enjoy the circus. I
averted my eyes and once more addressed the learned
judge, 'Of course,' I told him, 'the statements the defendants made to the police wouldn't be evidence against each
other.'

'But once they go into the witness-box in the same trial
and repeat them on oath, then they become evidence on

which the Jury could convict!' Bullingham added with relish.

'Your Lordship has my point.'

'Of course I do. You don't want your client sent down for armed robbery and grievous bodily harm, do you, Mr Rumpole?'

'I don't want my client sent down on evidence which may well be quite unreliable!' At that I sat down in as challenging a manner as possible and his Honour Judge Bullingham directed a sickly smile at Phillida. 'Mrs Erskine-Brown. Do you support Mr Rumpole's application?' he asked her in a voice like Guinness and treacle.

'My Lord. I do not!' Phillida rose to put her small stiletto heel into Rumpole. 'I'm sure that under your Lordship's wise guidance justice will be done to both the defendants. Your Lordship will no doubt direct the Jury with your Lordship's usual clarity.' When it came to buttering up the Bull our Portia could lay it on with a trowel. 'You may well warn them of the danger of convicting Mr Dennis Timson on the evidence of an accomplice. But, of course, they *can* do so if they think it right.'

'Oh yes, Mrs Erskine-Brown.' The Bull was purring like a kitten. 'I shall certainly tell them that. The Court is grateful for your most valuable contribution.'

So the two Timsons were ordered to be tried together and I thought that if only certain horses managed their races better than I was managing my case I might, in the not too distant future, be boarding an aeroplane for the Seychelles. In fact, that first day in Court was not an unmitigated disaster. As Hearthrug was drawing to the end of a distinctly unsporting address to the Jury, in the course of which he told them that the bankguard, Huggins, 'a family man, a man of impeccable character, who has sat upon his

local Church Council, was wounded by these two desper-
ate robbers, albeit in the foot', my client scribbled a note
which was delivered to me by a helpful usher. I opened it
and read the glad tidings: THE SCREWS TOLD ME, MR RUM-
POLE. PRETTY BALLOON WON BY A SHORT HEAD AT GOOD-
WOOD. One up, I thought as I crumpled the note and
looked up at Bullingham like a man who might not be in
his clutches for ever—one up and three to go.

I have it on the good authority of Harry Shrimpton, the
Court Clerk, that after he rose, Bullingham said to him, 'A
really most attractive advocate, Mrs Erskine-Brown. Do
you think it would be entirely inappropriate if I sent her
down a box of chocolates?'

'Yes, Judge,' Shrimpton felt it his duty to tell him.

'You mean, "Yes", I can?'

'No. I mean "Yes", it would be entirely inappropriate.'

'Hm. She hasn't a sweet tooth?' The Bull was puzzled.

'The Lord Chancellor wouldn't like it.' The Court Clerk
was expert on such matters, but the Judge merely growled,
'I wasn't going to send chocolates to the Lord Chancellor.'

Whilst the learned female Q.C. was being threatened by
unsolicited chocolates from the Judge, she was sitting, at
his express invitation, with Charlie Hearthstoke, in a quiet
corner of Pommeroy's Wine Bar in the company of two
glasses and a gold-paper-necked bottle in an ice bucket.
The ruthless counsel for the Prosecution, she was able to
tell me much later, had invited her there so that he could
tell her that my client, Dennis, possessed a firearm without
a licence, although it was unfortunately a shotgun and not a
revolver, and that he had done malicious damage with an
air rifle when he was fourteen. It was also thought that he
had rung the hospital to inquire about Huggins's health; an

event which, as interpreted by Hearthrug, showed not natural sympathy, but a desire to discover if he were likely to be charged with murder. All these facts were put at Phillida's disposal, so that she might be the better able to cut my client's throat. Then Charlie Hearthstoke told Phillida what a superb 'Courtroom technician' she was. 'The way you handled Bullingham was superb. He's dotty about you, naturally. Well, I can't blame him. I suppose everyone is.'

There was more of such flattery, apparently, and Hearthstoke made it clear that he wished he'd got to know Phillida better when he was in our Chambers, but of course she was always doing such important cases, and was 'very much married, naturally'.

'Not all *that* married,' Phillida now agrees she replied, and who knows what course the conversation might not have taken had I not hove to with Liz Probert, seen the bottle in the bucket, and asked Jack Pommeroy's girl, Barbara, to bring us another couple of glasses. 'Champagne all round, eh, Hearthrug?' I said, as we settled in our places. 'And I know exactly what you're celebrating.'

'I can't imagine what that could be.' Phillida tried to sound innocent.

'Come off it,' I told her. 'You're celebrating the unholy alliance between Cyril Timson and the Prosecution, with a full exchange of information designed to send poor old Dennis away for at least fourteen years."

'That's not fair!'

'Of course it's not fair, Portia. But it's true. And as the quality of mercy doesn't seem to be dropping like the gentle rain from heaven around here, we'll have to make do with Pommeroy's bubbly.' I pulled the bottle out of the bucket and looked at it with dismay. '*Methode Champenoise*. Oh, Hearthrug. You disappoint me.'

'Actually, Charles, it's quite delicious.' I saw Phillida smile at the odious Prosecutor.

'Grape juice and gas,' I warned her. 'Wait for the headache. You know Mizz Probert, of course?' Of course she knew Liz only too well, but I wasn't in a mood to make life easy for Cyril Timson's silk.

'Of course,' Phillida spoke from the deep-freeze.

'There's one thing I've always wanted to ask you, Phillida.' Liz being extremely nervous, started to chatter. 'Now you're a Q.C. and all that. But when you started at the Bar, wasn't it terribly difficult being a woman?'

'Oh, no. Being a woman comes quite naturally, to some of us.' She smiled at Hearthstoke who laughed encouragingly. 'Not that I had much choice in the matter.'

'But didn't you come up against a load of fixed male attitudes?' Liz stumbled on, doing herself no good at all. 'That's what made it all such tremendous fun,' Phillida told her. 'If you really want to know, I didn't get a particularly brilliant law degree but I never had the slightest trouble getting on with men.'

'Clearly not.' Hearthrug was prepared to corroborate her story. 'Oh, yes'—Phillida smiled at Liz in a particularly lethal way—'and there's one question I wanted to ask *you.*'

'About the exploitation of women at the Bar?' A simple-minded girl, Mizz Probert.

'No. Just . . . seen any good operas lately?' A deep old-fashioned blush spread across the face of that liberated lady Liz Probert, and I tried to help her by saying, 'You could have learned a great lesson from Portia today, Mizz Probert. How to succeed at the Bar by reducing Judge Bullingham to a trembling blob of sexual excitement. I've never been able to manage it myself.' Gazing idly about me, I saw Claude enter Pommeroy's, and I happened to tell his wife that he looked as though he'd lost her, a remark not lost on the egregious Hearthrug.

'Rumpole, lay off!' Phillida's aside was unusually angry. 'Are you going to lay off Dennis?' I was prepared to strike a bargain with her, but as she made no response, I invited Erskine-Brown to draw up a chair and sit next to Mizz Probert. He declined to do this, but squeezed himself, in a way welcomed by neither of the parties, between his wife and Hearthstoke. When we were all more or less uncomfortably settled, I asked Claude if I could borrow the copy of the *Standard,* which he was holding much as a drowning man clings to a raft.

'I went back to Chambers, Philly,' the unhappy man was saying. 'They said you hadn't been in.'

'No. I came straight here. I was discussing the case with prosecuting counsel.'

'Oh, yes.' Erskine-Brown was clearly cowed. 'Oh, yes. Of course.'

I wasn't listening to them. I was gazing like a man entranced at a stop-press item on the back of the *Standard.* The golden words read LATE RESULT FROM REDCAR. NUMBER ONE, MOTHER'S RUIN. Two down and two to go! Things were going so well that I suggested to Hearthrug he might order a bottle of the real stuff.

'Why? What are *you* celebrating?' Phillida asked.

'I don't know about you fellows,' I told them. 'But I've made a few investments which seem to have turned out rather well. In fact, my future is almost entirely secure. Perhaps I won't have to do this job any more.' I looked round the table, smiling. 'Suppose this should turn out to be Rumpole's positively last case!' At which point my learned friends, and one of my learned enemies, looked at me with a wild surmise, silent at a table in Pommeroy's Wine Bar, faced with what might well count as the most significant moment in recent legal history.

Events were moving quickly. Diogenes had won the Derby the previous Wednesday, and on Monday morning Henry had paid out my little bit of capital when I called into Chambers on my way to participate in *R* v. *Timson*. By Monday night, two of my favoured horses had brought home the bacon: Pretty Balloon at Goodwood, and Mother's Ruin most recently at Redcar. The speed of my success had somewhat stunned me, but I began to feel, as anyone must half-way through a successful four-horse accumulator, that I had the Midas touch. I had listened to Dennis's advice perhaps, but I could certainly pick them. As I settled in my armchair at the gas-fireside in the Gloucester Road area that Monday evening I had no real doubt that Hilda and I were bound for some easy retirement by a sunkissed lagoon. We should soon, I thought, be boarding an aeroplane for the Seychelles. 'I've got it, Rumpole.' She broke into my reverie.

'What've you got, Hilda?'

'What I've been wanting for a long time, that little hearthrug. It looks smart, doesn't it?'

'If that's what you always wanted, I think you might be rather more ambitious!' The new arrival at our 'mansion' flat seemed hardly appropriate to our new-found wealth.

'Just don't you dare throw your cigar ends at it!'

'Don't you worry,' I told her. 'I shall be chucking my cigar ends, my Havana cigar ends, my Romeo y Julieta cigar ends, at the sparkling ocean, as I wander barefoot along the beach in a pair of old white ducks and knock the sweet oysters off the rocks.'

'You're hardly going to do that in the Gloucester Road.' Hilda seemed not to be following my drift.

'Forget the Gloucester Road! We'll move somewhere far away from Gloucester Road and the Old Bailey.' I rose to get a glass of Château Fleet Street from the bottle on the sideboard. 'It's not *real* Persian, of course, but I think it's a traditional pattern,' Hilda told me.

'"Courage!" he said,'—I gave her a taste of 'The Lotos-Eaters':

'and pointed toward the land,
"This mounting wave will role as shoreward
    soon."
And in the afternoon they came unto a land
In which it seemed always afternoon.
All round the coast the languid air did swoon,
Breathing like one that hath a weary dream.'

'I have absolutely no idea what you mean,' Hilda sighed and turned her attention to the *Daily Telegraph*.

'It's not the *meaning,* Hilda, it's the sounds we shall hear: the chatter of monkeys, the screech of parrots in the jungle, the hum of dragonflies, the rattle of grasshoppers rubbing their little legs together, the boom of breakers on the coral reef. And we shall sit out on the hotel verandah, drinking Planter's Punch and never having to wear a bloody winged collar again.'

'I don't wear a winged collar now.' Hilda tends to think first of herself. Then she said, as I thought, a little sharply, 'I wonder if the bank manager will have anything to say about the hearthrug.'

'Hardly, Hilda!' I reassured her. 'I rather suspect that when I next run into Mr Truscott of the Caring Bank, he'll be inviting me for a light lunch at the Savoy Grill. I just hope I can make time for him.'

'The bank manager inviting *you* to lunch? That'll be the day!' She suddenly looked at me. 'You have *got* the hundred pounds for our hearthrug, haven't you, Rumpole?'

'"Fear not, Hilda...I do expect return/Of thrice three times the value of this bond."'

'That's all very well. But have you got the hundred pounds?'

Tuesday dawned with only the case and Yarmouth races to worry about, but soon a new drama was unfolding itself before my eyes. I got to Chambers a little too late for my breakfast at the Taste-Ee-Bite in Fleet Street, so, once trapped again in the robes and the winged collar, I went down to the Old Bailey canteen, took my solitary coffee and bun to a corner table and sank behind *The Times*. I was soon aware of voices at the next table. It was Phillida again, but this time her companion was Charlie Hearthrug, and they both seemed blissfully unaware of old Rumpole at the table behind them.

'You might come back into the fold?' I heard Phillida say, and Hearthstoke answered, 'Well, without Rumpole there, I don't see why I shouldn't find my way back into your Chambers at Equity Court.'

'That'd be something to look forward to. I used to think nothing would ever change. Marriage and building up the practice and having the kids and taking silk and perhaps becoming one of the statutory women on the Circuit Bench—Circus Bench, Rumpole calls it...' Phillida was clearly choosing this unlikely time and place to pour out her heart to Hearthstoke, who encouraged her by asking in soft and meaningful tones, like a poorish actor, 'Doesn't that seem enough for you now?'

'Not really. You know'—more confidences were clearly to come from Mrs Erskine-Brown—'sometimes I envy my clients getting into trouble and leaving home and doing extraordinary things, dreadful things sometimes. But their lives aren't dull. Nothing happens to us! Nothing adventurous, really.'

'Perhaps it will if this is really Rumpole's last case and we're in Chambers together. Almost anything can happen then.'

'Almost anything?' I saw Phillida's elegant hand, with its rosy nails and sparkling cuff, descend gently on to Hearthrug's. It was time to clear the throat, stand up and approach the couple.

'How are you enjoying our duel to the death, Portia?'

'Fighting you, Rumpole'—she withdrew her hand as casually as possible—'is always a pleasure.'

'Of course, you've got one great advantage,' I told her.

'Have I?'

'Oh yes. You've got an excellent Junior. Good old Claude. He's always behind you. Working hard. I think you should remember that.' And with a brief nod to both of them, I swept on towards the corrida for another day's battle with the Bull.

When I rose to cross-examine Inspector Broome, the Officer-in-Charge of the case, a glance up at the Public Gallery told me that Peanuts Molloy was still *in situ* and apparently enjoying the proceedings. My gaze lingered on him for but a moment and then I turned my attention to the Inspector as I had done over so many cases and confronted a middle-aged, somewhat sardonic man who was capable of rare moments of humour and even rarer moments of humanity. He looked back at me, as always, with a sort of weary patience. Defence barristers in general, and Horace Rumpole in particular, were not among the Inspector's favourite characters.

'Inspector Broome,' I began my cross-examination. 'I understand that no fingerprints were found on the gun.' At which point the Bull couldn't resist weighing in with 'I imagine, Mr Rumpole, that these gentry would be too...' —for a wild moment I hoped he was going to say 'experienced' and then I'd have him on toast in the Court of Appeal, but his dread of that unjust tribunal made him say 'too *intelligent* to leave fingerprints?'

Something, perhaps it was the success I was enjoying with the horses, emboldened me to protest at the Judge's constant interruptions at the expense of my client. 'My Lord,' I ventured to point out, 'the prosecution in this case is in the hands of my learned friend, Mr Hearthrug.'

'Hearthstoke.' The young gentleman in question rose to correct me. 'Beg his pardon. Hearthstone. I'm sure he needs no assistance from your Lordship.'

There was the usual pause while the Bull lowered his head, snorted, pawed the ground and so on. Then he charged in with 'Mr Rumpole. That was an outrageous remark! It is one I may have to consider reporting as professional misconduct!'

Of course, by the time he did that, I might be safely on my way to the Seychelles, but I still had to get through Yarmouth that day and Newbury the next. I thought it best to return the retort courteous. 'I'm sorry if anything I might have said could possibly be construed as critical of your Lordship...'

'Very well. Let's get on with it.' Bullingham suspended

his attack for the moment and I returned to the witness. 'Were the other areas of the strong-room examined for finger-prints, in particular the safe?'

'Yes, they were,' the Inspector told me.

'And again no fingerprints of either Mr Cyril or Mr Dennis Timson were found?' Bullingham roused himself to interrupt again, so I went on quickly, 'My Lord is about to say, of course, that they'd still be wearing their gloves when they opened the safe and that is a perfectly fair point. I needn't trouble your Lordship to make that interjection.'

'Isn't Rumpole going rather over the top?' I heard Phillida whispering to her husband, and she got the sensible reply, 'He's behaving like a chap who's got a secure future from investments.'

'No fingerprints identifiable as the defendant's were found, my Lord. That is true,' Broome told the Court.

'But no doubt a number of fingerprints *were* found on the door of the safe?' I asked.

'Of course.'

'And they were photographed?'

'Yes.'

'No doubt many of them came from bank employees?'

'No doubt about that, my Lord.'

'But did you take the trouble to check any of those fingerprints with criminal records?'

'Why should we have done that?' The Inspector looked somewhat pained at the suggestion.

'To see if they corresponded to the fingerprints of any known criminal, other than the two Mr Timsons.'

'No. We didn't.'

'Why not?'

'The two Mr Timsons were the only men we found at

the scene of the crime and we had established that they were wearing gloves.'

'Because they had gloves on them when you caught them,' Bullingham explained to me as though I were a child, for the benefit of the Jury.

'We are so much obliged to the learned judge for his most helpful interjection, aren't we, Inspector? Otherwise you might have had to think of the answer for yourself.'

Of course that brought the usual warning rumble from the Bench, but I pressed on, more or less regardless, with, 'Let me ask you something else, Inspector. When the defendants were apprehended, they were carrying about three thousand pounds worth of cash and other valuables from various deposit boxes?'

'That is so.'

'Was that the total amount missing from the safe?'

'No. No, as a matter of fact, it wasn't.' For the first time Broome sounded puzzled. 'That particular safe had been almost entirely emptied when we came to inspect it.'

'Were its entire contents valued at something over sixty thousand pounds?'

'Well over that, my Lord.'

'Well over that . . .' The Judge made a grateful note.

'You have no idea when the sixty-thousand-pound worth was taken? I heard Bullingham start with a menacing 'Perhaps . . .' and went on, 'My Lord is about to say perhaps they took it first and carried it out by the tunnel. That would be a sound point for my Lord to make.'

'Thank *you*, Mr Rumpole.' The Judge tried the retort ironical.

'Not at all, my Lord. I'm only too glad to be of assistance.' I smiled at him charmingly. 'But let me ask you this, Inspector. Your men came to the bank because an alarm went off in the strong-room?'

'That is so. The signal was received at Tooting Central at . . .'

'About 3 a.m. We know that. But it's clear, isn't it, that when your men invaded the bank they knew nothing about the tunnel?'

'That is quite right.'

'So they were admitted by the second guard on duty and went down to the vaults.'

'Yes.'

'No police officer ever entered by the tunnel?'

'Not so far as I am aware.'

'We all heard that evidence, Mr Rumpole. Or perhaps you weren't listening?' Nothing subtle, you see, about Judge Bullingham's little sallies.

'On the contrary, my Lord. I was listening most intently.' I turned back to the Inspector. 'And when your officers entered the vaults they found there two men running down a passage towards them?'

'That's what they reported.'

'Running *away* from the entrance to the tunnel.'

'Yes, indeed.'

'That is all I have to ask'—I gave Bullingham another of my smiles—'unless your Lordship wishes to correct any of those answers . . .'

'Hadn't you better sit down, Mr Rumpole?'

'Sit down? Yes, of course. I'd be glad to. Your Lordship is most kind and considerate as always . . .' As I sat I thought that dear old Ever So Grateful had better get a spurt on or I would find myself up on a charge of professional misconduct. These thoughts were interrupted by

Charlie Hearthstoke's re-examination of the witness.

'Mr Rumpole has asked you if you consulted criminal records on any of the fingerprints you *did* find on the safe.'

'Yes. I remember him asking me that,' Broome answered.

'Mr Rumpole no doubt felt that he had to ask a large number of questions in order to justify his fee from the legal aid.' Bullingham did one of his usual jokes to the Jury; it was a moderate success only with the twelve honest citizens.

'I suppose you *could* compare the photographs of fingerprints you have with criminal records, couldn't you?' Hearthstoke suggested, greatly to my relief.

'I could, my Lord. If the Court wishes it.' Inspector Broome turned politely to the Bench for guidance and the Judge did his best to sound judicial. 'Mr Hearthstoke has made a very fair suggestion, Inspector, as one would expect of a totally impartial prosecutor.' He said graciously, 'Perhaps you would be so kind as to make the inquiry. We don't want to give Mr Rumpole any *legitimate* cause for complaint.'

When we left Court at lunchtime, I followed the Inspector down the corridor in pursuit of the line of defence I had decided to adopt for Dennis Timson. When I caught up with him, I ventured to tell Inspector 'New' Broome what a thoroughly dependable and straightforward officer I had always found him. Quite rightly he suspected that I wanted something out of him and he asked me precisely what I had in my mind.

'A small favour,' I suggested.

'Why should I do you a favour, Mr Rumpole? You have been a bit of a thorn in my flesh over the years, if I have to be honest.'

'Oh yes, you have to be honest. But if I promised never to be a thorn in your flesh ever again?'

'Not making me and my officers look Charlies in front of the Jury?' Broome asked suspiciously.

'Never again.'

'Not letting the Timsons get away with murder?'

'Never murder, Inspector! Perhaps, occasionally, stolen fish.'

'Not getting my young D.C.s tied up in their own note-books?' He pressed for specific assurances.

'If I swore on my old wig never to do anything of the sort again. In fact, Inspector Broome, if I were to promise you that this would be positively my last case!'

'Your last case, Mr Rumpole?" The Inspector was clearly reluctant to believe his ears.

'My positively last case!'

'You'd be leaving the Bailey after this for good?' Hope sprang in the officer's breast.

'I was thinking in terms of a warmer climate. So if I were to leave and never trouble you again...'

'Then I suppose I might be more inclined to help out,' Inspector Broome conceded. 'But if it's that fingerprint business!'

'Oh, you won't get anything out of that. I just wanted to get somebody worried. No respectable thief's ever going to leave their prints on a Peter. No, what I was going to suggest, old darling, is something entirely different.'

'Nothing illegal, of course?'

'Illegal! Ask Detective Inspector Broome to do anything illegal?' I hope I sounded suitably appalled at the idea. 'Certainly not. This is only guaranteed to serve the interests of justice.'

• • •

After lunch, and after I had made my most respectful suggestions to the Inspector, Hearthstoke closed the prosecution case and Phillida called Cyril Timson to the witness-box. He agreed with most of the prosecution case and accepted the evidence, which we had heard, of Mr Huggins of having been shot at by some person and wounded in the foot. Phillida held the revolver in her hand and asked in her most solemn tones, 'Cyril Timson. Did you take this weapon with you when you tunnelled into the Penny-Wise Bank?' When he had, not unexpectedly, answered, 'No. I never,' I whispered a request to her to sit down and resist the temptation of cutting Dennis's throat. She was not in a temptation resisting mood.

'Did you ever,' she asked Cyril, 'have any idea that your cousin, the co-defendant, Dennis Timson, was armed with a pistol?'

'My Lord,' I objected, 'there is absolutely no evidence that Dennis was armed with anything!'

'The pistol was there at the scene of the crime, Mr Rumpole. *Someone* must have brought it,' Bullingham reasoned.

'Someone perhaps. But the question assumes . . .'

'Please continue, Mrs Erskine-Brown.' The Judge, ignoring me, almost simpered at Phillida, 'You may ask your question.'

'But you don't have to, Portia,' I whispered to her as I sat down. 'Remember the quality of mercy!'

'Did you have any idea that Dennis was armed?' She forgot it.

'No idea at all.' Cyril looked pained.

"And what would you have said if you had known?'

'My Lord'—I had another go—'how can this be evidence? It's pure speculation!'

'Please, Mrs Erskine-Brown.' Again, I was ignored. 'Do ask the question.'

'What would you have said?'

'Leave that thing at home, Den.' Cyril sounded extraordinarily righteous. 'That's not the way we carry on our business.'

'Can you tell us if Dennis ever owned a firearm?'

'I don't object, my Lord. All objections are obviously perfectly useless.' I rose to tell the Court and got a look from the Judge which meant 'And that's another one for the report'. But now Cyril was saying, 'Dennis was always pretty keen on shooters. When he was a kid he had an airgun.'

'And probably a catapult as well,' I whispered as I subsided.

'Did you say something, Mr Rumpole?' the Judge was kind enough to ask.

'Nothing whatever, my Lord.'

'In his later years he bought a shotgun.' Cyril added to the indictment of his cousin.

'Did you know what he used that for?' Phillida asked.

'He said clay pigeons, my Lord.'

'He said clay pigeons. Did you believe him?' the Judge asked and, looking up at the public gallery, I again saw Peanuts Molloy smiling.

'I had no means of checking the veracity of cousin Den's statement.'

'Thank you, Mr Timson, just wait there.' Phillida sat down, happily conscious of having done her worst, and I rose to cross-examine the witness. Bullingham sat back to enjoy further bloodshed.

'Mr Timson. When you were removing some of the property from the safe, you suddenly ran out of the strong-room into the corridor. Why was that?'

'We thought we heard a noise behind us.' Cyril frowned, as though he still found the situation puzzling.

'Coming from where?'

'He said "behind us", Mr Rumpole,' Bullingham reminded me.

'Thank you, your Lordship, so much! And it was that sound that made you retreat?'

'We thought we was being copped, like.'

'Why didn't you retreat back into the tunnel you came from? Was it by any chance because the sound was coming from that direction?'

'Yes. It might have been,' Cyril admitted.

'When you ran out into that corridor you were holding some boxes containing money and valuables.'

'Yes, I was.'

'And so was your cousin Dennis?'

'Yes.'

'You saw that?'

'Yes.'

'You never saw him with a gun in his hand?'

'No. I never saw it, like. But I knew *I* didn't have it.'

'Mr Cyril Timson, may I say at once that I accept the truth of that statement...' The Court went strangely silent; Bullingham looked disappointed, as though I had announced that throat-cutting was off and the afternoon would be devoted to halma. Phillida whispered to me, 'Rumpole, have you gone soft in your old age?'

'Not soft, Portia, I just thought it might be nice to win my last case,' I whispered back. Then I spoke to the witness, 'I agree that you didn't have the gun, and Dennis certainly didn't.'

'So where did it come from, Mr Rumpole?' The Judge gave me the retort sarcastic. 'Did it drop from the sky?'

'Yes, my Lord. In a manner of speaking, it did. Thank you, Mr Cyril Timson.'

I shot out of the Old Bailey, when Judge Bullingham rose at the end of that day, like a bat leaving hell. That was not my usual manner of departure, but careful inquiry at the sporting kiosk in the alley off Ludgate Circus had led me to believe that *The Punter's Guide*, out late on Tuesday afternoon, carried a full print-out of that very afternoon's results. If you can make one heap of all your winnings and risk it on one turn of pitch and toss, you will have some idea what I felt like as I hastened towards the news-stand and to what had rapidly become my favourite reading.

Meanwhile as Peanuts Molloy came out of the entrance of the Public Gallery, D.S. Garsington, an officer in plain clothes, peeled himself off a wall and followed at a discreet distance. When Peanuts mounted a bus going South of the river, the Detective Sergeant was also in attendance. This close watch on Peanuts' movements was something that the Detective Inspector had authorized on the understanding that I would be leaving the Bar after the present case and so would trouble the authorities no more.

While Peanuts was off on his bus journey with D.S. Garsington in attendance, I was watching the elderly, partially blind lady with the bobble hat try to undo the newly arrived parcel of *The Punter's Guide*, with swollen and arthritic fingers. At last I could bear it no longer. I seized the string and broke it for her. I fluttered *The Punter's* pages for the fly-away leaf of that afternoon's results, and there was the print-out from Yarmouth: 1.30 FIRST EVER SO

GRATEFUL. 'Oh, my God,' I said devoutly as I paid the old lady. 'Thanks most awfully!'

At about opening time Peanuts Molloy was in a gym used to train young boxers over the Venerable Bede pub along the Old Kent Road. Peanuts was neither sparring nor skipping; he was reporting back to another deeply interested member of the Clan Molloy. What he said, as later recalled by D.S. Garsington, went something like this: 'Like I told you. No sweat. They're still just blaming it on each other. There's one old brief that thinks different, but the Judge don't take a blind bit of notice. Not of him.' At which point the Detective Sergeant intruded and asked, 'Are you Peter James Molloy?'

'What if I am?' said Peanuts.

'I must ask you to accompany me. My Inspector would like to ask you some questions.'

'Oh yes. What about?'

'I believe . . .'—D.S. Garsington was suitably vague— 'it's about a fingerprint.'

Wednesday morning passed as slowly as a discourse on the Christian attitude to Tort from Soapy Sam Ballard, or an afternoon in a rain-soaked holiday hotel with She Who Must Be Obeyed.

First of all, Judge Bullingham had some applications in another case to deal with and so we started late, and then Phillida had some other evidence of a particularly unimportant nature to call. At last it was lunchtime and I was ready for the final throw; this was the crunch, the crisis, the moment to win or lose it all. I couldn't get away to Newbury to cheer Kissogram on, but I had decided to do the next best thing. Discreet inquiries from the Ushers at the Bailey had revealed the fact that there was a betting

shop recently opened by Blackfriars Station. I found it a
curious establishment with painted-over windows and only
a few visitors, who looked to be of no particular occupation, watching the television at lunchtime. They were
joined by an ageing barrister in bands and a winged collar,
who put a small cigar into his mouth but forgot to light it
while watching the one-thirty.

I find it hard to recall my exact feelings while the race
was going on and I suppose I have had worse times waiting
for juries to come back with a verdict. Somewhere in the
depths of my being I felt that I had come so far that nothing
could stop me now, nor could it—Kissogram pulled it off
by three lengths.

I hurried back to the Bailey repeating Dennis's magic
figure: 'Let's say, three hundred and thirty grand! Give or
take a fiver.' It was, of course, an extraordinary happen-
ing, and one which I intended to keep entirely to myself for
the moment or God only knew how many learned friends
would remember old Rumpole and touch him for a loan.
Uppermost in my mind was the opening speech I was due
to make of Dennis Timson's defence when the Bull, full of
the City of London's roast beef and claret, returned to the
seat of Judgement. It would be the last time I opened a
defence in my positively last case. Why should I not do
what a barrister who has his future at the Bar to think of
can never do? Why should I not say exactly what I
thought?

As I took the lift up to the robing room, the idea appealed to me more and more; it became even more attractive than the prospect of wandering along palm-fringed
beaches beside the booming surf, although, of course, I
meant to do that as well. Phrases, heartfelt sentiments,
began to form in my mind. I was going to make the speech

of a lifetime, Rumpole's last opening, and the Bull would have to listen. So, at exactly ten past two, I rose to my feet, glanced up at the Public Gallery, found that 'Peanuts' Molloy was no longer in his place, and began.

'Members of the Jury. You heard the prosecution case opened by my learned friend Mr Hearth—*stoke*. And I wish, now, to make a few remarks of a general nature before calling Mr Dennis Timson into the witness-box. I hope they will be helpful.'

'I hope so, too, Mr Rumpole. The Defence doesn't *have* to indulge in opening speeches.' The Judge was scarcely encouraging, but no power on earth was going to stop me now.

'Members of the Jury. You have no doubt heard of the presumption of innocence, the golden thread that runs through British justice. Everyone in this fair land of ours is presumed to be innocent until they're proved to be guilty, but against this presumption there is another mighty legal doctrine,' I told them. 'It is known as the Bullingham factor. Everyone who is put into that dock before this particular learned judge is naturally assumed to have done the deed, otherwise they wouldn't be there. Not only are those in the dock presumed to be guilty, defending barristers are assumed to be only interested in wasting time so they can share in the rich pickings of the legal aid system, an organization which allows criminal advocates to live almost as high on the hog as well-qualified shorthand typists. For this princely remuneration, Members of the Jury, we are asked to defend the liberty of the subject, carry on the fine traditions of Magna Carta, make sure that all our citizens are tried by their peers and no man nor woman suffers unjust imprisonment, and knock our heads, day in day out, against the rock solid wall of the Bullingham factor! For this we have to contend with a judge who invariably briefs himself for the Prosecution...'

During the flow of my oratory, I had been conscious of two main events in Court. One was the arrival of Detective Inspector Broome, who was in urgent and whispered consultation with Charlie Hearthstoke. The other was the swelling of the Bull like a purple gas balloon, which I had been pumping up to bursting point. Now he exploded with a deafening *'Mr Rumpole!'* But before he could deliver the full fury of his Judgement against me, Hearthstoke had risen and was saying, 'My Lord. I wonder if I may intervene? With the greatest respect...'

'Certainly, Mr Hearthstoke.' The Judge subsided with a gentle hiss of escaping air. 'Certainly you may. Perhaps you have a suggestion to offer on how I might best deal with this outrageous contempt?'

'I was only about to say, my Lord, that what I am going to tell your Lordship may make the rest of Mr Rumpole's opening speech unnecessary.'

'I have no doubt that *all* of his opening speech is unnecessary!' Judge Bullingham glared in my general direction.

'I am informed by Detective Inspector Broome, my Lord, that, after further inquiries, we should no longer proceed on the allegation that either Cyril or Dennis Timson used, or indeed carried, the automatic pistol which wounded Mr Huggins the bankguard.'

'Neither of them?' The Bull looked as though his constitution might not stand another shock.

'It seems that further charges will be brought, with regard to that offence, against another "firm", if I may use that expression,' Hearthstoke explained. 'In those circumstances, the only charge is one of theft.'

'To which Mr Cyril Timson has always been prepared to plead guilty,' Phillida stood up and admitted charmingly.

'Thank *you*, Mrs Erskine-Brown,' the Judge cooed, and then turned reluctantly to me. *'Mister* Rumpole?'

'Oh yes. Guilty to the theft, my Lord. With the *very greatest respect!*' I had said most of what I had always longed to say in Bullingham's Court, and my very last case was over.

'Ferrets! The Molloys said the Timsons were ferrets. They called it out after your wives in the street.' I was in the interview room again with Liz Probert and Mr Bernard, saying goodbye to our client Dennis Timson. 'I wonder why he used that particular expression. Ferrets are little animals you send down holes in the ground. Of course, the Molloys found out what you were up to and they simply followed you down the burrow. And after you'd got through the wall, what were they going to do? Use the gun to get the money off you and Cyril when you'd opened the safe? Anyway, it all ended in chaos and confusion, as most crimes do, I'm afraid, Dennis. You heard the Molloys and thought they were the Old Bill and ran towards the passage. The Molloys got their hands on the rest of the booty. Then Mr Huggins, the bankguard, appeared, some Molloy shot at him and dropped the gun and they scarpered back down the tunnel, leaving you and Cyril in hopeless ignorance, blaming each other.'

'But there weren't any fingerprints.' Liz Probert wondered about my cross-examination of Broome.

'Oh no. But the D.I. told Peanuts Molloy he'd found his and got him talking. In fact, Peanuts grassed on the rest of the Molloys.'

'Grassed on his family, did he?' Dennis was shocked.
'Bastard!'

'I'm afraid things aren't what they were in our world,
Dennis. Standards are falling. When you've got this little
stretch under your belt you'd do far better give it all up.'

'Never. I'd miss the excitement. You're all right,
though, aren't you, Mr Rumpole?'

'What?' I was wondering whether I would miss the excitement, and decided that I could live without the thrills
and spills of life with Judge Bullingham. 'I said *you're* all
right,' Dennis repeated. 'On the old four-horse accumulator.'

'Oh yes, Dennis. I think I shall be all right. Thanks
entirely to you. I shan't forget it. You were my last case.' I
stood up and moved towards the door. 'Give me a ring
when you get out, if you're ever passing through Lotus
land.'

I had looked for Gerald as I arrived down the cells, but
the gate had been opened by a thin turnkey without a sandwich. On my way out I asked for Gerald, anxious to collect
my fortune, but was told 'It's Gerald's day off, Mr Rumpole. He'll be back tomorrow for sure.'

'Back tomorrow? You don't know the name of his book-
maker by any chance?'

'Oh no, Mr Rumpole. Gerald don't take us into his confidence, not as far as that's concerned.'

'Well, all right. I'll be back tomorrow too.'

'Dennis Timson well satisfied with his four years, was
he?' the thin warder said as he sprang me from the cells.

'He seemed considerably relieved.'

'I don't know how you do it, Mr Rumpole. Honest, I
don't.'

'Well,' I told him, 'I'm not going to do it any more.'

I gave the same news to Henry when I got back to our clerk's room and he looked unexpectedly despondent. 'I've done my positively last case, Henry,' I told him. 'I shan't ever be putting my head round the door again asking if you've got a spare committal before the Uxbridge Magistrates.'

'It's a tragedy, Mr Rumpole,' my former clerk said, and I must say I was touched. A little later he came up to see me in my room and explained the nature of his anxiety. 'If you leave, Mr Rumpole, we're going to have that Mr Hearthstoke back again. He's going to get your room, sir. Mr Ballard's already keen on the idea. It'll be a disaster for Chambers. And my ten per cent.' His voice sank to a note of doom. 'And Dianne's threatened to hand in her notice.'

'I delivered you from Hearthrug once before, Henry.' I reminded him of the affair of the Massage Parlours.

'You did, Mr Rumpole, and I shall always thank you for it. But he's due here at five o'clock, sir, for an appointment with Mr Ballard. I think they're going to fix up the final details.'

Well why should I have cared? By tomorrow, after a brief bit of business with Gerald and a word in the ear of my man of affairs at the Caring Bank, I would be well shot of the whole pack of them. And yet, just as a colonial administrator likes to leave his statue in a public park, or a university head might donate a stained-glass window to the Chapel, I felt I might give something to my old Chambers by which I would always be remembered. My gift to the dear old place would be the complete absence of Hearthrug. 'Five o'clock, eh?' I said. 'Courage, Henry! We'll see what we can do!"

Henry left me with every expression of confidence and gratitude, and at five o'clock precisely I happened to be

down in our entrance hall when Hearthstoke arrived to
squeeze Ballard and re-enter Equity Court.

'Well, Hearthrug,' I greeted him. 'Good win, that. An
excellent win!'

'Who won?' He sounded doubtful.

'You did, of course. You were prosecuting. We pleaded
guilty and you secured a conviction. Brilliant work! So
you're going to have my old room in Chambers.'

'You *are* leaving, aren't you?' He seemed to need reas-
surance.

'Oh, yes, of course. Off to Lotus land! In fact, I only
called in to pack up a few things.' I started up the stairs
towards my room, calling to him over my shoulder, 'Your
life's going to change too, I imagine. Have you had much
experience as a father?'

'A father? No, none at all.'

'Pity. Ah, well, I expect you'll pick it up as you go
along. That's the way you've picked up most things.'

I legged it up to the room then and had the satisfaction of
knowing that he was in hot pursuit. Once in my sanctum,
he closed the door and said, 'Now, Rumpole. Suppose you
tell me exactly what you mean?'

'I mean it's clear to all concerned that you've fallen for
Mrs Erskine-Brown hook, line and probably sinker. When
you move into Chambers she'll be expecting to move into
your bachelor pad in Battersea, bringing her children with
her. Jolly brave of you to take her on, as well as little
Tristan and Isolde.'

'Her children?' he repeated, dazed. The man was clearly
in a state of shock.

'I suppose Claude will be round to take the kids off to
the *Ring* occasionally. They'll probably come back whistling all the tunes.'

There was a long pause during which Hearthrug considered his position. Finally, he said, 'Perhaps, all things considered, these Chambers might not be *just* what I'm looking for...'

'Why don't you slip next door, old darling,' I suggested, 'and tell Bollard exactly that?'

I must now tell you something which is entirely to the credit of Mrs Phillida Erskine-Brown. She was determined, once the case was over, to save the neck of her old friend and one-time mentor, Horace Rumpole, despite the fact that she had only recently been merrily engaged in cutting his throat. She had no idea of my stunning success with the horses, so she took it upon herself to call on the Bull in his room, just as he was changing his jacket and about to set off for Wimbledon to terrorize his immediate family. When she was announced by Shrimpton, the Court Clerk, the learned Judge brushed his eyebrows, shot his cuffs and generally tried vainly to make himself look a little more appetizing.

When Phillida entered, and was left alone in the presence, an extraordinary scene transpired, the details of which our Portia only told me long after this narrative comes to an end. The, no doubt, ogling judge told her that her conduct of the defence had filled him with admiration, and said, 'I'm afraid I can't say the same for Rumpole. In fact, I shall have to report him for gross professional misconduct.' And the old hypocrite added, 'After such a long career too. It's a tragedy, of course.'

'A tragedy he was interrupted,' Phillida told him. She clearly had the Judge puzzled, so she pressed on. 'I read the second half of that speech, Judge. Rumpole was extremely flattering, but I think the things he said about you were no less than the truth.'

'Flattering?' The Bull couldn't believe his ears.

' "One of the fairest and most compassionate judges ever to have sat in the Old Bailey"; "Combines the wisdom of Solomon with the humanity of Florence Nightingale"— that's only a couple of quotations from the rest of his speech.'

'But . . . but that's not how he started off!'

'Oh, he was describing the sort of mistaken view the Jury might have of an Old Bailey judge. Then he was about to put them right, but of course the case collapsed and he never gave the rest of that marvellous speech!'

'Florence Nightingale, eh? Can you tell me anything else'—the Bull was anxious to know—'that Rumpole was *about* to say?'

' "With Judge Bullingham the quality of mercy is not strain'd, It droppeth as the gentle rain from heaven." Rather well put, I thought. Will you still be reporting Rumpole for professional misconduct?'

The Bull was silent then and appeared to reserve judgement. 'I shall have to reconsider the matter,' he said, 'in the light of what you've told me, Mrs Erskine-Brown.' And then he approached her more intimately: 'Phillida, may I ask you one question?'

'Certainly, Judge,' our Portia answered with considerable courage, and the smitten Bull asked, 'Do you prefer the hard or the creamy centres? When it comes to a box of chocolates?'

After this strange and in many ways heroic encounter, Phillida turned up, in due course, at Pommeroy's Wine Bar, and sat at the table in the corner where she had formerly been drinking with Hearthrug. She was there by appointment, but she didn't expect to meet me. I spotted her as soon as I came in, fresh from my encounter with the young man concerned, and determined to celebrate my amazing good fortune in an appropriate manner. I sat down beside her and, if she was disappointed that it was not someone else, she greeted me with moderate hospitality.

'Rumpole, have a choc?' I saw at once that she had a somewhat ornate box on the table in front of her. I was rash enough to take one with a mauve centre.

'Bullingham gave them to me,' she explained.

'The Mad Bull's in love! You're a *femme fatale*, Portia.'

'Don't ask me to explain yet, I'm not sure how it'll turn out,' she warned me. 'But I went to see him entirely in your interests.'

'And I've just been seeing someone entirely in yours. What are you doing here, anyway, alone and palely loitering?'

'I was just waiting for someone.' Phillida was non-committal.

'He's not coming.' I was certain.

'What?'

'Hearthrug's not coming. He's not coming into Chambers, either.' She looked at me, puzzled and not a little hurt. 'Why not?'

'Henry doesn't want him.'

'Rumpole! What've you done?' She suspected I had been up to something.

'Sorry, Portia. I told him you wanted to move into his bachelor pad in Battersea and bring Tristan and Isolde with you. I'm afraid he went deathly pale and decided to cancel his subscription.'

There was a longish silence and I didn't know whether to expect tears, abuse or a quick dash out into the street. I was surprised when at long last, she gave me a curious little half-smile and said, 'The rat!'

'I could have told you that before you started spooning with him all round the Old Bailey,' I assured her and added, 'Of course, I shouldn't have done that.'

'No, you shouldn't. You'd got no right to say any such thing.'

'It was Henry and Dianne I was thinking about.'

'Thank you very much!'

'They don't deserve Hearthrug. None of you deserve him.'

'I was only considering a small adventure . . .' she began to explain herself, a little sadly. But it was no time for regrets. 'Cheer up, Portia,' I told her. 'In all the circumstances, I think this is the moment for me to buy the Dom Perignon. *Méthode Champenoise* is a thing of the past.'

She agreed and I went over to the bar where Jack Pommeroy was dealing with the arrival of the usual evening crowd. 'A bottle of your best bubbles, Jack.' I placed a lavish order. 'Nothing less than the dear old Dom to meet this occasion.' And whilst he went about fulfilling it, I saw Erskine-Brown come in and look around the room. 'Ah, Claude,' I called to him. 'I'm in the chair. Care for a glass of vintage bubbly?'

'There you are!' he said, stating the obvious I thought. 'I took a telephone message for you in the clerk's room.'

'If it's about a murder tomorrow, I'm not interested.' My murdering days were over.

'No, this was rather a strange-sounding chap. I wouldn't have thought he was completely sober. Said his name was Gerald.'

'Gerald?' I was pleased to hear it. 'Yes, of course. Gerald . . .'

'Said he was calling from London airport.'

'From where?'

'He said would I give his thanks to Mr Rumpole for the excellent tips, and he was just boarding a plane for a warmer climate.'

'Gerald said that?' I have had some experience of human perfidy, but I must say I was shocked and, not to put too fine a point on it, stricken.

'Words to that effect. Oh, then he said he had to go. They were calling his flight.'

What do you do if your hopes, built up so bravely through the testing-time of a four-horse accumulator, are dashed to the ground? What do you do if the doors to a golden future are suddenly slammed in your face and you're told to go home quietly? I called for Jack Pommeroy and told him to forget the Dom Perignon and pour out three small glasses of the Château Thames Embankment. Then I looked at Phillida sitting alone, and from her to Erskine-Brown. 'Claude,' I told him, 'I have an idea. I think there's something you should do urgently.'

'What's that, Rumpole?'

'For God's sake, take your wife to the Opera!'

During the course of these memoirs I have stressed my article of faith: never plead guilty. Like all good rules this is, of course, subject to exceptions. For instance, readers will have noticed that having got Dennis Timson off the firearm charges, I had no alternative but to plead to the theft. So it was with my situation before She Who Must Be Obeyed. I knew that she would soon learn of my announced retirement from the Bar. If I wished to avoid prolonged questioning on this subject, no doubt stretching over several months, I had no alternative but to come clean and throw myself on the mercy of the Court. And so, that night, before the domestic gas-fire I gave Hilda a full account of the wager I had placed with Gerald, and of the fat screw's appalling treachery. 'But Rumpole,' she asked, and it was by no means a bad question, 'do you mean to say you've got no record of the transaction?'

'Nothing,' I had to admit. 'Not even a betting-slip. I trusted him. So bloody innocent! We look after our clients and we're complete fools about ourselves.'

'You mean'—and I could see that things weren't going to be easy—'you lost my hundred pounds?'

'I'm afraid it's on its way to a warmer climate. With about three hundred thousand friends.'

'The hundred pounds I spent on the new hearthrug!' She was appalled.

'*That* hundred pounds is still in the account of the Caring Bank, Hilda. Coloured red,' I tried to explain.

'You'll have to go and talk to Mr Truscott about it,' she made the order. 'I don't suppose he'll be inviting you to the Savoy Grill now, Rumpole?'

'No, Hilda. I don't suppose he will.' I got up then to recharge our glasses, and, after a thoughtful sip, Hilda spoke more reasonably.

'I'm not sure,' she told me, 'that I ever wanted to sit with you on a hotel verandah all day, drinking Planter's Punch.'

'Well. Perhaps not.'

'We might have run out of conversation.'

'Yes. I suppose we might.'

She had another sip or two and then, much to my relief, came out with 'So things could be worse.'

'They are,' I had to break it to her.

'What?'

'They are worse, Hilda.'

'What've you done now?' She sighed over the number of offences to be taken into consideration.

'Only promised Detective Inspector Broome that I'd done my last case. Oh, and told the Jury exactly what I thought of the Mad Bull. In open Court! I'll probably be reported to the Bar Council. For disciplinary action to be considered.'

'Rumpole!' Of course she was shocked. 'Daddy would be ashamed of you.'

'That's one comfort.'

'What did you say?'

'Your Daddy, Hilda, has already been called to account by the Great Benchers of the Sky. I hope he was able to explain his hopeless ignorance of bloodstains.'

There was a long silence and then She said, 'Rumpole.'

'Yes.'

'What are you going to be doing tomorrow?'

'Tomorrow?'

'I mean'—and Hilda made this clear to me—'I hope you're not really going to retire or anything. I hope you're not going to be hanging round the flat all day. You will be taking your usual tube. Won't you? At eight forty-five?'

'To hear is to obey.' I lifted my glass of Pommeroy's Ordinary to the light, squinted at it, and noted its somewhat murky appearance. '"Courage!" he said, and pointed towards the Temple tube station.'

So it came about that at my usual hour next morning I opened the door of our clerk's room. Henry was telephoning, Dianne was brightening up her nails and Uncle Tom was practising chip shots into the waste-paper basket.

Nothing had changed and nobody seemed particularly surprised to see me.

'Henry,' I said, when our clerk put down the telephone.

'Yes, Mr Rumpole?'

'Any chance of a small brief going today, perhaps a spot
of indecency at the Uxbridge Magistrates Court?'

FOR THE BEST IN PAPERBACKS, LOOK FOR THE

In every corner of the world, on every subject under the sun, Penguin represents quality and variety—the very best in publishing today.

For complete information about books available from Penguin—including Pelicans, Puffins, Peregrines, and Penguin Classics—and how to order them, write to us at the appropriate address below. Please note that for copyright reasons the selection of books varies from country to country.

In the United Kingdom: For a complete list of books available from Penguin in the U.K., please write to *Dept E.P., Penguin Books Ltd, Harmondsworth, Middlesex, UB7 0DA.*

In the United States: For a complete list of books available from Penguin in the U.S., please write to *Dept BA, Penguin*, Box 120, Bergenfield, New Jersey 07621-0120.

In Canada: For a complete list of books available from Penguin in Canada, please write to *Penguin Books Ltd, 2801 John Street, Markham, Ontario L3R 1B4.*

In Australia: For a complete list of books available from Penguin in Australia, please write to the *Marketing Department, Penguin Books Ltd, P.O. Box 257, Ringwood, Victoria 3134.*

In New Zealand: For a complete list of books available from Penguin in New Zealand, please write to the *Marketing Department, Penguin Books (NZ) Ltd, Private Bag, Takapuna, Auckland 9.*

In India: For a complete list of books available from Penguin, please write to *Penguin Overseas Ltd, 706 Eros Apartments, 56 Nehru Place, New Delhi, 110019.*

In Holland: For a complete list of books available from Penguin in Holland, please write to *Penguin Books Nederland B.V., Postbus 195, NL-1380AD Weesp, Netherlands.*

In Germany: For a complete list of books available from Penguin, please write to *Penguin Books Ltd, Friedrichstrasse 10-12, D-6000 Frankfurt Main 1, Federal Republic of Germany.*

In Spain: For a complete list of books available from Penguin in Spain, please write to *Longman, Penguin España, Calle San Nicolas 15, E-28013 Madrid, Spain.*

In Japan: For a complete list of books available from Penguin in Japan, please write to *Longman Penguin Japan Co Ltd, Yamaguchi Building, 2-12-9 Kanda Jimbocho, Chiyoda-Ku, Tokyo 101, Japan.*

FOR THE BEST IN MYSTERY, LOOK FOR THE

□ A CRIMINAL COMEDY
Julian Symons

From Julian Symons, the master of crime fiction, this is "the best of his best" (*The New Yorker*). What starts as a nasty little scandal centering on two partners in a British travel agency escalates into smuggling and murder in Italy.
220 pages   ISBN: 0-14-009621-3   **$3.50**

□ GOOD AND DEAD
Jane Langton

Something sinister is emptying the pews at the Old West Church, and parishioner Homer Kelly knows it isn't a loss of faith. When he investigates, Homer discovers that the ways of a small New England town can be just as mysterious as the ways of God.
256 pages   ISBN: 0-14-778217-1   **$3.95**

□ THE SHORTEST WAY TO HADES
Sarah Caudwell

Five young barristers and a wealthy family with a five-million-pound estate find the stakes are raised when one member of the family meets a suspicious death.
208 pages   ISBN: 0-14-008488-6   **$3.50**

□ RUMPOLE OF THE BAILEY
John Mortimer

The hero of John Mortimer's mysteries is Horace Rumpole, barrister at law, sixty-eight next birthday, with an unsurpassed knowledge of blood and typewriters, a penchant for quoting poetry, and a habit of referring to his judge as "the old darling."
208 pages   ISBN: 0-14-004670-4   **$3.95**

You can find all these books at your local bookstore, or use this handy coupon for ordering:

Penguin Books By Mail
Dept. BA Box 999
Bergenfield, NJ 07621-0999

Please send me the above title(s). I am enclosing _____
(please add sales tax if appropriate and $3.00 to cover postage and handling). Send check or money order—no CODs. Please allow four weeks for shipping. We cannot ship to post office boxes or addresses outside the USA. *Prices subject to change without notice.*

Ms./Mrs./Mr. _____

Address _____

City/State _____ Zip _____

Sales tax: CA: 6.5% NY: 8.25% NJ: 6% PA: 6% TN: 5.5%